HANNAH CAPIN

FOUL IS FAIR

PENGUIN B

PENGUIN BOOKS

UK | USA | Canada | Ireland | Australia
India | New Zealand | South Africa

Penguin Books is part of the Penguin Random House group of companies
whose addresses can be found at global.penguinrandomhouse.com.

www.penguin.co.uk   www.puffin.co.uk   www.ladybird.co.uk

First published in the USA by St. Martin's Press
and in Great Britain by Penguin Books 2020

001

Text copyright © Hannah Capin, 2020

The moral right of the author has been asserted

Printed in Great Britain by Clays Ltd, Elcograf S.p.A.

A CIP catalogue record for this book is available from the British Library

ISBN: 978–0–241–40497–3

All correspondence to:
Penguin Books
Penguin Random House Children's
80 Strand
London WC2R 0RL

MIX
Paper from
responsible sources
FSC® C018179

Penguin Random House is committed to a
sustainable future for our business, our readers
and our planet. This book is made from Forest
Stewardship Council® certified paper.

FOUL IS FAIR opens with a violent assault (not depicted on the page) and follows a girl's ruthless pursuit of revenge.

She does not do what she "should" do.

She does not apologize.

She is not rendered powerless.

These narrative choices are deliberate.

There is a narrative many stories about sexual assault tell, especially in the realm of young adult fiction. It features a "good girl" who fits a certain archetype; in the aftermath, she is disempowered and struggling to regain her agency. This narrative is valid, authentic, and important, but it is not the story *Foul Is Fair* tells.

Despite its obvious relevance, I did not write *Foul Is Fair* in response to the #MeToo movement. The headlines that have informed this book are quieter and more quickly dismissed. Again and again, survivors who choose to come forward—survivors on the wrong end of the balance of power, and usually teenage girls—become subject to scrutiny, harassment, and victim-blaming. The tide turns, inevitably, to how unfair it is that a "youthful mistake" will "ruin a boy's life." Justice is scant.

I wrote *Foul Is Fair* for the survivors who have chosen to report only to be retraumatized by the media, the justice system, and the court of public opinion. I wrote it for those who have chosen not to come forward due to fear and self-doubt. I wrote it for those who have chosen to come forward years later, only to be accused of ulterior motives.

Even at a time when #MeToo has gained widespread support, a book that takes an uncompromising stance will raise questions.

Foul Is Fair will be a difficult book for some, but we need difficult books now more than ever.

To the survivors, to the silenced, to every girl who wants revenge: **this book is for you.**

Hannah Capin

For every girl who wants revenge.

THAT NIGHT

Sweet sixteen is when the claws come out.

We're all flash tonight. Jenny and Summer and Mads and me. Vodka and heels we could never quite walk in before, but tonight we can. Short skirts—the shortest. Glitter and highlight. Matte and shine. Long hair and whitest-white teeth.

I've never been blond before but tonight my hair is platinum. Mads bleached it too fast but I don't care because tonight's the only night that matters. And my eyes are jade-green tonight instead of brown, and Summer swears the contacts Jenny bought are going to melt into my eyes and I'll never see again, but I don't care about that, either.

Tonight I'm sixteen.

Tonight Jenny and Summer and Mads and me, we're four sirens, like the ones in those stories. The ones who sing and make men die.

Tonight we're walking up the driveway to our best party ever. Not the parties like we always go to, with the dull-duller-dullest Hancock Park girls we've always known and the dull-duller-dullest wine coolers we always drink and the same bad choice in boys.

Tonight we're going to a St Andrew's Prep party.

Crashing it, technically.

But nobody turns away girls like us.

We smile at the door. They let us in. Our teeth flash. Our claws glimmer. Mads laughs so shrill-bright it's almost a scream. Everyone looks. We all grab hands and laugh together and then everyone, every charmed St Andrew's Prepper is cheering for us and I know they see it—

for just a second—

—our fangs and our claws.

AFTER

The first thing I do is cut my hair.

But it isn't like in the movies, those crying girls with mascara streaks and kindergarten safety scissors, pink and dull, looking into toothpaste specks on medicine cabinet mirrors.

I'm not crying. I don't fucking cry.

I wash my makeup off first. I use the remover I stole from Summer, oily Clinique in a clear bottle with a green cap. Three minutes later I'm fresh-faced, wholesome, girl-next-door, and you'd almost never know my lips are still poison when I look the way a good girl is supposed to look instead of like *that little whore with the jade-green eyes*.

The contact lenses go straight into the trash.

Then I take the knife, the good long knife from the wedding silver my sister hid in the attic so she wouldn't have to think about the stupid man who never deserved her anyway. The marriage was a joke but the knife is perfectly, wickedly beautiful: silver from handle to blade and so sharp you bleed a little just looking at it. No one had ever touched it until I did, and when I opened the box and lifted the knife off the dark red velvet, I could see one slice of my reflection looking back from the blade, and I smiled.

I pull my hair tight, the long hair that's been mine since those endless backyard days with Jenny and Summer and Mads. Always black, until Mads bleached it too fast, but splintering platinum blond for the St Andrew's party on my sweet sixteen. Ghost-bright hair from Mads and jade-green eyes from Jenny and contour from Summer, almost magic, sculpting me into a brand-new girl for a brand-new year.

My hair is thick, but I've never been one to flinch.

I stare myself straight in the eyes and slash once—

Hard.

And that's it. Short hair.

I dye it back to black, darker than before, with the cheap box dye I made Jenny steal from the drugstore. Mads revved her Mustang, crooked across two parking spots at three in the morning, and I said:

Get me a color that knows what the fuck it's doing.

Jenny ran back out barefoot in her baby-pink baby-doll dress and flung herself into the back seat across Summer's lap, and Mads was out of the lot and onto the road, singing through six red lights, and everything was still slow and foggy and almost like a dream, but when Jenny threw the box onto my knees I could see it diamond-clear. Hard black Cleopatra bangs on the front and the label, spelled out plain: #*010112 REVENGE*. So I said it out loud:

REVENGE

And Mads gunned the engine harder and Summer and Jenny shrieked war-cries from the back seat and they grabbed my hand, all three of them, and we clung together so tight I could feel blood under my broken claws.

REVENGE, they said back to me. *REVENGE, REVENGE, REVENGE.*

So in the bathroom, an hour later and alone, I dye my hair revenge-black, and I feel dark wings growing out of my back, and I smile into the mirror at the girl with ink-stained fingers and a silver sword.

Then I cut my broken nails to the quick.

Then I go to bed.

In the morning I put on my darkest lipstick before it's even breakfast time, and I go to Nailed It with a coffee so hot it burns my throat. The beautiful old lady with the crooked smile gives me new nails as long as the ones they broke off last night, and stronger.

She looks at the bruises on my neck and the scratches across my face, but she doesn't say anything.

So I point at my hair, and I say, *This color. Know what it's called?*

She shakes her head: *No.*

I say, *REVENGE.*

She says, *Good girl. Kill him.*

THE COVEN

"What are you going to do to them?" Mads asks me.

They're in my bedroom, her and Summer and Jenny, when I get back. Summer and Jenny sit on the bed, one knee touching, and Mads stands lookout-sharp against the wall.

"Your hair," says Jenny. "It's short."

I sit down and Jenny reaches out and strokes one hand over the paintbrush ends. Little Jenny Kim from two houses over, still in last night's dress. Her cat-eyes are smudged to smoke but her lips are fresh pink, a tiny perfect heart on her perfect little face. She wears a rose-gold chain with one white pearl nestled under her throat.

She is so sweet it could kill you.

"I'm ready for war," I say.

"So are we," says Summer, next to Jenny. Summer, supermodel blond and supermodel tan and supermodel gorgeous, sunny and irresistible, enough garage-band songs about her to fill ten albums, the hottest virgin in California. Last year a football boy drove whiskey-fast up Pacific Coast Highway just to make her want him. Plunged his Maserati off the saw-blade cliffs. Summer went to his hospital room and left a lipstick kiss on the window so it was the very first thing he saw when he woke up. She never talked to him again.

He lived, but everyone knows he wishes he hadn't.

"Tell us what you want," says Mads. "We'll do it, Elle."

My parents named me Elizabeth Jade Khanjara. Everyone calls me Elle: they always have. Last night, I told the St Andrew's Prep boy with the dazzle smile and the just-for-me drink, *I'm Elle,* and he said, *Elle. Pretty name, but not as pretty as you.*

"I'm not Elle," I tell them.

Mads waits. She doesn't blink.

"I'm Jade," I say.

"Good," says Mads.

If I were the kind of girl who cries I'd cry right now for Mads, my favorite. Mads, my very best friend in all the world, since we were four years old together and she moved into the house on the other side of the fourteenth green. When her parents still called her by her deadname and the only time she could wear girl-clothes was when she was with me. Mads, who last night was the only one I could think about once I could finally stand without falling, and when I found her out back by the pool, tall and regal and lit up like a goddamn queen, that was when I could breathe again. Mads, who knew what happened without me saying anything, and found a pair of lacrosse sticks in the pool house and together we broke all the windows we could find, and the glass shattered and caught in the nets and our hands bled bright and furious.

Mads, my Mads, who once upon a time when we were eight and taping knockout-pink Barbie Band-Aids over skinned knees, looked at me and told me the name she wasn't and said, *I'm Madalena,* and I said, *Good.*

"Jade," says Jenny—

"Jade," says Summer—

"Jade," says Mads—

—and it's magic, dark magic. A spell from my three witch-sisters.

"Find them," I say, and I close my eyes because I can still feel it, almost, the poison the dazzle-smiled boy put in my drink last night so the world turned flashbulb bright but slow, so slow, until I couldn't fight anymore, and when I tried to scream they smashed their hands over my mouth and I bit and bit and my fangs drew blood and they said, *God damn, she's feisty.*

I open my eyes—now, this morning, here in my coven with Jenny and Summer and Mads—and they've done magic again. There on the screen Summer's holding, I see the boys we're going to ruin.

Summer prints it in color on the purring sleek printer my parents bought me to make sure I get into Stanford. They want me to be a doctor. I want to be the queen.

The paper looks like those WANTED lists in the post office, but instead at the top it says, *St Andrew's Preparatory School Varsity Boys' Lacrosse.* One smug smile after another. Secrets you can feel even on paper.

Mads finds a scarlet lip liner in her purse. I point at pictures and she paints bold circles onto the page:

Duncan.

Duffy.

Connor.

Banks.

Four boys from the room with the white sheets and the spinning lights, and four red circles in front of us now.

"We can kill them," says Mads, quiet, and she means it.

I look at Jenny in her baby-pink lace; Summer in her silky black shirt with the deadly plunging neckline; Mads with gold rings in her ears and fists ready to fight.

They are mine and I am theirs.

My nails are long and silver. Ten little daggers, sharp enough to tear throats open.

"Killing hurts worse if somebody you love is holding the knife," I say.

"So make one of them do it?" Summer asks. She's looking at the boys, the ones we haven't circled yet. She's hungry.

I nod.

Jenny smiles her pink-heart smile and says:

Fair is foul, and foul is fair

—another spell.

Mads hands me her lip liner. I look at every boy, one by one. Remember them from the party at Duncan's house, locking girls against the wall in the living room and pouring shots in the kitchen and smirking sidelong while I drank poison.

Today I choose who dies and I choose who kills.

There's one boy who wasn't at the party. Right in the middle of the page. Earnest eyes that trust too much. Innocent, he thinks, and he thinks he isn't one of them. He thinks he isn't lying when he says his prayers at night.

I carve a bloodred X across his face:

Mack.

CONFESSION

Summer says I have to tell my parents.

"No," I say, frostbite-cold.

"I'm not saying don't do the rest." Her eyes flick down to

the paper in her hands. "But what if you want to do something about them, later, and you need proof—"

And Jenny says, "Killing them isn't enough for you?
Damn, Summer."

And I say, "Thank you."

Summer looks at Jenny the way she always does. The way
everybody except Jenny can see. "I'm not saying cops. Or lawyers. Not yet."

And Jenny narrows her eyes and says, in her cotton-candy
bubblegum voice, "Not ever," because Jenny's father is the
sort of slick-haired lawyer who smiles at boys like Duncan
and Duffy and Connor and Banks and tells them he doesn't
want to know if they did it, he just wants to know who can
stand up and put one hand on the Bible and swear that *he's a
fine young man,* and then he takes their fathers' checks and
those boys walk out of court free, grinning guilt all over their
faces.

"I'm just saying, the hospital," Summer says.

I say it again: "No. Hell no."

So Summer says, "But what if—"

And I say, "Are you really going to tell me I can't say no?"

The words hang in the air and Jenny's eyes flicker bigger.

Then Mads says, "Jade."

She's still standing by the window, light slivering past the
curtains and sparking off her earrings and her shimmering
dark skin. Immovable.

"We're going to kill them," says Mads. "We're going to do
exactly what you tell us, until it's done."

And Jenny says, singsong, "Until the battle's lost and won."

And Mads says, "But this is insurance. You never know
what you'll need later."

And Summer takes my hand in hers and looks into my eyes and says, "Please, Jade, for us." It's so perfectly, perfectly Summer—her pool-blue gaze and her beach hair and that voice people would murder their mothers for—that I laugh, because if anyone knows exactly how to do what I need to do, it's her.

"I'll tell," I say. "But you have to do the rest." I nod at the boys in Summer's hands. "Find out everything. I need to know everything."

"Done," she says, with her megawatt smile. "Before sunset."

They watch me. Sisters, by something more than blood.

And Mads says, "Good."

They leave, because in the end this is all mine, and I put Summer's list under my pillow and brush my hair. Stare into the mirror until all that's left is the cold hard glint in my eyes. Dangerous eyes for a dangerous girl.

Then I go downstairs.

And here I am, standing in front of the fireplace we never use. Standing with my hands folded together in front of me, facing my parents.

"I'm going to tell you something," I say.

They wait. The silence hums loud in my ears.

"Don't be upset," I tell them.

"What is it?" my father asks. I can read it on his face: *poor grades*, he's thinking, *cheating on a test*. He's in his golf clothes, because plastic surgeons aren't the kind of doctors who work Saturdays. *She won't get into Stanford,* he's thinking. *She's ruined her chances.*

"I'll handle everything," I tell them.

"What *is* it?" my mother asks. She's in a brunch dress; perfect hair; fresh Botox. She's thinking *a boy*, but not in the way that's true. Thinking *heartbreak*, thinking about the boy she loved back when she was my age, the one her parents decided wasn't good enough for her. She loves my father. They're exactly right together: the goddamn American dream. But she still has a picture of the boy, the one who stayed out too late and called when she was studying. The one she left behind in Torrance when she packed her things for college, the way her parents said she should.

I hold my shoulders square. They see the little baby version of me: eyes too big for my face, tiny gold earrings, too much laughing. As soon as I speak they'll never see that same girl anymore, and knowing that makes my fingernails bite into my skin because I want it so hard, to rip those boys' faces open. Tear their hearts out and hold them, still beating, in my hands.

I'm not their little baby girl. I'm a cruel bitch and everyone knows it. Every teenage girl thinks she and her friends are the mean girls, the ice queens, the wicked witches, but Jenny and Summer and Mads and me—we're what they wish they were.

Savage.

And after all, little baby Jade waited patient at the top of the preschool playground castle the day Tristan Wilder pushed Summer on the sidewalk and made her spit blood. Waited for Tristan to climb grubby-handed up the ladder and teeter too close to the edge. Waited until the teacher wasn't looking.

Tristan Wilder went to the hospital the day he made Summer spit blood. And when the ambulance pulled away, Summer's eyes met mine and her face split into a smile and her teeth glowed red.

I've never been anyone's little baby girl.

"Yesterday," I say. "Last night."

I tell them.

But mostly lies. Because the real story is mine, and I already know what I need to do.

I tell them it was a Hillview party. I tell them I went alone; the girls weren't there; nobody knows but me. I tell them it was a Hillview boy. I tell them I'm not sure who.

I tell them I blacked out before it happened.

When I'm done the silence doesn't buzz anymore. It sits, vulture-quiet, on the mantel behind me.

My father stands up and walks out.

I can't look at my mother, so I stare at the painting on the wall and think of the very last act of this goddamn Greek tragedy. Four boys dead on the ground and me, standing over them with a crown in my hands.

Something shatters from the kitchen.

I see it where I'm not looking: my mother's face shattering, too. She says, *Elle, I love you, I love you* and then she's stumbling after my father, unsteady for the first time in her life. A broom brushes against the kitchen floor and crystal scrapes on marble. My parents speak too fast, two languages melting together, hushed and desperate: *it can't be, how could he, how can we, why did, who was—*

no.

My mother's voice gets so quiet I can't understand it even in the bone-crushing silence.

Then my father's voice spikes out, clear and loud:

kill the boy

—and I've never been prouder to be his daughter. My father, who spends his days slicing scalpels across cheeks and chests. My father with his expensive watch and his once-a-week haircut, who breaks people apart and sews them back together, better.

If I told him the truth, he'd take his scalpel and slice those St Andrew's boys' throats himself.

But this is all mine.

When they come back in my father's hands are fists and my mother's eyes shine.

"Tell us what you need from us," they say.

And I say, "Let me handle it myself. I need to. I will."

They look stronger when I say that. Like they know it's true.

Behind me, the vulture on the mantel spreads its wings, black and huge.

I say, "I want to transfer to St Andrew's."

CLINICAL

My mother goes with me to the hospital. *I want to go alone,* I told her and my father, but she took my hand in hers and said, *You're my daughter,* and that was the end of it. We drive my father's favorite car, the slut-red BMW convertible, three miles from our house to Cedars-Sinai. The sky is blue enough to drown in.

The nurses give me pills and ask too much. I swallow and lie. The doctor is tired and grave with eyes that dig too deep, and I float away from her white-gloved hands and wait like the vulture from the mantel.

They look at me like I'm something to be fixed.

When they say *do you want to talk to anyone* I tell them no, and they tell me to wait for a counselor anyway. Out in the hall my mother's voice edges sharper each time the doctor murmurs to her about police and reports and all the other things I don't want. My mother says, *She's my daughter.* My mother says, *No.*

I sit on the end of a white-sheets hospital cot in the black dress Summer let me borrow a month ago, for Valentine's Day, when all four of us crashed hotel bars downtown and smiled daggers at greased-up businessmen and collected martinis and waited for when the men got too close, and then we threw the drinks in their faces and ran back out into the night, stilettos clipping out gunfire, elbows locking us together. Summer's black dress and my silver heels. Holding my phone in both hands and texting Jenny, texting Summer, texting Mads. Dividing and conquering the St Andrew's boys. Piecing their whole lives together from their pictures and tags and reckless Connor's comments about *girls who won't remember.*

The woman they want me to talk to comes in so mousequiet I don't even know she's there until she says, "Elizabeth, right?"

I look up from my phone. My lips twist.

I say, "Wrong."

She flips a page on her clipboard and her eyebrows furrow. "Elizabeth Jade Khanjara?"

My phone buzzes. It's Summer: *You're gone. Full ghost,*

because I asked her to do it: erase every last trace of me so the boys won't find anything if they decide to dig where they don't belong.

My eyes meet the mouse's, and she's even more like prey when I bother looking her over. "It's Jade," I say.

"Jade, then," she says, and she offers up a careful smile, like if she shows too many teeth she'll shatter my poor fragile self.

I grin at her, glittering and wide.

She takes a step back and blinks three times, right in a row.

I text the coven, *They've sent an actual mouse to fix me. If I were broken, I'd be fucked.*

"First of all, Jade, I am so, so sorry," says the mouse.

Terrify her, says Jenny on my screen.

Almost too easy, I text back. *Almost not worth it.*

"So am I," I say with a lilt that should tell the mouse what I really mean, and the little twitch she does says she notices, but then she blinks again and decides I didn't mean it.

She has no idea.

"Jade," she says, sitting down in the ugly chair across from me, "what you need to know, before anything else, is that there's no wrong way to be a victim."

I look up for that. Straight into her mud-and-pity eyes. I flash my teeth again; let the light gleam off them. "I'm not a victim," I say.

She bows her head. "Survivor," she says, and that word is worse somehow, with its painted-false bravery.

Survivor, I text. *Fuck her. Is that the best she can do?*

"Not that, either," I say. There's more she wants to tell me, and the words cling to her like dust and rot: who I was and who I am and who I should be. I'm supposed to listen. I'm supposed to believe her.

"I—well, then," the mouse falters. "Well, what would you prefer?"

Tell her queen, says Summer.

Tell her killer, says Jenny.

Tell her justice, says Mads.

I won't let her read me her lines.

Fate, I tell the coven.

"Why do you need a word for it?" I ask, all mocking uncertainty.

"I don't—I don't know." She's grasping and too nervous. "What do you mean?"

My smile is lethal. "I mean those boys didn't turn me into anything I wasn't before."

She opens her mouse-mouth and closes it again.

I stand. Summer's dress blacks out the white sheets behind me. My heels are so high my arches curl into talons. I'm the huntress and she's the kill and she knows it now, too late to do anything.

I hold out one hand, palm up, and she places her mouse-hand into it like it's automatic.

"But I would prefer—" I say, and I lift her hand and kiss it. My eyes are still locked on hers. Her pupils shrink to tiny panicked pinpricks—

"Avenger," I say.

I drop her hand and walk out.

I am exactly the wrong way to be a victim.

RUN

I hate running. I always have.

Losers run, sweaty and red-faced. Glowing in neon or slumming in T-shirts. Flailing and obedient.

I hate running, but I run anyway, because my coven and me, we're the very best girls at Hillview. Running carves us hard as marble, and it means we can dance all night and fly fast away from the men who want their drink-money back when they don't get what we never promised.

So I run on Sunday, at dead noon. Alone, on the smoothed-glass sand where the waves wash everything away. In black on black with the ghost of my long hair shadowing me. The ghost of my hair and the ghosts from Duncan's party—

the things I remember, jabbing at my skin—

the things I don't, bubbling under it—

—matching my pace no matter how fast I run.

It's supposed to be two miles out and two miles back to my father's red car. But I don't turn even when I'm past the boardwalk, all the way to where the waves crash almost against the rocks. When the sand runs out I climb up and run on the road, straight up the coast and straight toward the traffic, until I can't feel my feet at all—

until it's only my black wings carrying me, reaching so wide the cars swerve into the other lane to make room—

until the hills stretch higher and closer, bare dark rock pressing in behind the houses—

—until my feet stop all on their own and I'm crashed

against the pavement and a truck roars past with its horn screaming in my ears.

Across the road a silver Lexus pulls over. The window comes down. Another car flies past, so close I can taste the exhaust. The traffic splits the car that pulled over into cut-up frames: a woman yelling something, sunglasses coming off, a door opening.

My wings are gone and my hair is gone and the sun blazes down too bright.

The woman is next to me, all of a sudden: "Sweetie, wake up—are you okay—"

She crouches down too close.

"Sweetie, can you hear me?"

Hey, slut, said Connor on Friday night, *can you hear me? Wake up—*

She touches my shoulder—

—and I push her so hard she falls almost into the traffic. She lets out a little cry and scrambles back on all fours, grinding freeway dirt into her white jeans.

I'm on my feet again. My shadow covers all of her. She cowers, wide-eyed and scared, and it breathes life back into me, and my hands find my phone and hold it straight out like a gun.

I leave her there, oil-streaked and trembling.

Mads finds me, twenty minutes later, straight down the cliff on a blade-thin crescent of sand the waves can't reach. She sits so close our arms seal together. The wide gold band halfway between her shoulder and her elbow is cold against my skin.

She doesn't say one single thing. She stares hard at the ocean. Gold-rimmed sunglasses and scarlet-orange lipstick.

She's the most beautiful girl in the world. I love her more than anything.

The waves rush in. Washing everything away, again and again, to clear blue nothing. The sun sinks just enough to shine straight into our eyes. White-hot and blinding.

I stand up and walk into the ocean. The waves are stronger than they look and cold enough to crack bone. I should fall, but I don't. I won't. I keep walking, steady, until my feet barely touch the sand and I float closer to the sun with every wave. Keeping my head above the water—

daring every fucking wave to try to drown me—

daring the sharks to find me—

daring the St Andrew's boys to come back—

—until my feet can't touch the sand at all and the waves are breaking all around me and the water washes out the sun. All I see is the biggest wave yet, blue and gleaming, closing in, and nothing else is real.

It breaks.

The blue goes black. I spin hard away from the light and skid through sand. My lungs burn and then they burst and the water rushes in.

I can't find the sky.

And then strong hands grab my arm and pull hard against the tide, and the sun comes shouting back.

We wash up on the sand. Mads and me, snarled together. I cough out water and blood. The sky is even brighter than before.

Finally Mads says, "You can't swim for shit."

We laugh, not like our siren call on Friday night, but raw and ripping open.

"Swimming fucking sucks," I say.

"Swimming is for flyover bitches on vacation," Mads says.

I cough again. There's water in my lungs; salt beating through my heart. "Swimming is for jock bitches who get up at five A.M. for practice."

"Swimming is for reality-show bitches who jump into pools in their bridesmaid dresses just to keep the attention on them."

I slither closer to Mads so my head is against her shoulder. Our hair blooms water into the sand. We laugh again, but there's something in it that isn't a laugh at all—

—something like a scream instead, hollow and full.

It dies but the echo doesn't.

I stare at the sun. "Did you see them?"

Mads's jaw shifts. "They were by that big window that looks out at the pool—"

"The one we broke?"

"The one we fucking smashed," she says. "They were together when we went out looking for Summer's boy."

It seeps in like the water in my lungs. The lights spinning through Duncan's house. Everything white, every room with corners hidden away, spotlights beaming down into secret alcoves with plaster-white statues of dead Roman kings—

—just enough space for a glowing girl and a dazzle-smiled boy to hide away right there with everyone watching.

"You and Jenny and Summer," I say.

"Me and Jenny and Summer," says Mads.

The silence hangs so heavy it drowns out the waves.

"We couldn't find you," she says. Her voice makes every inch of me sting.

We were together at first, Jenny and Summer and Mads and me, dancing and drinking and shining so bright the St Andrew's Preppers needed sunglasses to look at us. Then

Summer found a boy, and she chased after him and pulled Jenny with her, just their fingertips touching. We danced and we drank and we danced. The St Andrew's Preppers were everywhere, blond and tan and laced together with white powder and pills, and then Jenny was calling for Mads and me and a new song came on, loud enough to see it in the air, the best song all night. And everything was silver, and I spun away from Mads and into the middle of the biggest room. A sunken floor and a soaring ceiling with more lights beating down.

I danced. Alone. A whirl of platinum and white, too fast to catch, cutting the air and sending gold sparks flying.

And then when the song was over and I spun out to one of the niches with the dead-king statues—

I've never seen you, I've never seen anyone like you—

The dazzle-smiled boy, the only one who could watch me without going blind.

Mads grabs my hand. Pulls me back to her, to here, to now.

"I don't remember," I say. It feels like a scream, but it sounds like a whisper.

Her hand locks tighter on mine.

"The boy who gave me the drink—" I say—

I see white. Only white. The statues and the marble floor. The music. The spotlights. *What's your name?* he asked, faceless, and I said, *I'm Elle.* And he said, *Elle. Pretty name, but not as pretty as you—*

"I don't remember," I say, louder. I sit up, sword-straight, and so does Mads. The sun burns our skin so hot that the last drops of water boil to steam. "Did you see him?" I ask.

She knows who I mean. She shakes her head.

I take my hand back. It wants to shake but I don't let it. I count, one finger scarring the sand: "Duncan. Duffy. Connor. Banks."

The salt water in my lungs drips into my veins.

"The boy who mixed the drinks—Malcolm," I say. "The boy who guarded the door—Porter."

The salt water in my veins blisters through my skin.

"The boy who gave me the drink—"

Someone shrieks so piercing cold it takes my breath away.

"I have to remember," I gasp. "I have to know—"

Your eyes—he said, and then white, and the hallway, with my talons scraping the floor and the walls bending in, and Connor's iron grip—

The shriek tears the air open again.

"Jade," says Mads. "Jade, Jade, Jade—"

The shriek rips sharper. Cruel and ruinous.

"Jade," says Mads, again and again, until my shriek is a dagger that blots out the sun—

Jade, says Mads.

I stand up. My wings and my scream swallow up the sky.

BACKSTAGE

My father, the surgeon celebrities trust with their whole dead hearts, has connections.

My father, the immigrants' son who buried his father's accent so deep into the ground that political blind-callers read him the *college-educated white male* version of their script, knows how to be anyone he needs to be.

My father, the man who said *kill the boy*, will do anything to make sure his daughters get the very best lives money and sweat can buy.

I don't quite know how he does it, but when I get home Sunday afternoon there's a St Andrew's Prep uniform laid out on my bed.

I wake up so early on Monday that it still feels like night. And I text the coven even though they're sleeping, and I say, *Today St Andrew's meets its new queen.*

Mads texts back before I even set the phone down: *Take what's yours.*

The uniform is a white shirt, a blue-plaid skirt, and a blue-plaid tie. White knee socks and a navy blazer. I add my patent leather Mary Janes: Girl Scout buckles and round toes from the front, but deadly sharp heels from every other side. And I do the kind of makeup that makes boys look at you and think, *damn*, and girls look at you and think, *bitch*. Old Hollywood instead of the contoured Insta-goddess I was on Friday night. A villainess, not a heroine.

The scratches disappear with the kind of magic those lacrosse boys won't even suspect.

My lipstick is femme fatale red.

In the mirror I'm something from a two A.M. movie about Catholic schoolgirl vampires. Revenge-black hair, short and sharp; a face that says *she'll pull you to the dark side and you'll love every second of it.*

Summer texts me, *Ruin them.*

I pose and shoot until the girl on the screen has exactly the look she needs: a smile they'll read as inviting today, but tomorrow—whichever tomorrow finds them clutching at their throats and choking on blood—they'll look back and see the vengeance in it, and they'll wonder how the hell they ever missed it—

—and then they won't think another damn thing.

I post the picture to my fresh account, brand-new in person and online: *St Andrew's, you've met your match*. And I tag it just right, the same way those boys and their clinging groupie girlfriends tag everything, so they'll be talking about me before I even walk in the door.

Bold as hell.

I don't eat breakfast, but my mother gives me tea in a white cup threaded with gold, and she sits with me and lets me stay silent. When it's time to go, she hands me a heavy card. My father's handwriting loops across it under his letterhead: *Take the red car.*

My mother squeezes my hand so tight it's almost like we're only one person.

Then she lets go.

The car waits for me in the driveway, shining in the sunrise light, top down, keys in the ignition. There's a Tiffany box on the driver's seat with three lipstick kisses on the robin's-egg blue: Jenny's pink, Summer's rose, Mads's scarlet.

Inside, there's a silver crucifix on a silver chain. Bright and big and flashy.

I laugh. The noise jars the dead-stillness and a black cat streaks out of the bushes for the road.

Jenny texts me, *Bleed them dry.*

I will.

INTRODUCTIONS

I'm the very first St Andrew's Prepper in the door.

It's on purpose.

I've parked front and center, the best spot there is, so every-one walking in will see the red car and wonder who's new. St Andrew's wants to live in the Middle Ages, somewhere craggy and cloud-covered, instead of soaking in the almost-summer sunlight of SoCal in March. So behind the same sky-bound palm trees as every other building in town, there's a gray stone fortress with jutting angles and diamond-pane windows. When the door claps shut behind me I could al-most believe I'm withering away in some castle with bats in the eaves and snakes under the foundation. Secrets in the walls and girls half-dead and locked in the attic.

I'm ready.

It's dark, but not like nighttime streets or a club when the lights black out before the bass drops and shocks everyone alive. Like a crypt instead. Chandeliers drag down from the rafters and incense hazes the air. My Mary Janes click out a warning to the class pictures on the wall: row after row of sepia-tone fuckboys grinning through glass.

I go to the office first. Good little new girl. *Hello I'm Jade, I'm so beyond excited to be here, what an amazing opportunity.* They eat it up and lick their lips.

Then I swing back into the hall and hit every classroom on the schedule the thousand-year-old secretary sent to my phone. I introduce myself the exact same way each time: *Good morning,* brash enough to make them look up but polite enough that they have to smile. And then, before they can answer, *I'm the new girl. Jade Khanjara.*

They nod. They all look the same—Dr. Farris from biology, Magistra Copland from Latin, Sister María de los Dolores from religion. Books stacked like battlements and eyes that do skittish sideways glances and then settle back to blank. They're playing defense already, always, because here the students run the show. Boys like Duncan and Duffy and Connor and Banks have fathers who can pay enough to erase any ugly little blemish on their records, the same way their fathers' fathers did a generation ago.

The teachers know it's not worth saying no at St Andrew's.

But I smooth my smile out enough that they can think to themselves, *good manners, that new girl. Well-behaved.*

So they can think I'm on their side, as much as any St Andrew's girl can be.

The teachers say, *Jade, excellent, excellent,* and make neat notes on their lists, and just like that I'm Jade and Jade only, from the first time they call roll.

And someday, soon, when I'm standing in front of this castle with the palm trees and the gaudy-bright California flowers that clash hard with gray stone—

when I'm holding my long knife as it drips blood—

when the snakes slither out from under the foundations—

when Duncan and Duffy and Connor and Banks are dead and I'm queen, terrible and savage—

—all these teachers, they'll say, *oh, Jade? Jade Khanjara?* They'll pause.

And then they'll settle back into that look they're giving me this morning, and they'll say:

Lovely girl. She'd never do a thing like that.

NEW GIRL

When all the beautiful vain St Andrew's Preppers spill into the castle I'm waiting in the common hall. Right in front of the Virgin Mary statue where the lacrosse boys' girls take pictures, one after another: *#StAPstunners #blonde #prepschool-life*. The boys roll up the minute before the last bell, but the girls come in early to stand guard with Mary, full of grace. Slice and dice: who-and-who hooked up last night, who looks like a skank today, who's drinking where tonight. Unsheathe mirrors and front cameras, *oh my god I look so VILE*, and tap the screen and post the shot: *#pretty #model #LAgirl*.

Not that I'd know anything about it.

Not that I'd know all their names already. Who they hate and who they're afraid of. Who's fucking which *#StAPlax* boy. Who went to the party Friday night and watched *that little whore with the jade-green eyes* when she drank that just-for-her drink too fast and had to grab that dazzle-smiled boy's arm when the room got slow and fast and dizzy.

I'm just the new girl.

I wait by the statue with her shy downward gaze. Half a smile playing on my lips. Phone out, scrolling, not waiting for anybody.

Innocent little flower with a silver crucifix.

They show up all at once, bursting around the corner in a cloud of laughter and sick-sweet perfume. Six of them, a whole flock—fluttering and flitting left-right-left, orbiting the girl in the middle. Starlings with hollow bones and skinny legs and voices that tilt up-up-and-away—

"Oh my god did she *really*—"

"What a fucking tart—"

"Can you spell *trash*—"

They laugh too loud, a show for all the plodding not-it girls.

"Just, god, that was a party—"

"Well, what did you expect, it's Duncan we're talking about—"

Their elbows wing in, toward the girl in the middle: Duncan's girlfriend. Their queen for today, the tallest and the prettiest. She's beautiful in that about-to-break way, like a Russian runway model who lives on cigarettes and other girls' jealousy. Ice-blue eyes and flax-white hair. Her Hollywood tan almost covers up the hollows in her face.

Almost. Not quite.

"Still can't believe you blew it off, Lilia—"

—and that's her name, not Lila or Lily or Lillian: Lilia Helmsley, missing last Friday. She gave her girls a neat excuse on all their party pictures, *so bummed I'm missing it, my mom is such a Nazi for making me do this spa weekend, she's the worst*, but she's lying. She was hiding from a boy she doesn't like but can't dump because he's the king and she's the queen and she has to stay perfect.

Besides, if she dumped him, he'd tell the whole world she's a slut-dyke-cheater-prude, and he'd slam her skull against the wall until she couldn't remember he made it all up.

She's afraid of him but she can't tell him no or enough or good-bye.

She'll never stop him.

"—and I'm just saying, make sure Dunc doesn't forget what you look like, or what you can do for him. Like, I'm not saying anything *happened* Friday, but—"

Another elbow flies and the blabbermouth girl squeals, but shuts up.

"He won't," says Lilia, wan, both hands clutching her Starbucks cup. She notices me before the rest of them do. Her eyes are dead-blank but the truth sits right there anyway: she knows Duncan fucked someone else at the party.

She's glad.

I smirk.

She stops walking and her flock stops, too. The starling on her right sees me: "Who the fuck is that, and who does she think she is?"

Lilia sips her coffee and blinks slow. "New girl."

Her right-hand girl scoffs. "Let's get rid of her."

Lilia starts walking again, toward me.

"God, you're too nice," says her right-hand girl, and everyone else shrills *for real,* but they hurry up next to her anyway. What this weak little spindle-queen says, goes, as long as she's Duncan's.

Lilia floats in front of me, smiling veneers and black coffee. "You're new," she says. "I'm Lilia."

I spin my coven's crucifix between two fingers. "Jade," I say.

"You're in our spot," says the right-hand girl with a toss of honey-blond hair. Her eyes say, *get out,* and her stance says, *I'm next in line and God it's my turn,* and all Summer's online stalking says, *industry parents, smarter than most, not afraid to fight dirty.*

I spin the crucifix again. "I didn't see the sign."

Three of the minion-girls go wide-eyed and drama-starved. A fourth falls onto Lilia's arm and says, "We love her."

"Adore," the rest of them chorus.

"Jade," says Lilia. "Welcome to St Andrew's."

Then they swoop in, all of them, skirts and feathers and *hi oh my God you're going to love St Andrew's, you're lucky we found you, no offense but we're the only girls worth knowing, everybody else is just jealous, love the necklace—Tiffany, right?*

Inside. Just like that.

But the right-hand girl hangs back. "Jade," she says, tapping out the end of it with the tip of her tongue. Her left hand hooks against her hip, two fingers resting on the handle of her sabre.

Piper Morello, Duffy's girlfriend, freshly on-again after their Friday night fight. She's clawed her way up to where she is: Lilia's lady-in-waiting, captain of the fencing team, a junior who tells seniors what to do. A girl who carries a sword on her hip even in the off-season, no guard, swinging from a tie she's looped around her waist, shining sharp on her skirt and her skin. It's against all the rules and that's why she does it. So everyone knows the rules don't apply to her, in the halls of St Andrew's or the locked-tight rooms at Duncan's house.

I could love her if I didn't hate her so much.

fine, go fuck some roofied slut, said Piper Morello on Friday night—

see if I give a shit, said Piper Morello in the doorway harping at second-place Duffy—

you're worthless anyway, said Piper Morello while everything spun and I tried to separate up from down, tried to scream, tried to rip my arm out of Duncan's grip, got a hand around my throat for the trouble—

you deserve each other, bon fucking voyage and I hope you get chlamydia, said the same Piper Morello who won last semester's Outstanding Citizenship award.

"New girl," says Piper Morello now, Monday morning in the common hall with her sabre slivering the air into jagged little pieces. "Where'd you come from?"

"Hell," I say before I can stop myself.

Lilia blinks again. The flock nudges like they're not sure if they should laugh.

"Boarding school," I say. "New Hampshire. Boring as shit. Cold as shit. They kicked me out." I spin the crucifix once more: third time's a charm. "*Deo gratias*, honestly."

The First-Communion-purest of them gasps but Lilia giggles a tiny high-pitched trill and then they all join in.

Except Piper. "Kicked out," she says. "Keep it classy." And then, "Why?"

I shrug. "Fucked a teacher."

This time they all gasp, but it's a shivery-excited gasp. A *this-girl-doesn't-mess* gasp.

Piper stays steady. "You'd think he'd be the one to take the hit for that. Not you."

And I say, "You'd think."

Lilia takes a long sip of coffee. Leaves a barely-there coral crescent on the lid. She says, "No, you wouldn't."

But nobody hears it, not one single girl, because they're all hissing and giggling back and forth about bold-bitch Jade.

Except Piper, narrow-eyed, two more fingers on her sabre now.

"You fence," I say before she can make her next move.

"I'm captain of the girls' team," she says. "State champion."

I smile. "For now."

She laughs and her amber eyes spark. "Find someone who

can beat me. Nobody can. Not even the boys." Her grin sharpens. "Unless you're saying you can."

She's fiercer than I thought she'd be and I'm glad. She'll fight hard. "It's the off-season."

"It's never the off-season," she says, and her fingers tap down one-two-three-four on the handle. "Not for winners. I'll take you on whenever you think you're ready."

I tip my chin and say, "*Prête.*"

And her grin goes thrill-white and she says, "*Allez.*"

"Piper," Lilia sighs out—everything she says is a sigh. "You *exhaust* me."

Her flock flutters their yeses.

Piper claps one arm around Lilia's shoulders and Lilia stumbles a step. "Everything exhausts you, babe," Piper says, antifreeze-sweet. "You do too much."

"Probably," says Lilia. "But so do you."

I like her a little more because of that.

Piper gives Lilia a look that says, *I can't wait until you're over.* Then she shifts back to me: "Did you fence for—what was your old school?"

"No," I say. I don't give anything away. In ten minutes when she's sitting in English, she'll get my last name from someone in my biology class and she'll stalk me like we stalked her, but she won't find anything. I'm invisible now.

And anyway, it's true. I never fenced for Hillview. Never joined Latin Club or the Indian Student Association. My days and nights and weekends went to my coven: lounging across Summer's king-sized bed, all four of us tangled together, long arms and long legs and wearing each other's clothes, scrolling through gossip and lies. Or sitting high up in the bleachers watching Hillview boys play football or lacrosse.

Or flying up the coast in Mads's Mustang, loud music and knotting hair and restless dauntless boredom.

After-school activities are for losers with curfews.

"Then where?" Piper asks.

"France," I say. Let her figure out I'm lying, eventually. Turn her paranoid and let everyone else decide she's a bitch with a vendetta. They'll side with me when I'm done with her.

"Paris?"

I stay coy. "Does it matter?"

Her beading gaze locks tighter. "I know you."

I laugh at her.

She bristles. "I do. I know you."

"I'm sure you don't." I slip a glance to the rest of them and they shift and smirk. They want her cut down almost as much as she wants to climb even higher.

"I know you," she says again, blind to them. "I'll remember—"

"*Piper*," Lilia breathes out in a long limp rush of air. "Chill."

"Yeah," says one of the flock-girls. "Chill."

That makes Piper turn. Leaning forward, so her sabre swings in front of her. She gives the flock-girl a look that's fire and scorn, right in front of Lilia's face while Lilia's buried in her phone.

If Lilia wasn't standing right there, a fragile paper peace-keeper, Piper would send that flock-girl to the guillotine this second.

"You too, sweetie," says Piper.

Lilia looks up and Piper settles back into line. "Well," she sighs out, and then she pauses so long her starlings almost suffocate holding their breath for her. "Jade doesn't want to be late on her first day."

"Maybe she does," says Piper. And then, "Let's wait for the

boys. You know they're going to love a girl like Jade." Her eyes track down my body and back up again: *Slut.*

Exactly what I want her to think.

But she slides a look to Lilia, too, and says, "Besides, you want to see Duncan." She turns it into a test: *you're avoiding him, aren't you? Shitty girlfriend. Shitty queen. Count your days.*

"I'll see him at lunch," she says. "Come on, Jade. I'll walk you to class."

I'm not ready to go yet. Not until I see the golden boys with their curling smiles and their crooked ties. A crosse clipped to each backpack. Ready to swing and hit and kill.

"Whatever you say, Lili," says Piper with a smile so plastic I can't believe Lilia swallows it without choking. "I'll kiss Dunc for you."

Lilia's eyes catch mine for a second again: *do. And keep him.* "You're the best," she tells Piper, and she links her elbow with mine, bone and nerve and frozen-slow blood. "Come on, Jade—"

The boys come in.

The whole room changes. All the St Andrew's Preppers clustering around the columns in the common hall, all the chitter-chatter energy and show-off laughter—it all goes quieter, stiller, watchful. The floors glow hot and the chandeliers flare from gold to blue-white—

—earthquake weather and earthquake light—

—and there's a tremor, but only barely. Just enough that everyone pretends they don't notice. But they do.

The boys swing around the corner the same way the girls did. All at once and inseparable. But the girls were a flock of birds, and the boys are a pack of wolves. Their smiles are bolted into place and their teeth are so square-straight it jars.

Duncan. Duffy. Connor. Banks.

The crowd parts for them. They stalk straight toward Lilia and Piper and their girls. Next to me, Lilia freezes to stone.

"Duff!" Piper squeals, and the flock prisses, and the boys yell louder than they need to.

Duncan shoves Duffy. "Still haven't taught her how to shut up yet, huh, Duff?"

Piper laughs on demand. Fake, but they don't care.

Jesus, Duff, Duncan said on Friday, *shut the bitch up—*

My skin fires so hot Lilia thaws.

"Come on, Jade," she says, the third time now, and out of nowhere she's stronger than Piper and dragging me off to the left, through a vaulted entryway, into an empty hall. Shoving all her featherweight nothing against a door and pulling me after her.

The door claps shut.

She locks it.

We're alone in a girls' room with a slanting ceiling and a too-big mirror, magnified, so we can see our flaws up close.

She still has my hand. Our arms are pressed together, inside-wrist to inside-wrist. Her pulse flutters too fast. We watch us in the mirror.

Then: "God," she says. "God *damn.*"

"What the hell?" I say, because new-girl Jade doesn't know anything.

She says it again, louder, and then she frays into a high uneven laugh that lasts too long.

this bitch almost makes me miss Lilia's starfish shit, said Duncan on Friday night.

give her a minute, said Banks, *she'll be gone—*

"God!" says Lilia, and she cuts off her laugh and pulls her hand out of mine. Her palm drips thin blood. I've cut three claw-marks into her skin.

We both look back into the mirror. The blood runs down her hands. Each streak takes one finger: index, middle, ring. Her eyes measure the silence.

I smile my St Andrew's smile and say, "Stigmata."

She scatters into giggling gasps again. "Jade."

I take her wrist and pull her to the sink. Three red drops bead up on her fingertips and fall all in a row onto the porcelain.

"Pretty," Lilia breathes, so soft she's mostly thinking it.

"What the hell?" I say again.

"Just—" she starts, and then she goes quiet for a second. "I'm alive, that's all."

I spin the faucet handles and they screech. The three drops wash away and my hand guides Lilia's under the water.

She finds me in the mirror again and says, "*We're* alive."

"Lilia," I say, "you're fucking crazy."

Her fingers twine into mine, wet and cold. "So are you."

I don't tell her she's wrong.

Her eyes drift wider and float and focus sharp at last. She says, "I can tell."

REUNION

"You chose the perfect boy," says Summer, after school.

"Too perfect," says Jenny.

"The perfect target," says Mads.

We're standing against the south wall of St Andrew's, shadowed in a stone alcove, looking down the golf-course-grass slope to the field. Dark sunglasses and internet intel. "I know," I say.

"But like, *really*," Summer tells me, scrolling. "He's totally spotless, reputation-wise."

Jenny wrinkles her nose. "You're doing him a favor, getting him to kill all his friends. He's boring as fuck right now."

"Not boring," says Summer. "Honorable."

The rest of us laugh. Jenny says, "God, Summer, you're such a romantic."

"He *is*," says Summer. "He's the least asshole boy on the whole team."

Jenny runs her tongue over her teeth. "The whole team roofies girls."

"I'm just saying, if everyone he knows does this shit, if they've been doing this shit since before it was even them, and it's just—the way things *are*, but he doesn't, he *won't*—"

"It's not a fucking *cult*."

Summer's eyebrows arch. "Close enough, don't you think?"

"No," says Jenny with a little scoff.

"Look." Summer holds her phone out to us. She has a whole album saved already, the grid filling up the screen: *GOLDEN BOYS*. She clicks on a post: Duncan and Duffy and Connor and Banks at a party, arms draped over each other's shoulders, a liquor bottle gleaming in Duncan's hand. Duffy's caption says, *To the nights we won't remember.* Connor's comment, right below, says, *we will, she won't.* It's not from Friday; it's not even from this year.

"Okay, fine, so call it a cult," Jenny says, nudging against Summer. "And our boy still rolls with them."

"He doesn't do what they do." Summer scrolls and scrolls, past Duncan and Duffy and Connor and Banks, past Duncan's little brother who mixed the drinks on Friday night, past boys from last year and the year before, off studying prelaw and economics now. All slinging comments and collecting hearts on every post. "He won't. He'll never really be one of them."

"He doesn't stop them, either," says Jenny. "Very fucking honorable."

A breeze curls around us in the shadows, hot pavement and freeway exhaust. "He wants to be honorable, but not as much as he wants approval," says Mads, staring down at the painted-green field. "He'll sell out enough to stay in with them, but he can still pretend he's innocent."

The first few St Andrew's Preppers are winding down the path to the bleachers. The away team bus pulls up: tinted windows, shiny red-white-blue paint, VIKINGS blazing along the side. "He'll sell out to take Duncan's place," I say. "He's ambitious."

"He's weak," says Jenny, and she steals Summer's phone, and Summer lets her.

"Both," says Summer. "Once Jade gets in his head, he'll do anything she tells him to do."

I'm smiling too wide but I don't care.

"Jade has an eye," says Mads. "She could see all that just from the picture. Before we spent all weekend digging up their secrets."

My smile stretches wider.

Jenny laughs into whatever golden-boy portrait she's flipping past. "God, I love it."

"Just," says Summer, "are you sure?" She's lip-biting the way she does whenever she's worried about something.

"That's cute," says Jenny, and her eyes linger on Summer's until Summer does a movie-perfect blush. "Cute that you feel so bad for this asshole and not for all those boys you've black-widowed."

Summer still blushes. "That was different."

"Damn straight it was different. You were just bored. Jade's crusading."

"I *know* the boys I ruin," says Summer.

"And I know the boys I'm about to ruin," I say. Lilia's name lights up on my screen: *Meeting at the field in five, see you there?*

"Not him," says Summer.

Mads finally looks away from the field. "If Jade says he's a target, he's a target."

I leave Lilia on read and face them, all three of them, against the gray stone. "He's a target," I say.

Mack, the honorable sellout. Strong—and ambitious—and brave—

—but still so fucking weak it turns my stomach.

"Are you in?" I ask even though I don't need to.

"Yes," says Jenny.

"Yes," says Summer.

"Yes," says Mads.

The breeze curls up again, hot and greedy. "Go," I tell them. "Exactly like we planned it."

We clasp hands for one heartbeat. All four of us, ready for war.

I walk out into the sun, alone.

VARSITY

We sit in the very front row, on display. Lilia, the queen about to shatter. Piper on her right. New-girl Jade on her left. The flock fanning out on either side and one row back, whispers and laughing and unbuttoning one-two-three lower than they can get away with in the hall.

I unbutton one more than that and loosen my tie so the knot hits just under the made-you-look V. My silver crucifix glows against my skin.

New-girl Jade is brazen and brash and everybody already knows it.

"Game day on your first day. Lucky bitch," says a flock-girl, poking between Lilia and me. "Have you ever—"

"The boys." Piper cuts her off, so much sugar in her voice that Lilia's lips do an anxious little twist. "Let's tell her about the boys."

"She's going to meet them right after the game," says Lilia.

"Seriously," the first flock-girl says. "So thirsty, Piper. God."

Piper doesn't bother turning to whoever said it. "I've already got Duffy," she says. "Just looking out for the new girl. In case she'll slum it with a high school boy."

"If I find the right one," I say.

"Oh!" says Lilia, not even a sigh. Awake enough that I check her hands first, for blood. But she's sifting through her bag and she comes back out with a lipstick that uncaps to rotting bright St Andrew's blue. She draws one line on each cheekbone, under her eyes. Then she paints her right-hand girl, and Piper preens like Lilia's anointing her.

"We're going to kill them," says Piper.

Lilia turns to me, on purpose, a spark almost like life in her dead eyes. *So are you,* she said when I said *you're fucking crazy.* Like she already knew. Like she knows I'll be the one who does the killing.

But then she stripes the lipstick across my cheeks, left-right, cold war-paint.

She doesn't know anything. She's dead and empty.

Past her, Piper says, "Doesn't take much to get on your good side anymore, does it?"

"It's not a *competition,*" Lilia sighs.

Piper nudges her too hard. "Everything's a competition, sweetie. You know that better than anybody, don't you?"

Lilia can swat away the rest of Piper's needling bites, but this one lands. "Piper, God—" she starts, but then—

The St Andrew's boys run out onto the field, fists and crosses, yelling loud. The whole flock flies up, and everyone behind us, too.

Right this blistering second the little field feels like a whole goddamn colosseum.

I'm on my feet. Screaming in my blue war-paint. Screaming with Lilia and Piper. Screaming so hard my throat bleeds.

Duncan—

—the alpha boy, leading the charge, eyes a startling piercing gray that sears everything he looks at even with his helmet in place. The boy whose father ruled this field once upon a time and whose brother will rule it next. The boy who holds all the power, the same way his family does, and decides who joins the pack. The best, the fastest, the one they all watch and obey—

Next to me, Lilia slips and grabs at Piper's arm. Piper wrenches away and her sabre slashes the space between them and glances off Lilia's thigh. She stops screaming to look down, and there's a hair-thin red line on her skin. She screams again, louder.

Duffy—

—the favorite, the one who'd hide the body for Dunc if he killed. *If.* Piper's perfect match. She shrieks so shrill for him that he turns and sees her and raises his fist. Piper stops for a breath and catches my arm behind Lilia's back and says, "Jealous yet?"

Connor—

—the worst of them. The ugliest, the one everybody knows does the kind of shit only blond boys with director-producer fathers can get away with, the one who came so close to admitting it on Duffy's Friday-night picture, *damm banks, the slut did some cat scratch shit on ur arm, fukkin wild,* that I can't believe the rest of them haven't taken him out themselves to keep their own names clean—

Banks—

—the biggest, towering tall and broad-shouldered. A defenseman. The kind of hair-trigger brute who can slam his fist against the spot where your ribs join together and you'll forget how to breathe—

The rest of them: Porter, the goalkeeper, the one who guarded the door. Malcolm, Malcolm Duncan, the skinny sophomore who told his big brother *yeah, I'm sure they'll work, made the fucking drink myself.* Ross and Lennox and Seward and O'Donnell: nobodies who don't matter.

And Mack. Square-shouldered and clean-cut and *honorable,* eyes right ahead.

The boys from the white-sheets room on my sweet sixteen. All of them, and their ride-or-die brothers. Charging across the field in blue and white and battle yells.

I'm supposed to be afraid of them. Forget everything I thought I felt and collapse right here, weaker than Lilia.

I scream louder.

The boys circle together next to their benches, right in front of us. Close enough that if I wanted to, I could jam Piper's sword into Connor's throat before anybody could think about stopping me. If I went fast I could get Duffy, too, before the rest of them threw me down.

For a second everything flashes red. Stains that bloom from their chests and turn the whole field warm and metallic.

I raise one fist, just like Duffy did, and I scream with all my might. The boys crush close, yelling, crosses up and cracking together. Duncan and Duffy and Connor and Banks.

I know it better than I've ever known anything: every second in my whole life has just been practice for what I'll do to these boys.

This is why I'm alive.

THE BATTLE

Summer was right. I was right.

Mack is perfect.

Duncan's the best on the team. Flashy and bold. An attack-man who gets the goals and the glory. Duffy is his faithful eager dog, right there with every assist. Banks and Connor level the Vikings on the other end of the field, harder than they have to, and they slam chest-to-chest themselves just as hard every time the calls go their way.

But Mack runs the whole field. In better shape than all of them, even Duncan, and hungrier than all of them, even Duffy. He's where they need him to be before they figure it out. And he's the kind of good-game good-boy who puts out a hand for the boys from the other team when they're gasping at the sky from one of Banks's hits.

The crowd doesn't notice him like they notice Duncan and Duffy and Connor and Banks. But Duncan and Duffy and Connor and Banks notice, and by the third quarter they're punching him so hard I can see the proud bruises through his jersey.

When it feels right, I lean over to Lilia and say, "That boy," and point. "Who is he?"

They shriek, all of them: *Jade oh my God I knew it!*

"Mack," says Piper before anyone else can. "Well, I mean, you shouldn't call him that. Not yet."

"Yeah, same," chirps one of the flock-girls, but Piper doesn't bother with her.

Lilia takes my arm again. "Andrew Mack," she tells me. "He's good."

"You'd know," says Piper.

Lilia turns toward me so one sharp shoulder cuts in front of her right-hand girl. "The boys," she says. "You have to watch yourself with them. But not him."

Piper's never-shutting-up next to her, *damn, Lili, you're such a drama queen, like you haven't fucked the whole team, like you ever do anything except forget the way things actually happened so you can keep on playing Sister Holier-Than-Everybody,* until finally Lilia snaps, "God, Piper, just shut *up* for once, okay?" and she docs.

Then Lilia turns to me again. "He's single," she says.

I know.

"He's smart. In all the honor societies."

I know.

"He's a damn good middie. He might even beat Duffy out for captain next year."

I know.

"You can trust him."

I could, but I won't. So I tilt my head and ask, "Why isn't he one of them?"

She blinks shutter-fast and looks away. "I don't know what you mean."

"Yes, you do," says Piper, acidic. "And to answer your question, new girl, because he won't put the team first."

So I quote Lilia: "I don't know what you mean."

Her gaze lingers, ember and spite. "You will."

"*Piper,*" says Lilia. Watching the boys; watching Duncan, but not because she loves him. "Don't." And then, to me: "I'll introduce you to Mack. After. He'll like you, I think—"

Duncan swerves past a Viking and scores again and everyone jumps up to scream his name.

Mads texts me, *Ready.*

When all the girls settle back in, I say, "I'll be right back." Lilia flutters up again and I wave her off and pin her in place with a smile.

I walk around to the back of the bleachers. At the corner, leaning against the wall with one baby-blue high-top hitched up against the stone, there's Jenny texting. Sunglasses so dark you can't see where she's looking. She doesn't say anything and neither do I.

I round the next corner, and there's Summer in floaty silver chiffon walking figure-eights by the bathroom doors, purring into her phone, "I told you I'll be there. Twenty minutes, okay?" She almost walks into me, and she puts one hand up to her lips and goes, "Oh my god, I'm so sorry! I didn't even *see* you," and disappears back into the call: "No, nothing, just some girl—"

In the bathroom, I fake-fix my hair. It doesn't need fixing. It's shiny and unruinable. But I run my hands through it anyway, until a cluster of lower-school girls trips in spilling he-said she-saids and one of them whispers too loud, "That's the new girl. Lilia loves her."

My alibi.

I text the coven, *Ready.*

The lower-school girls slam their stall doors. The locks click into place: one-two-three.

Jenny says, *Clear.*

Summer says, *Clear.*

Mads says, *Clear.*

I walk out, long strides, light slashing across my eyes. Past Summer telling next week's ex, "—black lace, yeah, new, yeah, soon, if you're good." Around the last corner. Mads waits by the tennis courts in whitest-whites, spinning a killer-blue racket in one hand.

She nods.

I open the door set into the stone with VARSITY nailed over it. Unlocked, because no one would fucking dare.

The locker room is dark except for the light from two narrow windows high-up. I snake through their things: ties and shoes and a liquor bottle not even hidden. They have polished wood shelves and brass hooks but everything belongs to them, so everything spills out onto the benches and the floor.

Connor's pile is the last one at the end. A blue-and-white team bag and a satchel with his monogram branded into leather so soft my skin crawls. I want to slash it open. Rip the leather apart, and then the whole locker room.

But I have to be patient.

His phone is buried under textbooks and a stray cuff link, getting ruined. He doesn't have to give a fuck. He can smash anything he wants, be careless and violent and dirty, and tomorrow he'll have something new to break. He's the kind of fuckboy prick who doesn't even bother looking for his phone if it goes missing. The kind who doesn't lock it, because he's spilled all his secrets already.

The kind who doesn't check to make sure he has everything when he heads out after a game.

Besides, nobody trusts him. He's the one who lets the boy-talk leak out of the locker room; the one who pulls out bribes in broad daylight; the one who isn't dazzle-smiled or square-jawed enough to smooth things over. He makes the rest of them uneasy. Duncan only keeps him around for blunt force, on the field and off. And—

if I'm right, and I know I am—

—because good-king Duncan, *damn-she's-feisty* Duncan, knows someday he'll need a boy to blame.

He's got one.

On Saturday, after all the St Andrew's Preppers had stumbled home, after all the best pictures were up, Connor said on some second-string boy's blurring dance-floor shot—

another party, another slut down lol

The second-string boy wrote back: *get your trophy?*

And Connor said, *always do.*

The second-string boy said, *pics.*

Connor said, *dunc would kill me lmao.*

The second-string boy said, *dm me?*

And Connor said, *done.*

Here I am, two days later, with his phone in my hands. Standing in their hazed-dark secret place and opening his message to the second-string boy.

He said, *u cant tell dunc u know.*

And the second-strong boy said, *bro you were yelling about her all night.* Then, *pics, u promised.*

And Connor said, *u think im fukkin high? no phones in the room. dunc's rules.*

The second-string boy said, *bet Dunc's rules say no trophies too.*

Connor said, *dammm.* And then, *tru tho.* And then, *check it out lmao.*

He sent a picture, off-center but searing clear: an old St Andrew's tie, hanging crooked over a bookshelf. The silk scarred with a constellation of earrings. A white pearl, a silver hoop, a gold stud. Half a dozen of them.

The one at the bottom, centered between the points, is gold and crystal and mine. He plucked it off of my ear before we were even in that white-sheets room. Porter, at the door, said something that melted down the walls, so I couldn't understand it, and Connor said, *fuck what Dunc says.*

I zip Connor's phone into my purse. Then I take out the other gold-and-crystal earring, the one still left when they left me.

Connor's this-year tie hangs halfway through his collar and halfway across his duffel bag. I poke the earring into the bottom of the tie, right between the points. Exactly like the one in the picture.

He won't even notice.

Poor Connor.

He'll be the first to die.

When I stand up everything looks exactly how I found it. I take one step toward the door and my phone buzzes. Jenny says, *Someone's coming.*

I don't have time to get out. He'll see me coming around the corner.

I text, *Who?*

My eyes flurry around the half-dark. I want to hide where I can see him, but there's nothing out here besides the benches and the shelves and all their wolf-pack debris.

Summer sends a picture: one lone boy passing her post, blurred and looking over his shoulder. It's Malcolm, the good-king's little brother, shorter and skinnier but with the same glittering gray eyes and almost-black hair. The same fucking smirk.

Malcolm, the boy who bought the poison and mixed the drinks.

Mads texts, *Get out!*

I say, *Staying*, and I slip around the corner to the showers.

There's nowhere to hide.

No dividers. No curtains. Just a stretch of smooth white tile, and four showerheads poking out of the wall to the left, and four sinks to the right under a high window where the light bleeds in. And at the other end of the room, two urinals and one stall.

The locker room door bangs open. I fly across the tile, weightless and gliding on my toes so my heels don't click. Slide into the stall and pull the door almost-shut. Step up onto the porcelain, on just my toes again, left hand balancing me against the wall. Tap my phone over to silent and press the screen against my skirt so it won't light up and give me away, crouched and waiting in the shadows while a boy I'm not afraid to kill fucks around one wall over.

He's mumbling to himself. Unzipping a bag and knocking something to the floor.

made the fucking drink myself, said Malcolm on Friday night. Grinning from the doorway, leaning in front of zit-faced Porter.

you know I trust my dealer, said Malcolm, flashing his teeth, flashing a gleam in his gunmetal-gray eyes, *you know his pills are always what he says they are—*

"Jesus, I called you now, didn't I?" says Malcolm on the other side of the wall. "In the middle of the fucking game, too. Coach is pissed, and all because you won't just let me text, or just give me a minute—"

give her a minute, said Banks to Malcolm on Friday night, *she'll be gone—*

"Fuck," says Malcolm right now. "Don't even read that shit. It's Connor, man. He's sloppy but my brother keeps him in line. Sure as hell won't come back on you when you're just the fucking dealer. And anyway, the bitch won't say any-

thing. They never do." He laughs at nobody and my nails bite
into the wall so hard they almost stick. I'm this-damn-close
to falling; this-damn-close to knocking the door open and
shouting Malcolm's name—

Or better: whispering it. Murmuring it, a low sweet call.
Luring him in.

A room this white needs a little blood to wake it up.

But that's not the plan. And I'm not ruining the plan for a
boy like Malcolm.

I dig my claws in and keep my balance.

He mumbles under his breath. He takes his time, lets his
dealer go off, because good-prince sophomores have all the
time in the world. Humming to himself, almost. I watch the
end of the shower room, the space where his wolf-song bends
around the corner, and think, *soon, soon, soon.*

Not soon enough.

The humming stops. Everything stops, for a dead-bloated
second. Silent enough that I could think I was alone again.

Then his shoes yelp on the tile and there he is, a long thin
slice of him in the crack between the hinges, ambling over
to the second sink and spinning it on to fill a bottle too fast,
phone crammed against one shoulder. Humming again. The
light from the high window catches in his hair and gives him
a silver-white halo.

He's ten feet away from me. Maybe twelve. Gulping water
fast and careless with his dealer in his ear.

Him and me. Alone. And he's the weakest of all of them—

He stops humming again.

He turns and scans the back of the room. For a second he
stares right at me. His eyes linger too long. His teeth chew at
his bottom lip, star-bright and unsettling.

I don't blink. I don't breathe. I'm predator-still in the shadows, and he's half-blind from facing the windows, and I know what I'm up against and he doesn't.

"Yeah, and I'm done with you, too," Malcolm says into the phone, trying on his brother's voice. "Yeah, fuck you, too. Later."

He hangs up and walks out. The door bangs open-shut and I lose my balance and clatter to the floor.

When I'm sure he's gone I push the door open and check myself in the same mirror Malcolm used. St Andrew's Prep Jade is still perfect, from her war-paint to her crucifix to her slutty unbuttoned blouse. Not quite tall enough to catch a halo of light, even in my heels.

Good.

My phone lights up. *Clear,* says Mads.

Clear, says Summer, a second later.

Clear, says Jenny, finally.

I tell them, *Done. Your turn.*

PROPHECY

Our golden wolves win, a victory at the very last second—

—Mack flying down the field so fast not one single Viking can catch him, hurling the ball to Duncan; Duncan slipping through two defensemen and leaving them to crash into each other while he runs for the goal and scores right as the clock runs out. They come in bloody and shouting, right in front of us again. The whole pack shining with sweat and glory.

Lilia breathes out, "Thank fuck."

The boys push Mack and Duncan into the middle of the pack. The good-king hits Mack hard across the back. "Damn, that was a beautiful assist. Saved our asses from all the shit Connor let by."

Connor's lips curl. He hits Duncan harder than he needs to and his almost-black eyes hitch over to the flock-girls and he says, "Luck's a whore. She fucks us all eventually."

Then Duncan and Duffy come over and sweep Lilia and Piper off their feet. Lilia's shoulders go rigid but Piper wraps python-tight around Duffy, her spray-tan against his sweat, his crosse and her sabre swinging.

The rest of the starlings hover around the boys they like best, big-eyed and high-pitched. A whirl of flattery and plans for after until the coach yells at the pack to hit the locker room, and then they run off, spinning to look back at the girls, helmets loose in their hands. Connor drags behind. He's last-place and he knows it.

I keep my eyes on him until he notices. Until he stares back. Until he rakes his almost-black eyes across every inch of me; until his lips curl again.

I don't look away. The girls flit beside me and behind me, *Lilia, Lilia, I'm riding with you, right? It's my turn,* but I'm still and unblinking and watching Connor hold onto the stare for longer than he should. Until the heel of one cleat catches and he stumbles, and his sneer turns to a snarl, and he spits one last narrowed-eye glare at me and disappears after his friends—the ones who don't trust him.

"Jade, you're with me," says Lilia in her smoke-thin voice. But still a command.

Piper sucks air between her teeth and says, "Fucking hell, Lili. When did you start giving to charity?"

Lilia blinks, mascara-heavy hummingbird wings. "When did you start telling me who my friends are?"

The rest of them breathe in the drama so hard their lungs almost burst.

I say, "I'll drive myself."

Their shiny bird-eyes flick back and forth, Lilia-me-Lilia-me, waiting for her to knock me back down to where new girls belong.

She smiles, faint. "I'll text you the address."

Piper laughs loud and grabs my arm with one quick hand. Her fingers press into the bruises under my sleeve—Duffy's fingerprints, her next-in-line boyfriend, the one who said on Friday night, *shit, who knew there was a bitch out there worse than mine?*

"Jade," says Piper. Just that one word.

"Piper."

They're leaving now, the rest of them, gathering up their things and pecking out texts and jostling for the place closest to Lilia. Piper is the only one who isn't falling over herself to beg for Lilia's right-hand seat.

She waits until they're ten steps toward the gate—until Lilia looks over her shoulder and says, "Piper? You're with me."

And Piper levels me a hard amber stare. "You know I am."

She wings up next to Lilia. Their elbows link. The breeze slices across the field and swirls their hair together, blond on blonder, and the sun glints off Piper's blade. They glow, all of them, brighter than they should.

I watch them go—

—and I wait for Mack.

But first it's my coven's turn. Everything has to happen exactly the way I want it.

I text them, *It's time.*

Then I climb the bleachers, to the highest row on the right-hand side, nothing behind me and nothing below. I don't see Jenny or Summer or Mads, but I'm not supposed to. Not yet. And I know they're exactly where I told them to be, waiting.

The moment bleeds out: golden light playing across the field and shadows growing on the lawn. The air clings close. The last St Andrew's Preppers are gone and I'm alone.

I slip Connor's phone out of my purse.

Duncan and Duffy are the first boys out of the locker room, passing almost underneath me, so close I could drop my long knife straight down and sink it into their shoulders. Connor trails behind them, and then Porter.

I find Banks's texts on Connor's phone, *Bank$* with a dollar sign. The last message Connor sent was Saturday noon, *last nite was wild, shoulda got her fukkin number,* and Banks wrote back the second he got it: *Keep your mouth shut or I tell Dunc.* And Connor again: *chill.*

I text Banks—Connor texts Banks—*lost the slut's earring in the locker room.*

The reply pops up with no pause: *You better be joking.*

I text back, *nah.*

Banks says, *You're so close to dead.*

I say, *you too if you don't find it.*

He says, *Fuck you.*

I say, *no thx.*

He says, *Dunc's gonna give you hell.*

I say, *worth it.*

And then I scroll until I find *Mack* further down Connor's messages. I tell him, *show this to banks.*

I send the same picture Connor sent the second-string boy: his trophied tie. One text to knot Mack together with the wolves before they all fall apart. One picture to crack Connor's secrets open.

The screen goes black.

Banks fires back, like clockwork: *FUCK you, you'll pay.*

Exactly as furious as I want him to be with boasting shameless Connor.

Malcolm and his second-rank pack walk out, and the last stragglers. Banks and Mack are the only boys left in the locker room.

A minute passes and then another. Past the front lawn, a siren shrills.

Then Mack walks out with Banks. Their heads are conspiracy-close but I catch Banks's words, high and tight: "—when Dunc gets him alone—"

Mack cuts him off: "I'll talk to him."

And Banks laughs, and it echoes under the bleachers. "You don't know shit."

They're almost to the corner now. I set Connor's phone down and text the coven on mine: *Now.*

And then they appear, all three of them, almost out of nowhere, and stand three-in-a-row across the path to the parking lot. They wear the same St Andrew's colors they wore when they hid in plain sight all through the game: Jenny in her blue crop top, Summer in silver, Mads in crisp white.

The same, except for the masks. White satin and jeweled and matching, left over from the party Summer threw last

New Year's Eve. Turning my coven as faceless as the dazzle-smiled boy.

They stand unmoving. In the almost-sunset light their shadows are long and wicked.

Banks stops hard.

They say it together, Jenny and Summer and Mads, their voices floating up to me—

Mack, their time is up

—and Banks takes a step back and says, "What is this shit?"

They speak again:

Mack, your time is here

—and the boys look at each other, and Banks remembers who he's supposed to be. He bites off a laugh, hard and mocking. But he's nervous: I can see it wavering on the air like summer heat. "Somebody's fucking with you," he tells Mack. "Come on, let's—"

"Connor will fall," says Jenny.

"You'll take his place," says Summer.

"And then you'll take Duncan's," says Mads.

Banks starts in on another dig, but Mack takes a step forward, shoulders strong and straight. "Who sent you?"

"To the nights we won't remember," says Jenny: the words from that Friday night picture.

"No," says Summer. "*They* will—"

And Mads says, burning cold: "She won't."

Banks stops laughing.

"Who sent you?" Mack asks again. "Are you—"

"Get the hell out," says Banks. "Or—"

Tires squeal and Duncan's white Escalade slams to a stop at the gate and Duffy yells, "Banks, we're leaving your ass!"

Banks's head jerks up and he hisses out, "Watch your backs, you and whoever sent you." And he shoves past them and jogs for the car. The back door swings open for him and he slides in and slams it hard and yells, "Fuck that shit, Mack!"

They're gone.

I pick up Connor's phone again and text Mack:

she won't.

He looks over his shoulder, just the way he's supposed to. Looking for Connor, even though he knows Connor is gone. Looking for whoever heard the coven's coiling words.

I stand up, here at the top of the bleachers, and the sun sets me on fire.

My coven disappears as spirit-smooth as they came in, melting into the shadows while Mack stares up at me; while I take each step down the bleachers with the kind of watch-me walk he couldn't look away from even if he wanted to. While he puts one hand up to shade his eyes even though I'm the one looking straight into the sun.

He doesn't break the stare and neither do I until I get to the bottom of the steps and the wall at the edge of the bleachers blocks him out. And then I take one spun-out second to let the adrenaline soak in and stay. Let the blood rush hard under my skin but keep the smile airbrush-smooth on my face.

I turn the corner and there he is, closer than before, waiting for me. Golden Mack. Our eyes lock—

My breath catches in my throat.

I don't fall for boys. Not at first sight, not dancing close, not ever. I don't believe in love or meant-for-each-other or *chemistry*, whatever that means, when Summer talks about the look some oily-eyed thirty-year-old is giving her from across the club. *It's called lust, that's literally it*, Jenny told her, two days before the football player drove over the cliff, and I said, *exactly, and it's all you,* because it was and she knew it. We all know it, my coven and me, and every girl who's ever walked into a room and made every head turn: how to make boys think we want them, so then they want us, too. How to make them do anything we say.

It's power.

And we decide it, us girls, if we know anything about anything.

I decide who wants me. And I'd never be weak enough to want them back. Never be weak enough to want them for anything more than what they can get me. The night I want. Or the answers to the test I didn't study for because I was running wild with my coven instead. Or the key to ruining all the boys who need ruining.

I decide how it ends.

Every night except one.

But right now—

swimming in the gold-dust light, with my eyes and his locked together, staring into the earnest leaf-green sea-green summer-green and seeing the golden boy I'm supposed to see instead of the wolf he is—

—I could forget that this is all just a plot. Make myself fall for him, if I wanted to. The same way I'll make him fall for me. The same way I'll make him fall.

But I don't forget.

It's a spell, but only for him. On him.

He'll speak first. I decide that.

I count it in my head, *one-two-three,* and then he says, "Jade." I smile—I let myself smile. And his cheeks go a little red. "Lilia's friend. Right?"

"Just Jade," I tell him. I'm nobody's friend here. "And you're Andrew."

"It's Mack," he says, even though Piper told me *you shouldn't call him that. Not yet.*

"Mack," I say, and I take one more step, so we're almost toe to toe. I have to look up to keep the gaze, and I do: a proud chin-tilt that makes the chopped ends of my hair brush back across my blouse. I look straight into his eyes and I say, "You won the game."

"It was all of us," he says.

"Don't be so modest."

"Dunc got the points. Banks kept them down. Duff went hard. Connor—"

"Connor almost lost it for everybody. Until you saved them."

He stays quiet.

"You won the game," I say again. "Duncan said it, too."

He's trying not to admit it, but I can see the pride about to break through his loyal-soldier mask.

My fingers graze his arm. The shock electrocutes us both and the sky flickers brighter for one shattered second.

"You won," I tell him: third time's a charm.

He smiles, finally, and it lights him up—

green eyes and ruddy-tan skin and blond hair a little too long and tangling, and tall and strong and ready to take Duncan's place as soon as I can make him want it—

—and I will. I know I will. And then I'll ruin them, every

last one of them, and the more they beg and fight and try to run, the more I'll make them wish they were already dead.

My hand locks over his. "Say it."

He says, "I won."

THE FIRST KILL

We walk in together. The golden boy and the new girl, turning gold now, too. Alchemy by association.

Our entrance is so good I couldn't have made it any better even if I'd planned it. We're at Lilia's house, perched up in the hills looking down on everybody else. It juts glass corners out of a stone lawn where every plant is pale and spiny. I parked my father's car too close to Duncan's: a bullet hole against the concrete drive.

The front doors swing on their hinges, unguarded. The first floor is bare and waiting, stark except for the trail of bags and blazers and crosses they all shed on their way in. Duncan's pack and Lilia's flock sprawl dirty and drunk on three white-leather sofas that stare down at the skyline.

They look. All of them. At Mack and me, at *us,* together. And they all go silent.

"Damn, new girl, you work fast," says Duncan. He's at the center of the biggest sofa, a careful space on each side of him and Lilia but no space between them. His left arm locks her against him. Her eyes are mirror-blank.

"Only when I know what I want," I say.

They laugh. Duncan glossy and on-purpose. Duffy because Duncan did. Banks with a little edge, like Duncan without the polish. Connor too hard and hungry: enough to get caught.

"This is Jade," says Mack with his yes-ma'am manners.

And Piper says, "We know."

Duncan's eyes stay on Mack and me, because Piper wants everything too much: Duffy, and all the things Lilia has, and all the things Duncan can hand out. "Heard you got kicked out of boarding school," he says. "Is that true?"

"Heard you throw unforgettable parties," I tell him. "Is that true?"

"Sometimes the girls forget," says Connor. He's still Duncan's third choice, sitting third-nearest after Duffy and Banks with the two stupidest flock-girls hanging close even though they know better.

Banks's laugh cracks open. "Watch yourself."

"Or what?"

They share a loaded look that drags too long.

Duffy breaks the standoff. "God, Banks, you're tense. Gotta do something about that."

One of Connor's girls reaches over and swats the girl closest to Banks and she goes pink on purpose. Banks slides one hand farther up her thigh, but he says, "Shutting Connor up would do the trick."

And Duffy grins. "It's those three bitches in the masks, isn't it?"

"I still think you're making that shit up," says Connor. "I didn't see anything."

"Cute, Banks," Piper cuts in, curling closer to Duffy, swirling an almost-empty bottle. "Imaginary girls. The only way you're getting any this century."

Connor's black eyes glisten and he laughs again. He's back in his St Andrew's shirt, with the collar unbuttoned and his tie hanging loose and uneven. "Maybe not the *only* way—"

"Try me, Connor." Banks shoves the girl away from him. "Go ahead. Tell Dunc what you told me after the game. Show him what you sent to Mack. Go for it. We're all waiting."

But Connor doesn't stand up. "I didn't send shit to Mack."

I look at Mack for the first time since we walked in—since his golden wolf-pack started facing off one-to-one. I make my eyes say *innocent, innocent, innocent.*

He nods. Just for me. Just enough that the rest of them will miss it.

He trusts me.

Knowing it jolts hard under my ribs. Because it's working: Mack is almost mine already; the plan is almost real already; the boys are almost dead already—

"You better watch yourself, Connor," says Banks, and he gets up and stalks over to the bottles jumbled across the island. He grabs one, not even looking, and drinks.

The room is betrayal-quiet. They're all watching Banks, because Duncan might be the one who tells them what to do, but Banks is the one who tells them how to feel. The good-times boy. The one with enough real charm to run for office and win someday, because he's almost-but-not-quite as perfect as Duncan. Just rough enough and still magnetic. Banks, last in the room on Friday night, hanging in the doorway, yelling back to somebody. Laughing. Turning—and he faded darker and brighter but I could still see his whole face change. Campaign trail to kill room.

"The fuck is it so quiet in here?" says Banks. He slams the bottle down and laughs. Fake, but everybody else laughs, too, and then it turns real. It's a party again, because Banks says it is.

"That's more like it," Duffy says. "Damn." And one of the flock-girls gets up and links her phone to the sound system and music spills out of the speakers, and Mack puts a hand on my arm and leads me over to the rest of them, and we sit. The girls chatter about nothing. The boys pour another round.

Nobody looks at Connor. Not even the stupid girls next to him.

And he catches me watching.

His jaw gets tighter. "What's your fucking deal?"

I glance at Mack next to me. Point back at me and my crucifix. "Me?"

"Yeah, you. Crazy bitch."

I laugh.

Banks laughs.

Everybody laughs.

And Connor looks hard at me and says, "Fuck you," and then he pushes a too-close flock-girl off of him and sneers at Banks. "You're not so innocent, either."

He cuts past him to the bags by the door. Everyone watches him now, but they're laughing, because Banks is laughing and Duncan isn't stopping them.

They have a boy to blame.

Connor digs through his bag and straightens back up. "Going to smoke on the roof," he says. "You coming, Duff?"

Duffy looks sidelong at good-king Duncan. Duncan grins square teeth and vodka at Banks.

"Later," says Duffy.

I don't even realize I'm grabbing for Mack's hand until I feel our fingers braid together. I hold tighter than I should, because it's realer every second—

because Connor is alone now, peeled off from the pack—

because even if I can't take down all of them at once, I can take down one lone wolf at a time—

because Connor will be the first kill, and that's exactly how it should be.

Connor's eyes cut back toward me, but he looks at Mack instead. "Never trust a bitch," he says. Then he's gone.

A door slams upstairs, and Banks says, "So anyway, welcome to St Andrew's, *bitch*." He crosses back over to the rest of us, another bottle in his hand. Sits down heavy and takes a drink. Smiles wide and holds the bottle out to me—

and his smile is too bright—

and his charm is too true—

—and his voice claws and claws behind my eyes, *pretty name* instead of *bitch*.

I take the bottle. I raise it high and unshaking. "*Crazy bitch*," I say. I drink too much too fast. My veins heat up.

Banks laughs, but I watch Duncan. He lets me wait just long enough that maybe, without the liquor, without Connor trapped up on the roof, I'd be nervous.

I'm not.

"To the crazy bitch," says Duncan. He tips his drink toward me.

"To the crazy bitch!" they all chorus.

Duncan drinks.

We drink—all of us.

I'm one of them now.

When everyone settles back into everything, Banks slides over to where Connor was and leans in. "You saw those girls, Mack," he says.

He nods.

"You know what I'm thinking," says Banks, "I'm thinking Connor sent them."

"Great theory, dumbass," says Duffy. "Why would he bother?"

Banks laughs with all of them, but then he says, "Because Mack's getting all the glory lately. Connor's fucking with us, all of us, about—"

"Careful," says Duncan, his fingers digging a little harder into Lilia's shoulder.

Banks blinks. "Chill, Dartmouth." But he grins when he says it, and Duncan lets him get away with it. "Connor's messing with us, and he's messing with Mack, because he knows Mack's got his spot if he fucks up any more. Especially after—you know." He lets the words hang, loaded down.

"Careful," Duncan says again, colder.

But Banks nods anyway and says, not turning, "What do you think, Mack?"

Next to me, Mack hesitates. "Connor wouldn't go that far."

Banks drinks again and reaches over to scruff Mack's hair. His arm is six inches from my face. Marked guilty with three long red scratches.

"God, golden boy," says Banks. "You're too fucking pure."

"Seconded," Piper chirps from Duffy's lap. "Good thing he's got the crazy bitch to corrupt him."

I know Mack is turning red again without even looking. And then I look, and he is, and he looks back at me for long enough that Banks catches it and hoots at him.

So I blush, too. On purpose, just like Banks's flock-girl, because I'm supposed to be a flock-girl too. Stupid and unseeing and ready to fall for him, for them, for anything.

"What did they say?" I ask Mack. So innocent I almost bleed white.

His eyes stay locked on mine. "They said Connor would fall," he says to me. Only me.

Lilia says, a whole world away, "If Connor sent them, why would—"

"It wasn't him," Duncan cuts in.

I'm still looking at Mack. "Is that all they said?"

"We need to shut Connor up," Banks says.

"Banks—" Duncan warns—

"Kidding." Banks laughs. He's the life and death of the party. Once Duncan is dead, he'll be the one in control. Duffy will be nobody when he doesn't have Duncan to lend him a little taste of power. A taste he's allowed to have, because he could never pull off a mutiny.

But Banks—

Banks could turn them all against Duncan if he wanted. Friday night, that muddy half-second before his face changed and he took the last step in and slammed the door in Porter's face and said *fuck, Dunc, you know how to pick them*—

if instead he said *fuck, Dunc, let her go*—

—everything would have been different.

And Mack—

—he could turn them all, too. Duncan sees it, I think, and so does Duffy: this too-pure boy, the one who won't quite obey, is only on the outside because he's the biggest threat of all to their fucked-up nailed-down order.

"You know what, I'm going to go talk to him," says Mack.

"You kiss all the wrong asses," Duffy says through Piper's hair.

"Yeah, and you know all about ass-kissing, right, Duff?" Banks says. They howl at him, the whole pack.

But Mack gets up. He still has my hand. Flock-girl Jade isn't supposed to let go, so I don't. I follow him up the silver-steel stairs. The door at the top is all glass. All light, like staring heaven in the face.

Heaven or death.

Mack stops at the door and turns to me. "Connor texted me," he says all at once. "Right before those girls disappeared. He said . . . he said, 'She won't.'"

I laugh, but I turn it light as air. "Does that mean something?"

He trusts me. He shouldn't. "That's what those girls said, too. 'She won't.'" He leans closer. "She won't remember.'"

My hand tightens on his. "Who?"

"I don't know," he says. "Connor's . . . you can't trust him."

I shouldn't push it too far. I should let it play out. Be patient.

Should.

I say, "What does he have on Banks?" When I say his name another shred of static sloughs away and I see Banks there at Duncan's house, cutting through the dance-floor crowd, closing in with a drink in his hand to where I stood all alone—

Mack checks over his shoulder, out to the roof. "Not just Banks. Dunc and Duff, too."

"What is it?"

His lips get tight.

I laugh again. A disarming glittery laugh. "I won't tell."

Finally he says, "Dunc had a party Friday. Something happened."

I'm holding his hand almost too tight. "What—"

"Whisper, whisper," Piper shouts from downstairs. "Just fuck her already. God."

His face goes white and then red, but I laugh as bright as Mads on Friday night—like blinding sunset light and the moment Piper ruined. I push the door open and Mack almost falls and I almost fall with him.

Then we're outside, spinning around the corner.

The roof is gray and razor-smooth. The second floor is glowing glass off to the side, and the edges drop straight to nowhere. Connor sits with his feet hanging off into thin air. Blocking out the skyline.

"Fuck you, Banks," he says.

"Not Banks," says Mack.

Connor turns around. He's dropped his things behind him on his way across the roof: shoes, a lighter, an empty bottle. "Fuck you too, Mack."

Mack lets go of my hand and starts toward Connor. "You're pushing your luck."

Connor takes a hit from his joint. He turns his back again before he breathes the smoke out.

"Banks and Dunc," says Mack. "They're—"

"Being pussies? No shit."

"They think you're going to get them caught."

His laugh drips venom. "Even if I did, nobody'd believe the slut."

"Believe what?" I say, uninvited. Jade the flock-girl, flighty and stupid.

Connor turns again. "Shouldn't have brought the crazy bitch, Mack."

I do the breathy little giggle he wants. I'll make him say it. "Believe *what?*"

He looks straight at me. "Doesn't matter." His grin gets wider. "She wanted it."

"Stop," says Mack. His voice is hard. A flicker of the king he needs to be.

"Or what?"

"Don't make it like that."

Connor throws the end of his joint over the edge. "Stay out of this. It's Dunc and Duff and Banks and me. You're not one of us just because you had a couple good games."

They're both facing the skyline. The light is changing behind me, from blinding gold-white to dusk red. I slip Connor's phone out from between my skin and my waistband.

I take that picture, the one he sent the second-string boy. His old tie and his trophies. And then a second: the one I snapped in the locker room after meddling Malcolm left. Today's tie, pinned through with my earring and Connor's fate.

I tag Duncan and Duffy and Banks.

I write a caption that will kill him in his very own words: *another party, another slut down.*

And I post it for the whole damn world to see.

Then I swoop toward them, let the phone fall next to Connor's lighter, take Mack's arm, pull him away from the edge so he's looking back toward where the sun used to be. "Let's go," I say.

"Back downstairs?"

I count the seconds. Long enough for Duncan and Duffy and Banks to see what Connor's done. "Anywhere," I say.

"Your friend's being a dick anyway. You deserve better, don't you think?"

He doesn't answer, but he doesn't have to.

"They should kick him out and bring you in," I say.

Connor snorts.

And I lean closer and say, "Soon."

Then the door slams open and Banks comes around the corner, furious and drunker than before, with Duncan behind him and Duffy and Piper hurrying to catch up.

"Get up," says Banks.

Connor swings one leg back onto the roof and gives him a lazy smile.

"Get *up*."

"Chill." Connor pushes up so he's facing them—

—*us*.

Banks is grinning. He's all kill-room now. "Where is it?"

Connor's eyes shift to Duncan and back. "Where's what?"

And Banks lunges at him and grabs his shirt. "You're so fucking close right now—"

"Banks," says Duncan, even. Warning.

"Right." Banks shoves Connor almost back to the edge—

and his tie swings, and the red sunset light catches on my gold-and-crystal earring—

—and this is it.

This is when they all know Connor is dead.

"For fuck's sake," says Banks. He grabs Connor's tie and pulls it free. "Going to stop me now, Dunc?"

The tie hangs in front of him and Duffy and Piper. Piper laughs nerves and thrill.

"Shut her up," Duncan tells Duffy without looking at him. He crushes the tie in his hand and says, "Start talking."

Connor's eyes shift again. The sky behind him is as dark as dried blood. "I didn't do shit."

"You just fucking posted," Banks spits out, but Duncan raises one hand, barely, and Banks steps back in line.

"I don't even have my phone."

Ass-kisser Duffy points. "Then what's that?"

Connor looks at the phone by his feet—

at Duncan's fist around the crushed-up tie—

at his pack's hungry eyes—

—and now he knows it, too.

"Fuck you," says Connor. "Fuck your setup. I didn't do shit."

Duncan takes one step closer. "You did plenty." Next to him, Banks lunges for the phone; swipes it open; deletes the post. Deletes Connor's whole account.

"*Fuck* you," Connor says again. "I'm not taking the fall for this. You and Duff and Banks did the exact same shit."

"Except they aren't broadcasting it to everybody in America," says Piper.

Duffy grabs her arm too hard. "Shut *up*."

"I'm not the one who cheats with some roofied slut—"

"Get her out of here," says Duncan. His voice stays even.

"I'm not leaving if the new girl gets to stay."

"She's leaving, too."

For a second nobody speaks. Behind Connor, the sky burns down to dirty gray and the lights slide brighter.

"Come on." I pull at Mack's hand. "Let's go."

"Mack stays," says Duncan.

Piper snickers. "Damn, Mack, look at—"

"*Enough,*" says Duncan, deadly hard, and Piper clamps her mouth shut.

"Just give us a minute—" Duffy starts.

"Fuck off." She yanks free and looks at me. "Coming, new girl?"

I give Mack one last look and whisper *Soon* again, so soft it isn't even a sound.

But I know he hears it.

I let go of his hand and follow Piper back across the roof. At the very last second, right before I turn the corner, I look back.

They're circling closer—the golden wolves. The pack. Connor takes a step back, almost to the very edge.

Caught.

"What the *fuck*," Piper hisses. She's inside already, propping the door open with one hand. Her skin puffs red where Duffy grabbed her. "You're twisted, you know that?"

And then I catch my reflection in the glass. I'm smiling.

"They're going to fucking *kill* him," she says.

A flock-girl wouldn't smile. A flock-girl would be downstairs with Lilia, giggling and blushing and drinking until she couldn't remember why the boys went up to the roof.

"He asked for it," I tell her.

I grab the door and step around her and go back to the starlings and the second-string. Malcolm stands blessed but uneasy at the counter, lining glasses up in too-even rows. Not quite smiling. Not quite ready to rule the way his brother does.

Not like Mack.

I sit down where I was before, across from Lilia. She hasn't moved. She has both hands around a bottle and she's staring out at the city with her eyes glazed over.

Piper sits and grabs the bottle. "Turns out your new girl's a sadistic bitch," she says.

Lilia smiles. "Good."

It's almost dark out, but the only lights on in the living room are the gallery lamps shining on three canvases on the wall. They're thick with silver-blue paint.

In the half-dark, they drip like shining blood.

The music swells. Piper drinks. The skyline glows bright and brighter, filmy white-gray.

The boys come back.

First Mack. Then Duffy and Banks. Then Duncan, pausing halfway down, his shadow darkening the space behind him.

"Out," says Duncan. "Everybody. Her parents will be home soon."

"Where's Connor?" a flock-girls asks. Wide-eyed, with one hand trembling near her lips.

"Up on the roof, drunk off his ass." Duncan's voice is satin.

He waits. He doesn't ask again.

Malcolm's second-rate boys cave first, and then the girls. The music stops. They trickle back out onto the concrete and thorns.

Then Banks.

Then Duffy, scared and sweating, one hand tight around Piper's shoulder with her shrugging him away.

"Mack," says Duncan when the rest of them are gone. Across the room, Lilia sinks deeper into the white leather. The shadows wind around her. She could almost be a ghost.

"Thanks for keeping their story straight," says Duncan.

Mack waits at the front door. He looks taller. Different.

I go to him. He takes my hand—

like we've been together for years—

like it's instinct, the two of us—

—like he's mine and I'm his, already.

"Connor," says Mack. "You're really going to do it?"

Duncan nods, once and certain.

And Mack says, "Are you sure?"

On Friday night, when the room twisted in on itself and the sound and the light bled hot together, Connor was the first one to grab my wrist. To lock his arm around me and pull me down the hallway to where Porter stood by the door at the end, melting into the floor, melting into the wall.

Then I knew.

And I fucking fought.

But his grip was steel and everything else was smoke and he pushed Porter out of the way. Took my earring and talked back. The room was all white and sparkling, dizzying, glittering. And I sunk my claws into his arm and my heel into his foot and he laughed. Outside the door, Porter said, *are you sure?*

I bit down hard. Sunk my fangs into Connor's skin. He pulled his hand free and I said, *you picked the wrong girl—*

He threw me down and I tasted blood: his and mine.

He said, *yeah, I'm fucking sure.*

Tonight, right now, I look at Mack and his king, and I say, "Yeah. He's fucking sure."

Duncan's teeth shine in the dark. "Don't let that one go," he says. "I'll see you tomorrow."

We pick up our bags from next to the door. Only Connor's

things are left—his wrinkled blazer, his too-soft leather bag, his crosse.

"Lilia," says Duncan. "Come up."

She's almost invisible. "No," she breathes out.

"That wasn't a request."

Light catches on a bottle as Lilia tips it back. She drinks for a long second, and then she lets the bottle fall and shatter on the floor.

Duncan doesn't move until his queen is next to him. She's fading. When he puts one arm around her, she almost disappears. "Dunc," she says, "I don't want to watch."

"Yes, you do," he says.

Mack and I walk out into the night. He reaches back to shut the door that's been open since before we were here—

—and good-king Duncan turns. "Mack?"

"Yeah?"

Duncan says, "You're one of us."

They disappear up the stairs. Mack shuts the door behind us and we cross the driveway, together and silent. My heartbeat is so loud I can hear it. The whole night shines, from the concrete to the sky.

We get in the car. On the roof two silhouettes stand dark against the last red glow over the hills.

Two wolves. Moving closer and closer to the edge.

"Connor will fall," says Mack, so quiet it's almost reverent. "They said—"

I don't pretend to be a flock-girl. I take his hands in mine and we shift closer together until his eyes are all I see.

Golden-boy Mack. Noble Mack.

"He can't," he says.

"He will," I say.

And he says, "The girls in the masks. They were right."
The air goes so still I almost can't breathe.
I kiss Mack.
Lilia screams.
Connor falls.

LOYALTIES

"What the fuck," says Jenny. "What the actual fuck. You *like* him."

We're in Summer's room, the four of us, drinking wine from the Horowitzes' cellar, so dark red it's almost black. Or Summer and Jenny and Mads are drinking it. I'm drunk enough without it, on Lilia's vodka and Mack's kiss and Connor's blood.

"Stop it," says Summer. "I think it's beautiful."

Jenny grabs the bottle out of her hand. "Right. Because you know all those boys who got all stupid over you turned out so well. You know they totally could've held themselves together to finish another three murders—"

"Come on," says Summer. "That was boys. This is Elle."

That name pulls me out of the warm night haze. "It's Jade," I say, dagger-sharp. "And I've known him for five hours. I don't *like* him, Jenny."

She drinks. "Yeah. You better not. You better just be drunk."

I turn my back on them and cross back past Summer's bed and out to the landing. From the railing I look down on the living room and the lazy crawl of people out to the patio and back. Circling with champagne flutes while a man in a white tux and a bronze tan clatters jazz on the grand piano. It's Monday night—still, somehow—but every night is a party at the Horowitzes'.

I stand on the landing in my St Andrew's blue, staring down at them. Nobody looks up—

—nobody even thinks that maybe there's a girl looking down on them, fresh off the kill.

"You did it," says Mads, low. She's next to me now, quiet but coiled to spring. Always, and especially now. Especially since Friday night.

"Thank you," I say, because she's the first one to even say it. That I'm one day into St Andrew's and already, nestled safe in Hollywood Hills, there's a bloodstain Lilia's father's gardener will never be able to power-wash out of the concrete.

Downstairs Summer's stepmother, twenty-seven years old and straight off a reality show, squeals as obvious as a freshman flock-girl. She needs them to believe that she's holding court. That she'll last longer than the other two wives, or at least long enough to lock down the alimony to keep her in Beverly Hills. She'll never be a good enough actress to pull it off, or Summer's father would've bothered to get her something better than a reality show. He's a producer. She's no one.

"Connor," says Mads. Without even turning I know her eyes are on me, ringed with gold shadow. Red-orange lips, like always. Hair in Bantu knots. "It's good he was first."

I nod.

"Duncan next?" she asks.

I nod again. I'm still looking down at the party instead of back at her. I know exactly what I'll read in her eyes.

"Oh, come on," Jenny yells from Summer's room. "Don't be a bitch. It's actually really fucking entertaining to see you in love."

"Oh my god, it's not love," says Summer.

"Like you'd know," Jenny shoots back.

And it shuts Summer up, because all the boys and the girls she's destroyed have always been nobody. Just for sport. Except she's only playing the game because she'll never tell Jenny the truth and Jenny won't ever see it. Because Jenny is Jenny, loud and blunt, and Summer is sweet black-widow poison—

—or that's what she wants us to think, but Jenny's the only one who doesn't see through it. We've known, Mads and me, for so long I can't remember not-knowing.

Summer loves Jenny and only Jenny. She'll never settle for anybody else.

And right now Mads is looking at me the same way she looks at Summer when Summer pretends Jenny doesn't matter.

"Mads—" I say, but I still can't look. Downstairs, Summer's stepmother spins in a circle. Her dress is fringe and thirst.

I start again. "Duncan's easy. Mack already wants to take his place. He just doesn't know yet." Mack, not Mack. Their golden boy. He might think he's noble, but he'd kill just like any of them would if he wanted it enough.

"He thinks he has his honor," I tell Mads. "He has to be

able to tell himself what he's doing is the honorable thing. He hates who they are."

"Does he?"

I think of the way Mack's eyes went dark when he said, *Dunc had a party Friday night. Something happened.* The way he flinched, pride and shame and rage all at once, when Duncan told him, *You're one of us.*

Mack has never done the things that bind the wolves together in rule and ruin. And Duncan let him in, still and at last, because Mack found his own way: standing steady with Connor's fate spelled out between them.

But he didn't find his way. I found it for him.

"I can make him do whatever I want," I say. "Trust me, you know I never lie—"

She laughs.

I turn so my back is against the railing and we're shoulder to shoulder. Lean back and look down. The marble floor is straight under me with nothing to stop me from falling as hard as Connor did.

I look at Mads. She blinks a slow flash of gold.

"I don't lie when it matters," I say.

She doesn't answer.

"I'm not lying now."

She shrugs. "Not about the plan."

Mads never lies, ever. No matter what the consequences are for telling the truth.

"I don't like him," I say.

"It doesn't matter either way," says Mads. "You're still going to kill them. You're still going to make him take the fall."

"Of course I'm going to kill them," I say, and the hot thrill comes back as sharp as Lilia's scream cutting through the almost-night and Connor's shadow plunging hard and fast to hell.

"Jade, come back. Jade," Jenny whines from Summer's room. "We're supposed to be planning how you're going to get your precious Mack to murder somebody. Not fucking around on balconies like we're in a fucking movie."

Mads tips her head toward mine and I do the same. Until we're foreheads-together, eye to eye, no room for lies. "You tell me when you need me."

I say, "I don't need anyone."

She laughs, but it's the most beautiful sound in the world. She says, "I know."

We go back to Jenny and Summer and settle in close. All four of us, pressed together on a comforter the same color as Summer's lipstick. Jenny scrolls through trash-news with blurred zigzags of light in front of Lilia's driveway.

Cops + paps outside composer John Helmsley's house. Blood + body bag. Guess who?

"Guess who," says Jenny, and she laughs. "I fucking love this town."

Summer elbows her.

"Oh, shut up," says Jenny.

I lean closer. "Are there pictures?"

"Jesus, Jade, wasn't it enough to see it in person?" Jenny grins at me, and her eyes glow with the light from her screen.

"I didn't see all of it. He wasn't dead when I left."

"Okay, but can't you trust this Z-list update shit? They said body bag."

"I need to see it," I say.

"It's such a beautiful story," says Summer, and Jenny shrieks laughter in her face. "For real. It really is a movie—"

My phone lights up. Summer is still talking, screenwriting Connor's fall even though he doesn't deserve even a fine-print line at the very end of the credits, but I'm not listening, because the message on my screen is from Mack.

He's dead.

Just two words, but the best two words I've ever read.

"Jesus." Jenny cuts Summer off. "That's him, isn't it?"

I can't look up from those two perfect words. "Who?"

She crows. "Mack. God, you're fucked."

I stare at the words for one more second, and then I hold the screen up for her—for all of them. They crowd in.

"Well, I'm not wrong, am I?" says Jenny with a smirk.

"Fuck you," I say, but I'm smiling broad and brilliant.

"Jade," says Summer, and she throws herself back into her ten pillows and sighs a beautiful deep sigh that warms up the whole room. "I knew you'd do it." She pushes her hair out of her face. "You better tell us we can wear those masks again."

I nod. And I take my phone back and steal one more look at Mack's words: *He's dead.*

I type, *He deserved it.*

"Are you sure—" Mads starts to say, but I send the text before she finishes.

"That's one way to play it," says Jenny. "I hope he likes sociopaths."

"It will work. I know it," I say.

Summer is still staring up at the ceiling. "You always know everything."

"Of course she does," says Jenny. "Just ask her."

My phone lights up again: *They're terrible. You don't know how terrible they are.*

I text him back: *Take Connor's place. You're better than he ever was.*

"Duncan," says Mads, to bring us back. "When?"

"Soon," I say, the same as I said to Mack this afternoon.

"How soon?"

I look at my coven. Summer is sitting up now, and they're all watching me—bright eyes, lips just barely parted, drinking everything in.

"As soon as I can turn Mack into exactly who he wants to be," I tell Mads.

"Who you want him to be," says Jenny, proud. "You evil bitch."

"But really," Summer says, "you're almost there, right? With Mack."

My phone blinks on again. Mack says, *I will.*

And a second later he says, *WE will.*

Under the fake nails from Saturday morning, my claws grow a little. They'll be back soon, longer than before.

I feel fucking high—

better than the second before the wave closed over my head and crushed the air out of my lungs—

better than when I looked into Connor's eyes and saw a dead boy looking back at me—

better—or close to better, at least—than when Lilia screamed and Mack's kiss went from careful to triumphant.

I tell Summer, "Almost."

EULOGY

By Tuesday morning everyone knows.

I'm early again, but when I get to the Virgin Mary statue the whole flock is already there. Lilia and Piper stand a little apart. The rest of them are a nervous gleeful knot.

"Jade, did you hear—" one of the starlings says, all in a rush. I walk past her, to Lilia and Piper.

"So apparently you're inner circle material now—" Piper starts.

Lilia cuts her off with one blink. Her glass-blue eyes are shot through with red and circled twice as dark as yesterday. She tips her coffee cup back, but it's empty. She lets it fall. Piper snaps her fingers and a flock-girl shimmers over and snatches the cup from next to our feet.

Lilia looks at Piper and me. "He killed him. He *killed* him."

"God, say it a little louder," says Piper.

Lilia's hands scrabble at her purse. She pulls out a pack of Parliaments and flicks her lighter.

"*Lili,*" says Piper. "Get it together."

She breathes out a thin line of smoke. "He didn't die right away," she says. "He was lying there—he was bent all wrong—Dunc wouldn't let me call 911 until we knew he was dead—and he was breathing like there was a knife in his neck—and there was so much blood—"

The cigarette falls out of her hand. She lights another one and leaves the first on the floor, trailing haze.

"Jade," says Piper, staring. "What the fuck." She glances at Lilia. "Your new girl's getting off on this, by the way."

I'm breathing too fast. I slow it down, count it off—

Duncan, Duffy, Connor, Banks—

—hear Connor's broken lungs rasp and see his eyes wide and scared and searching, and then finally empty.

I smile at Piper. "He deserved it."

"Fuck you," she says. "And fuck whatever Mack told you. You didn't even know Connor."

Lilia's fingers tremble on her cigarette. "But it's true."

Piper's mouth drops open and she turns it into a laugh so harsh the flock-girls peek over their shoulders to see. "God," she says. "Everybody's losing their shit this week. Ever since that stupid party—"

The boys come in.

It's exactly like yesterday, and nothing like it at all. Today the lights don't flicker: they blaze brighter and stronger, so everyone squints. Today they're not laughing, but their silence is ten times louder than anything they said yesterday—

Duncan—

—sharper edges overnight, still the good-king, more the good-king than he's ever been, eyes fading from gunmetal-gray to pure silver, something fast and fatal in the way he walks, something that makes the not-it girls bow their heads—

Duffy—

—trying so hard I can smell it like burning oil, three razor-nicks on his jaw, squaring his shoulders on every step but still with his face blanched white and circles under his eyes, because yesterday was a test and he failed and he knows it—

Banks—

—all heat where Duffy is cold, liquor on his breath and a dangerous spring in the way he walks, not SS-tight like

Duncan but loose and loping and ready to kill again if he has to, or maybe even if Duncan tries to collar him too hard—

Mack—

Mack.

Not Connor, because Connor is frozen in the morgue with his chest cracked open. Ugly Connor. First-in-the-door Connor. Connor is dead because of me, and Mack is in his place because of me.

—and he wears it better than any of them. Not sick and shaking like Duffy or drunk from it like Banks. Not polished past perfect like Duncan. Still with that golden-boy glow all over his face, and glowing even brighter with the ambition no one else could see until I saw it.

"Shit," says Piper. She takes a step back.

They stop in front of us. I can feel the rest of the commons watching. Everything stands still: Lilia trailing her forgotten cigarette, Piper with her hand on her sabre, the boys in their same wolf-pack formation like Connor never existed and it was always Mack.

Duffy breaks first. He flinches toward Piper. She dives for him, puts her hands on his shoulders, presses her lips to his. He kisses her back but his eyes stay haunted.

Banks laughs. "You're losing your touch, Piper."

She jerks back and scowls. "Maybe Duff just has some fucking decorum."

Shutting bitches up is my specialty, said Duffy on Friday night when Duncan told him *shut the bitch up*. And he locked his hand across my mouth and even when I bit he didn't let go. Not like dead Connor.

I smile wide at Banks. "Duffy's a gentleman. Show some respect for the dead."

Then I take Mack's hands in mine and stare hard into his eyes and everything twists, but not the way it does when I look at the other boys. He doesn't look away. He's afraid, because of Connor, but not as afraid as he wants to be.

This time he kisses me first. The boy who let Connor die. For a second—

—*blinding summer light and Malibu sunsets, and leaning my head out the window with my hair streaming out behind me and screaming wild into too-fast turns—*

"Damn," says Banks. "That's more like it. I'll take her when you're done with her, golden boy."

The summer light splinters into scraping white marble and poison.

I pull back, but I don't let go of Mack's hands. And I smile at Banks again, but different this time. My innocent-little-flower smile. "You'll never have me," I say.

Duncan lets it land, and then he takes another step in. Closing off our inner circle from the rest of them. "We're clear," he tells us, instead of asking. "No texts about what happened. No talking to the rest of them." He nods toward the flock-girls and Malcolm's second-rank, hanging back.

"They know," says Piper. "Everybody knows."

Duncan's eyes are so silver-bright he makes Piper blink. "They know Connor can't keep it together when he's crossfaded. It's a real blow to the team. We'll miss him. We'll remember." He leans on the last word.

His pack takes it in and stays quiet, even Banks. Piper's lips twitch.

Lilia brings her cigarette up, ash crumbling off the end, and takes a drag.

"Jesus, Lilia," says Duncan. "Get rid of it."

She doesn't say no, but she doesn't move, either.

Duncan takes the cigarette out of her hand and drops it. His heel grinds it into the floor. "We're going in," he says to Duffy and Banks and Mack.

"Where?" Piper shifts for her blade.

"Chapel," says Duffy, dry lips and faking it. "So they can tell us about Connor."

Right as he says it, a cluster of baby-bird freshmen flitters past with a banner bigger than they are, carved with Connor's name.

Piper's eyes narrow. "Fucking shitshow."

Duncan measures out a look. "We're going."

They leave the way they came in: united. Blood-bound. Strides almost matched.

But Mack looks over his shoulder—

—at me.

Only me.

Piper scoffs. I don't care.

Bells toll from the chapel, the same as yesterday, but today there's something better about them. Deeper and darker and weighted, warning-heavy. The rest of them—all the St Andrew's Preppers who won't ever be as good as Duncan and his wolves—fall in line behind them. Filing past us until it's only Lilia and Piper and me with two spent cigarettes on the floor.

"God," Lilia sighs, and she starts for the chapel.

Piper stops me from following: a half-step in front of me with her hip jutting out so her sabre catches against my skirt.

Lilia looks back. "Coming?"

"Just need a minute with the new girl, sweetie."

She shrugs and drifts around the corner.

Piper waits, like maybe I'll break. Like I'll spill my darkest secrets to her right here with Mary gazing down at us and Lilia's first cigarette still pluming smoke.

I wait right back. The hall stretches bigger, all shining planks and perfect arches. Sister María de los Dolores slips out of the shadows and crosses the hollow space corner-to-corner, almost gliding, eyes cast down the same as the statue's.

When she's gone Piper pushes too close and says, "Why are you here?"

"Ask my parents."

She laughs. "I'm not Lili. You can't bullshit me like that." She shifts even closer. "You're nowhere. You don't even exist."

I spin my phone between my fingers. "You followed me yesterday." And she did, with her thousands of sunbleached selfies she never captions and her thousands of followers she never follows back. Piper Morello, the better version, angled just right and filtered into the queen she thinks she'll be when Lilia stumbles one time too many.

Her lips pinch and unpinch. She doesn't say, *You made that account yesterday, too.* She says, "Jade Khanjara. Is that even your real name?"

I keep my voice exactly as light as it needs to be. "Of course."

"Where were you before St Andrew's?" she asks. "Exeter? St Paul's?"

I don't answer. My heart skips faster, but I'm glad. I want her to fight. I want her to know I'm lying, and not to be able to prove it.

"You're not on anybody's records," she says. "So where was it?"

"Why does it matter?"

"Why won't you tell?"

"Non-disclosure agreement," I say. "From the settlement."

"There's no case anywhere."

I tip my chin just the slightest bit. "I was fifteen."

"There's nothing from this year about a fifteen-year-old-girl and a teacher at any of the boarding schools in New Hampshire," she says, all her gloss gone now. Closing in.

So I laugh. "Stalk much?"

"Like you don't," she tosses back, and I don't deny it. "You're hiding something."

"Everyone's hiding something."

She goes still when I say that. In her eyes I can see her thoughts spinning fast. "What did Mack tell you?" she asks.

"Nothing I didn't already know." I pause. "Not yet."

She steps back, straighter. Her filtered sunbleached good-citizenship self is back in place. "You're not getting away with it. Whatever it is."

I tap my phone open and flip to the front camera. Check my lipstick—for her, not for me. "Neither are you."

We leave it like that. A draw.

But she walks away first.

IN MEMORIAM

I'm the very last St Andrew's Prepper through the door.

Piper is just ahead of me, passing the freshman girls' banner and Connor's team portrait without looking. The same portrait Mads circled in scarlet on Saturday.

The chapel doors swing shut behind us. The air is hot and hazy and every pew is full, blazer shoulders lined up tight. Sister María de los Dolores stares heavy-eyed at Piper. I smile innocent and she softens just enough and waves us toward the space behind the last pew. We slip in and stand with our backs to the stone. Piper elbows me and nods past the sister: a man stands against the wall, in plainclothes but with a gun on his belt. His eyes rove to Piper and me.

Sister María de los Dolores turns, stern, and puts him back in his place.

At the front of the chapel the dean tells Duncan's lies. The good-king and his wolves sit in the very first row, four together, and the second-rank boys fill in the row behind them. Malcolm glances over his shoulder and meets my gaze for one stilted instant. He chews his lip again, nagging forgotten and familiar.

It's not a funeral. It's not even a memorial. Even the dean isn't captive enough to try to turn Connor into anyone we should miss. Everything he says is cut and dry and courtroom-perfect.

The dean's words bleed together and swirl up like smoke to the rafters. I don't listen. I don't care. I don't want to stand still, caught here between Piper and Sister María de los Dolores and the detective, not checking my phone and not watching Duncan and not next to Mack.

I don't want to wait.

Every second Duncan stays king is too long.

When the dean finishes reading the lawyers' speech everyone stands to file out. The whispers start. First the freshman banner-girls and then the ugly boys who stand at the farthest side of the commons and stare at Lilia and Piper and their flock with bitter jealous hate.

Piper and I don't cut in front of them. We wait for our boys.

Outside the doors, somebody gasps and the whispers weave tighter.

"Fucking freshmen," Piper mutters.

Sister María de los Dolores pretends she doesn't hear.

The voices get louder. The line surges forward and bunches up at the doors.

Piper slips a sideways glance at me. I keep my eyes on Duncan and Duffy and Banks and Mack, at the very end of the line, not talking.

"It's not *okay*!" comes a banner-girl's voice, whining up. "It's nasty and lies and—it's *vandalism* anyway—"

"You just think Lilia's going to blame you. No more prom princess." It's one of the edge-of-the-commons boys, his words glee-greased and simmering.

And the voices swell loud again.

Sister María de los Dolores pushes into the crowd and out through the doors. Her words cut ruler-quick: "Move along! Get to class!"

Piper shifts closer to me, eyes darting across the crowd. She wants to cut in, I can tell. But Duncan is watching. She hisses, "You brought the storm with you, new girl."

Then Malcolm's boys pass us, and the starlings, hovering off-balance without their queen.

Piper's glare clips all their wings at once. "Where's Lilia?"

"She—" three of them say together, and then they all go quiet. Finally the prettiest one says, "She fainted—"

"She didn't faint," another one breaks in. "She fell. She *almost* fainted—"

"Close enough," says the prettiest one. "She was blacking out. So Rosie and Calla took her to the nurse—they practically had to *carry* her—before the dean started, and they never came back, so—"

"I don't need a fucking novel," Piper snaps. She checks her phone and says to me, so the rest of them can't hear, "Did she text you?"

"She barely knows me. She's your best friend . . ." And I leave a little pause with an almost-question hiding in it. "She'd text you first."

Piper ruffles. "Lili plays mind games," she says, and then she pushes past the flock-girls and hooks her elbow into Duffy's. They fall back, the two of them and Duncan.

Mack is right in front of me, with Banks. He holds out his hand and I take it and fold in next to him. Look up into his eyes.

"Get a damn room," says Banks.

I smirk at him and bring my other hand to Mack's so both my hands lace together around his. "Are you all right?" I ask—

—and I keep my voice low and warm and red, and I mean more than I say.

"I am now," says Mack.

Banks snorts out a laugh. "Whatever the hell you two have going—"

But he cuts himself off and his face goes as marble-white as Duffy's. Then it goes red and he's laughing harsh and pushing through the doors and grabbing the banner hard enough that the stands it's tied to crack against the floor.

All the beautiful vain St Andrew's Preppers have stopped

moving again. Started talking again. Banks tears hard at the banner but it won't rip apart. One lone girl giggles, high and desperate.

Banks whirls. His eyes are rage and his hands are striped with blue. "*Move,*" he barks out, and they do. Like rats out of a sinking ship.

Across the banner, cutting through Connor's name, bold blue letters say GUILTY.

"Porter," Banks shouts, and he grabs his shoulder. Porter spins wide-eyed and so scared I have to bite the inside of my cheek so I don't smile and ruin everything.

"I didn't—I'm not—" Porter tries to say. Sweat on his lip and his forehead shining.

"Knife," Banks says, low, crushing the banner in on itself. The metal stands shriek against the floor.

Porter digs into his bag and holds out a leather-sheathed knife. His hands shake and he drops it and yelps. Banks snatches up the knife before Porter can move. He slashes once—

Hard.

The banner slices in two and crumples down. Two white flags waving.

Banks throws the knife back without its case. Porter barely catches it, handle-first but only by luck, and then he runs.

The door swings open again. Sister María de los Dolores steps out of the chapel with the dean and the detective close behind her. Duffy sees his gun and almost gags. The detective stares too long.

"His teammates," says the dean, smooth and unbothered.

Duncan nods at the detective. Says, so practiced I can see it in print, "He'll be missed."

The detective's gaze slides over each of us in turn. Holding on until the dean catches his shoulder and eases him away and says, "Well, then, the sister and I will show you out—"

Then it's just us: Duncan and Duffy and Banks and Mack, and Piper and me with Lilia nowhere, and Connor's team picture watching, and the banner broken on the floor.

We wait for Duncan to speak. The silence gleams dark blue.

His jaw clenches twice, fast.

He smiles his same slick smile from yesterday's end-of-the-match good-game line.

"Get rid of it," he says to Banks. And then, to all of his pack, "See you at practice."

They leave, all four of them, with Banks ripping the banner off the stands and burying it in a trash can. It's just Piper and me left behind.

I take down Connor's portrait. Stare into his dead eyes.

I don't feel anything now that he's gone.

"Jade," says Piper.

I turn.

She swoops to the floor and back in the same nimble little dive the flock-girl did when Lilia let her coffee cup fall. Holds up a bullet-black lipstick tube. Uncaps it and twists it up.

It's crushed almost to nothing, but we'd both know the color anywhere. The same as the letters scrawled across the banner. The same as the streaks our queen painted on our faces before the game.

Lilia's war paint.

COURTING

After school I stop in Dr. Farris's classroom and linger too long with my eyes bright and my chin tipping just-so. Asking questions and not listening to the answers. Waiting for him to ask me about Connor, so I can bring out my innocent-little-flower face for him and for the not-it senior with the electric-blue hair grading quizzes at a lab table. Piper would never give her a single glance, but the story will get back to her in an hour anyway: *that new girl, the one who fucks teachers? She's trying it again.*

Once the halls have drained themselves empty and Dr. Farris knows how very sad I am about poor dead Connor, I give the senior girl a zipped-lips wink and make my exit.

Next is Piper.

All day she's been chained to her phone, double-texting me every chance she gets even though next-in-line Piper never texts first unless it's to Lilia. But today Lilia was nowhere, and Lilia didn't text back. So Piper chirped and chirped at me: *Did you hear from her, Did anyone say anything, Shut them up, Tell me everything.* I texted back often enough to keep her interested, but I waited long enough to make her hate herself for begging.

She's silent now, finally, as I walk down to the athletics building on the other side of the tennis courts. The plaque over the second door says COMBAT.

I prop the door open and watch without stepping in.

The room is long and half-lit. There are two of them on

the strip farthest from the door. They're white-armored with masks on. Their sabres flash too fast to see.

It's almost an even match. Piper has her back to me, honey-gold ponytail bouncing with every lunge. She's shorter than the boy she's fighting but she attacks first every time. She's grace and ferocity. Springing and slashing toward the end of the piste. Finally her blade slices across the other fighter's chest and she shouts a pure wild scream that fills up the narrow room and pushes around me and out the door.

She spins and throws her mask down.

"New girl," she says, strung tight. She gleams and paces. Behind her, two real sabres—the kind that win blood, not points—hang in an X against the white wall. A trophy from a war where someone's great-great-grandfather cut other men's throats and earned medals for it. A warning for anyone who faces St Andrew's on the piste.

Piper quits pacing. "Are you here to fight?"

I say, "No."

"Why not?" She presses forward: another attack. Now that I've seen her fight, I can see her next word in the air before she says it: "Afraid?"

I let the silence say, *You know I'm not.*

Her smile fades half a shade.

I say, "When I'm here to fight, you'll know."

I let the door swing shut before she can answer.

Next is Mack.

They've been texting me about him all day, Jenny and Summer and Mads. As fast as Piper, but not as thirsty.

Stay in control, Jenny said.

And I said, *I am.*

And she said, *We don't fall in love*.

Summer said, before I could say anything, *Why not?*

And Jenny said, *It's a fucking rule, okay?*

Then Mads said, *There are no rules*.

That ended it.

We're meeting again tonight, in Jenny's father's library with its floor-to-ceiling legal books and three giant monitors blinking at one desk like department store mirrors. We're meeting because I called it.

I want Duncan dead before it's been a week.

They think I'm too impatient. But they won't stop me if it's what I want, because they're mine and I'm theirs.

That's a rule. That's the only rule.

I cross the tennis court where Mads stood guard yesterday. Come out by the bleachers and climb the steps to the very top. The field is alive again. The wolves run drills and crash hard against each other, on the kill even in practice. The coach shouts and Duncan shouts back.

There isn't a missing space for Connor. Someone else is in, some hungry second-rank boy who knows enough not to ask questions.

Mack is all glory. Better than before. Better than ever. Duncan sees it—I can tell by the way he tries not to look.

Duffy sees it, too. I can tell by the way he stumbles.

They play—

they fight—

—and it's beautiful from up here, circling high enough to understand everything. Banks yells so loud I can see it in his throat—both hands tight on his crosse, smashing fearless into the boys who trust him. And then laughing just as loud a second later when he throws one hand down to pull them back up. Duncan flies smooth and unstoppable, so it looks easy. Duffy reads Duncan with every step.

They're power and boasts. Invincible.

But everyone can break.

When the coach sends them in I sit taller. Today I don't need to stand.

Mack sees me—

puts one hand up to shade his eyes—

slows down without thinking—

—and Banks looks where he's looking and laughs. Mutters something into Mack's ear and claps him on the shoulder and jogs off.

Mack climbs up to where I'm waiting. Each step sings out on the metal.

He smiles. "Jade."

"Mack."

He drops his helmet and gloves and crosse and sits down next to me. We kiss, just hello, but still warm enough that I almost forget again.

When we sit back he says, "I'm glad you didn't get here even one day later."

I laugh. "I wouldn't have wanted to miss yesterday, either."

He remembers to look ashamed. By the time Duncan is dead, he won't remember at all. "No. God, you know I hate that you had to see that."

"I can handle it."

"Yeah. I can tell," he says. The light is in his hair and in his eyes. He's more golden than he's ever been. "You seem like you can handle anything."

I smile for him. "I'm glad you noticed."

He looks out at the field. Green and perfect, like there's

nothing to hide. "I mean," he says, "these days. Today and yesterday. They're my best days this year even with Connor. Because of you."

"Connor's nothing," I say. "Connor was always nothing."

"See, that's what I mean." He ducks his head. "It's not just, you know, I played well yesterday, I played well today, I'm falling for this girl the way I thought was just movie bullshit."

I look down, flock-girl shy, but only for a second, because if Mack is who he needs to be he doesn't really want a flock-girl. He wants the queen.

"It's because you'll say that. You only knew Connor for half a day but you could see who he was, and you'll *say* it. You won't step around it because his dad's important." He leans back against the railing. He smells like mud and sweat but I don't care. It's a battle smell. A winning smell. "You make it so nobody can pretend things aren't the way they are."

"I don't believe in lies," I tell him. And I'm hidden so deep—

behind the murder-bright flowers, under the wood and the stone—

—that I almost believe it.

Mack says, "Neither do I."

I kiss him again. This time I let it last. When our lips are still close and everything is still washed-out, I whisper, "This entire school is going to be ours."

"Next year?" he asks. His eyes are all I can see.

"Next month," I say. "Next *week*."

"Dunc's not going anywhere."

"You didn't think Connor was going anywhere, either, did you? And now—" I run one nail across his throat.

"Jade!" His face is all terror.

I swallow down a scoff. He's weak. The boy who runs swift into the fray. The boy who took his almost-brother's place before he was cold. The boy with vaulting ambition that burns in his eyes—

—but not a wolf like the rest of them. Still human. Still *kind,* or close enough that it's dulled his teeth.

I'll change him. He'll be wicked, too. Like we'll need to be to burn St Andrew's to the ground and rebuild it from the black ashes, new and ours.

"Jade," says Mack, one hand on mine.

I turn my hand palm-up and clasp his the way I'd hold a sabre. "Connor will fall," I say. "You'll take his place. That's what they said, isn't it?"

His face changes again. He turns away so I won't see it, but I do.

He isn't as weak as he wants to be.

"They were just girls. Just messing with Banks and me."

Just girls, says the boy with teeth that won't cut. *Just girls,* about Mads with her foot slamming the accelerator all the way into the floor, hands that know how to fight, nerves that know how to kill. *Just girls,* about Summer's poison lips, about Jenny's whiplash temper that could destroy anyone before they even knew she was swinging for them.

Just girls, like me, and without me noble Mack will never even pick up a knife.

"That's what they *said,*" I say again, and the *s* hisses through my teeth. "Isn't it?"

He turns back to me. Challenge and uncertainty.

"Isn't it?"

He nods.

"Connor will fall."

He nods.

"You'll take his place."

He nods.

I wait. The words claw against my throat.

"And then I'll take Duncan's," says Mack.

I can feel my eyes blazing too bright—wildfire galloping up the hills and choking the sky. I should put it out or look away. But I don't, because that little second of hating him is over and right now he's everything I want.

"You believe them," I say.

"Of course not."

"But you think they're right."

He waits this time. And then he says, "They made it come true, with Connor."

I breathe it in. "What do you mean?"

"You were up there on the roof. You didn't see him with his phone out, either, did you? He didn't post anything."

Pride swells up in me, dark and glowing. "You think it wasn't him?"

He doesn't answer.

"You think it was those girls, and not him, and you let Duncan—"

"Stop," he says, stranglingly urgent. "You can't say it."

I stand up, all wings, looking back up the hill to the school. The sun throws my shadow so long that I don't look like *just a girl* at all. And I laugh for him, a stinging whetted laugh he won't understand. He's *innocent, innocent, innocent* without even trying, except he isn't—he just thinks he is.

I know better.

I touch down on the metal seat, so close my rolled-short skirt pleats over his leg and I can feel his heartbeat through his skin. "I'm not scared of Duncan," I say.

"You should be."

I kiss him, to stop the warning I don't need. To stop the spinning white and the good-king's voice, *that little whore with the jade-green eyes*—

And I pull away and whisper, "You're scared enough for both of us."

He says, out of breath, "I'm not scared."

I say, "Yes, you are."

He says, "I'm not scared. I just don't want them hearing you say that—I don't want them thinking you *want* something to happen to Dunc, too—"

I laugh him blind and snake my arm around him and up his neck, into his hair. "God, no, that's not what I meant."

"I know," he says, and he doesn't. Not at all. Golden-boy Mack with his faith in fate. "But you know how far Dunc will go—"

"Duncan is nothing," I say, just air.

"I'm not scared," says Mack.

"Prove it."

He kisses me the way he kissed me when Connor fell. Everything fades and it's only Mack and me high up above the field, above everything, flying into the sun, shadowing St Andrew's and LA and the whole fucking world to nothing under my wings.

NIGHTFALL

Dark comes faster today.

Yesterday it was sunset forever, hanging on until the very end. Tonight one minute Mack is climbing the bleachers to sit with me and then—

before I can even blink—

—it's night. The sky is clearer than I've ever seen it: true black, not dirty and buzzing. The stars shine diamond-bright on the empty field.

It's just us, Mack and me, at the top of the bleachers and on top of the world. Talking about everything and nothing. Lies and truths and the line between is blurred so gray I'm not sure which is which.

I told him, *Everything's different for me here.*

(Truth.)

I told him, *It's because of you.*

(Lie.)

I told him, *I've never met anybody like you.*

(Truth. I think.)

We're curled together now, leaning against the railing, looking up.

"Are you sure we never met before?" says Mack.

I say, "Never."

He says, "It feels like I've known you for so much longer than a day."

"It was a day that mattered."

"Yeah." He pulls us closer. "But it's more than that. It's like you already knew me, too. Better than anybody. Better than Banks, and we've been best friends since we were kids."

"Maybe I did," I say.

(Truth.)

"Maybe it's because we're the same," he says.

"Maybe," I say.

(Lie.)

"I know what I want," he says. "So do you. Together we could be great."

"We *will* be," I tell him.

(Truth. Truer than anything I've told him all night.)

"Partners in greatness," he says, so bold and stupid and right that I grin into the starlight.

"We'll take what's ours," I say.

Now that it's dark, he doesn't blink it away. "Yesterday," he says, "when you said Connor didn't deserve what he had—"

"He didn't. You did."

"You think—" He hesitates. "Do you think I deserve what Duncan has, too?"

"What *does* he have?" I ask, and I trace a C for *captain* over his heart. "A letter on his jersey? Duffy kissing his ass?"

"It's not just that," he says. "It's power. He decides what's right and wrong. He decides who they are—who *we* are."

He leaves it there on the line, raw and too honest.

"You deserve it," I tell him. "More than anyone."

His eyes stay uncertain.

"I don't know why it isn't already yours," I say. "I don't know why you weren't one of them before, or why all of it's even his at all—"

"They do terrible things. Dunc and Duff and Connor and even Banks, and everybody knows."

"Like what?" I ask.

He looks away.

"What do they do?"

He shakes his head, and he's a coward, and I hate him for it. *Everybody knows,* he said, and he knows, too. But instead of the truth, he says, "You saw what Dunc did to Connor."

"Connor deserved it."

"Maybe, but that doesn't make it right."

I watch him. "You let him do it."

"Nothing I said would've stopped him."

"You let him do it, and he let you in."

It's the truth. I know it and he knows it.

"You could've stopped him," I say, and the dead-dark sky skips bright.

It digs into him, the thing he still won't say out loud, but he swallows it back. "You can't just kill someone because they have dirt on you."

I let my head rest against his chest. His heart beats steady and strong. "If he didn't kill Connor, Connor would've ruined him."

Mack's face flickers darker. "He ruined himself," he says. "They all did. They think they can get away with anything—I mean, they *can,* that's the thing."

"So can you."

"But I *don't,*" he says, and I see it again, like I did yesterday. A little shift—

a twist nobody else would notice—

—another glimpse of the king he'll be once I've finished whispering everything to him. Pouring the fearless ruthless spirit he needs straight into his ears and his blood.

"I'd never do what they do. I want a *future,* Jade. Not just the things we were already going to get because of our parents. I want to earn it. Be better than any of this. Not just use it to get away with—"

He stops.

"Get away with what?" I say, and I sweeten every syllable. Honey and light.

Mack is still staring at the sky. Like it's not just me that knows everything about him. Like it's the stars, too.

My fangs scrape against each other and prick my lips. I taste blood again. "What happened on Friday?"

"I don't know."

"You're *lying*. You said you don't lie." I pull away.

"I don't know. Not everything," he says. He takes my hands in his. "I'll never lie to you, Jade. Never."

(Truth. I think.)

"They won't tell me," he says. "But—"

"You know," I tell him.

It's on his face, all of it. "There was a girl," he says. "They won't tell me what happened. But Dunc and Duff and Connor—even Banks—"

My claws dig into his skin, but he's holding my hands as noose-tight as I'm holding his.

"They did something. They hurt her." His eyes are darker than yesterday. Summer-green hardening to first frost.

And it's there, in words, real.

The truth.

"Duncan doesn't deserve any of this," I long-*s* hiss. "You're the only one who can change anything."

He pulls me close again. For half a second the dark flashes white and I grab for his arm to slash him away—to scream into the empty battlefield—

Then the night is back and the little silver daggers on my hands stop before they tear him apart.

"The sky's too dark tonight," says Mack. "It's never this dark."

"We don't need light," I say.

"It's just—the stars." He looks up, straight up, at everything he wants. "It's like they can see what I want. And—"

I hold my breath so I won't speak. So I won't scream.

"You're the only one I'd tell," he says.

I know.

He looks at the stars and then into my eyes.

He wants what I want.

"Maybe I'm not good," he says. "Maybe I'm worse than any of them."

SWORN

The drive home is perfect. Dark and stars and the wind in my hair, and the cars fly fast and I weave through the glowing lights. Cutting too close.

Just once, I scream into the stream of red and white—

scream for Connor's broken neck—

scream for the dagger we'll slash into Duncan's throat—

scream for Mack, good and evil and all mine—

—for *that little whore,* for *crazy bitch,* for *queen.*

I can still taste Mack's kiss and his promise. Our pact.

Partners in greatness.

Hancock Park is asleep under the trees. I slide into our driveway with my wings lifting me up, already ready for tomorrow—

Jenny stands exactly in my path. The headlights cast her shadow huge against the center garage door. Hands on hips. Eyes on fire.

I stop in front of her. "What the hell, Jen."

She slams both fists against the hood. "What the hell, yourself."

I kill the car and step out onto the driveway.

"Nice of you to text," she says. Her hair has gone from pure black to pink, pastel-bright in the spotlights ringing the house.

I haven't checked my phone since Mack looked up from the field to my perch. I didn't meet Jenny and Summer and Mads at Jenny's house. I didn't even look to see what time it was when we finally walked back to the empty parking lot, hands holding us together in the dark.

"Don't even try to say you don't like him," she says.

"I don't."

"You're fucked." She sits down on the hood of the car and her doll-short skirt fans out. "And go for it, have fun with your Stockholm shit, have fun playing house with a fucking accomplice, have fun pretending this is a normal crush and not some fucked-up proving-something—"

I flare. "Are you done?"

"Hell no," she says. "Have fun. But don't even try your lies with me. Don't you fucking tell me this isn't going to ruin your plan. Because it is, and when it does, I called it. And I don't *want* to call it. We're murdering those boys and your Mack obsession isn't going to fuck that up, okay?"

We stare for a frozen second. The spotlights blink out and back on so quick I'm not sure if it's real.

I slap her across the face.

"*Fuck* you," she says.

My handprint glows on her cheek. "Fuck *you*," I say.

She leans back onto her elbows and says, "That's better."

I watch her for another lit-up breath. "I know what I'm doing."

"No, you don't."

"I'm a St Andrew's girl now," I fire at her. "I'm one of them and Connor's dead."

"You didn't kill him."

"I made it happen. Just like I'm making Mack mine."

"You really think he's going to kill his best friend just because he wants to fuck you?"

My hand twitches. I want to slap her again, but if I do she'll win.

"It doesn't mean anything that he wants you. You know what it meant to his *friends*—"

I lunge for her. Pin her arm against the car with two nails digging deep between the bones in the back of her hand. She yelps. Her eyes light up. She sparks pain and pride.

"Don't you ever forget who I am," I say.

"Exactly," she says. She's still pinned to the hot metal, but she doesn't pull away. "I didn't. But you can't, either. You don't want Mack. You want to kill them."

"I *know*."

"It's not just going to happen. You can't be so fucking cocky."

"It's *working*."

"Duncan already wanted to off Connor. You barely had to do anything."

"Yes, I did. I had to turn into one of them. I had to make him think—"

"Barely anything," she says. "Not compared to the rest of this. Duncan was ready to kill. Your golden boy isn't."

"He will be." My words are iron-solid.

Jenny watches me, still caught in my claws. Her brand-new hair splinters the same way mine did Friday night. She still smells like bleach, even painted as princess-pink as her kindergarten crayon drawings.

"You can't lose your focus," she says.

"I'm not."

She blinks her giant circle lenses. Tonight her eyes shine silver, the same color as Duncan's. She reaches out with the hand I'm not pinning down and brushes her fingertips against the chopped-off ends of my hair, the same way she did on Saturday morning.

"Don't trust him, Jade," she says.

"I don't."

"Don't believe him."

"I don't."

"You're alone," she says. "When we're not there you're alone. Don't forget that."

Finally I let her go. "I'm going to do it," I tell her. "Don't try to tell me I don't remember why I'm there."

And I tip my chin back. Show her my neck, guillotine-ready, with Duncan's bruises bleeding through the makeup. Give her one-two-three seconds. Let my hair fall—

REVENGE

—and step back and fold my arms behind my back, the way my father does when he's pacing in the living room on the phone, forgetting where he is.

"We're here," says Jenny. Not sweet like Summer or steady like Mads. Too fast, but lit up from inside. "You need us."

My hands grip tight onto my skin. "You need me, too."

"Exactly," she says. "It's a rule."

"There are no rules."

She rests one heel against my father's car. My car now, I think. Now that I'm sweet sixteen. "It's going to be harder than you think," she says.

"I'm ready."

Jenny stands up. Cups her hands under my jaw so her pinkies rest cloud-light over the bruises. Rises up onto her tiptoes and kisses my cheek in the same place where I slapped hers.

She says, "Don't lie."

WATER

When Jenny flies off into the night the warm breeze dies all at once, so the whole street is a cold dead void.

My cheek burns where she kissed me. My hand burns where I slapped her.

She said, *Don't trust him, Jade.* I said, *I don't.*

The breeze comes back again, breathing close around my neck and teasing at my too-short hair.

I won't trust him. I won't.

I spin and the breeze scatters away. Then I'm inside with the door locked iron-sure against the night, and skimming up the stairs in the dark, and standing straight and still in front of the same mirror that watched me slash hard with my knife.

When I blink my hair flashes long and platinum.

Jenny said, *Don't trust him.*

I go to the tub and turn on the water. It runs hot and hotter until steam fills the whole room and clings cloying to my skin. The water rises, clear and hot, until it sulks away into the little drains along the top of the porcelain. Until it seeps over the edge and pools shallow around my feet.

I stand in a lie-white towel with my eyes burning green. My hands grasp at the dead ends of my hair. I want it back—

the dark unrepentant black—

the long shining cape that matched me better than my best dress—

—the way it was before I told Mads to turn it St Andrew's blond.

The water boils and bubbles and I kneel beside it and let my fingers drag deep.

Then my mother's hands are in my hair, as gentle and unasking as when I was her little laughing daughter with the too-big eyes. Brushing the dull painted-black a hundred times and a hundred more. Weaving in oil that soaks into every strand from the roots to the knife-sliced ends.

She gathers all my short hair together and sweeps it smooth over my shoulder. Her fingers find the bruises on my neck.

The room is white and hot and choking. My eyes close tight—

shutting out *Don't trust him*—

shutting out *I'll never lie to you, Jade, never*—

shutting out *God damn, she's feisty*—

—and my hands come up out of the water so fired-red I can feel it all the way to the bone.

My fingers find hers over the dark blue spots that mark my skin.

We stay that way, together, until the water runs cold.

CHAPEL

Wednesday morning, Lilia is back.

Except she isn't. Not really.

She slouches in front of the statue, cheekbones jabbing close under her skin, eyes sinking into bruise-blue shadows. Pupils blown too big. No trace of the dying-desperate nerve that made her paint Connor's guilt where everyone could see it.

"Whatever the fuck you're on, it better keep you quiet," says Piper.

Lilia leaves her empty stare exactly where it is. I can almost see through her throat.

Piper's starling-call laugh sings across the commons. "You're over," she says. "Dunc knows you wrote on the banner. And almost got that cop on the damn case, too."

Nothing.

"He's tired of you anyway. Give up."

Nothing.

"Fine," says Piper. "Stay with him. Let him do what he'll do."

Less than nothing.

Piper shakes her head and locks in on me. "New girl," she says. "You and Mack—"

"Me and Mack," I say, as alive as Lilia is dead.

"I never thought there was anything interesting about him until you showed up," she says. Her eyes are beady-bright. "He never even cut class. And now he's the kind of boy who makes out with sluts he barely knows the morning after somebody—" She catches herself just in time. She'll never say it out loud, not as long as Duncan's still king and she and Duffy are still groveling at his feet. "Falls," she says, after a broken little pause. "The kind of boy who doesn't answer when Dunc texts him."

"He doesn't have to listen to Duncan," I say.

Piper glances at Lilia. Her eyes gape huge and vacant. When Piper looks back at me, her whole face says, *She's over, and when I'm in her place—*

"You're going to fall so fast, new girl," says Piper. There's something strange and slipping in her smile. "Mack's going to get sick of you. Dunc's going to get sick of Mack. You're going to end up where every other girl like you ends up."

She thinks she can scare me. She doesn't know anything at all.

"A girl like you," she says, and her voice goes feather-soft so none of the flock-girls can hear. "Who thinks she can come in and take whatever she wants—"

Friday night shimmers between us, a static-white scrap coming back: Piper pushing past Porter right on Duffy's heels, tripping into the room, grabbing for her second-place boy, shrieking, *You can't just take whatever you want like I'm not even anything—*

And Duffy said, *You're not.*

"None of this is yours. You're just the entertainment of the week," says Piper. "They'll throw you out when they're done with you, unless you learn how to follow the rules. You don't even know what they'll do to a girl like you—"

Fine, said Piper on Friday night. Following the rules, seething and powerless and still shrieking at Duffy, and Duffy's hand came down hard against my face and crushed my skull down. And Piper said, *Go fuck some roofied slut—*

"Piper," says Duncan's purring charming voice right beside us. "Stop."

We both step back.

"Jade," says Duncan. "Let's talk."

He takes a step closer, and behind him the wolves close rank. I steal a glance at Mack. He's soldier-faced like the rest of them but I can read his eyes. He's watching Duncan as much as Duffy does now, but instead of scrambling ready-to-serve he's measuring out what Duncan has to lose.

I smile at Duncan. Perfectly, shiningly innocent. "Let's," I say.

He puts one arm behind me, not quite touching my back but doing everything he can to own me anyway. Walks away from the rest of them without even one look at Lilia.

I want to spin around and grab the arm he's caging me with and break it. Hear the bone crack and see the splintered white rip through his skin. Watch his face fold in pain and his body crumple. Listen to him beg for mercy.

Instead I bite my cheek until blood coats my tongue, and I keep my heels clicking even.

Duncan takes us to the chapel. He pushes one door open and lets the wood and iron swing back heavy after us. Dull light seeps through the stained glass. At the far end of the room, a huge gold crucifix hangs behind the altar. Christ looks up instead of down at us. Crowned with thorns. Hands dripping gold blood.

"New girl," says Duncan with a flash of teeth. "Jade Khanjara." He pronounces it exactly right and oiled-smooth, like it's natural on his lips.

"James Duncan," I answer.

He laughs. His eyes flicker fast across my face. We're at the doors, under the stone arch, and he stands just right so he can pretend he isn't locking me into the corner on purpose.

"What's your story?" he asks.

"Everyone already knows it," I say. He's dialing up his good-king charm, the same sheen he wore at his party, so crafted-perfect he looked like one of his plaster statues breathed to life. When Summer saw him she said, *Damn, I can see why he's their king,* but Mads said, *Don't try it. Not even you.* And then Jenny was pulling us hand-in-hand-in-hand-in-hand through the crowd, but I dragged back and kept my eyes on him because Summer was right: there was something in the way he was watching the whole party that said he ruled it all.

For a second his eyes met mine. For a second his teeth flashed white. Then his chin tipped down and he said something to the boy in his shadow, and the shadow-boy's smile flashed bright, too.

"Piper doesn't trust you," he says now. Easy smile, easy stance, easy laugh. But it's not easy at all. Up close, I can see all the whirring first-place effort underneath.

"I've noticed," I say.

"She says I shouldn't, either."

I lean into the cage he's built around me so the bars bend and strain. "I didn't realize you took orders from Duffy's girlfriend."

He scoffs and then he gives me a little nod, the same way the boy Piper was fighting yesterday nodded when she got her final touch. He knows I've won the point. "Piper's insecurities don't matter to me," says Duncan.

"Likewise."

He leans one hand against the door: a third wall closing me in. "Mack's losing his mind over you."

I say, coy, "We're a good match, don't you think?"

"You and Mack?" He shrugs. When his shoulders settle back down, he's the slightest bit closer than he was before. "Not bad. You and me? Better."

I laugh. Flock-girl flattery. "You're with Lilia."

"There's an expiration date on that," he says, and I laugh again because he's right for exactly the wrong reason.

"If Lilia's your type, I'm not," I tell him.

"Lilia's everyone's type." His eyebrows edge up just enough to finish the sentence for him. "But you're different. You're not a St Andrew's girl."

"Not yet."

"Not ever." He shifts closer. "You'll be good for Mack."

"I know."

He shows his marble-hard smile again. "You know a lot."

I nod.

"You know what happened to Connor."

He's close enough now that I have to tip my chin back to look into his eyes. "I do."

He waits for me to say more, but I don't. Outside the stained glass, shadows flutter and breathe.

"I trusted him," Duncan says, finally. Lying.

"That was a mistake." I say it sweeter than sweet.

He grins. "Never a St Andrew's girl." Then, "He confessed, you know."

I see them on the roof, circling closer to the edge in the blood-red sunset.

"He admitted everything. Maybe he thought I'd let him get away with it."

He's still lying.

"Of course it didn't change what he did. Betrayal doesn't get you anywhere around here."

It's a warning.

"Still—" And this time he makes it obvious when he leans closer. The play he's been plotting since we walked out on his pack. "He died well, don't you think?"

"Yes," I hiss before I can stop myself.

"There it is," he hisses back, so close I breathe in cold mint and aftershave. The dusky stained-glass light blows out to white—

God damn, she's feisty—

I jerk away and my head hits the stone wall. I'm back in the chapel, back in the almost-dark, but Duncan still pushes too close. He leers victory all across his face.

"We'd be good together," he says, his lips so close to mine it's almost a kiss. "We'd be power. You'd like it."

I flatten my hands against the stone. Cold and unfeeling and jagged. He hasn't won. He won't. "So would you," I say, and I leave my murder-red lips parted and I don't flinch. Not again.

His breath catches.

I pounce. One hand off the wall and onto his arm, silver skimming over the dark blue of his blazer. I say, clear and bright, "I'm with Mack."

He grabs my arm. It takes everything in me not to scream. Not to fight. Not to kill him right here with his gold god watching.

"For now," he says. "Until he finds out who you really are."

I won't ask him what he means. I won't.

"I'm watching you, new girl," he says. He smiles his practiced smile.

I smile mine back. His hand on my arm burns like a brand.

"You and me," he says. "Soon."

He walks out.

REVELATIONS

I have to find Mack.

The bells in the tower over the chapel are ringing already, with Duncan barely gone, with me alone in the dusk breathing his scent and digging at the air instead of his skin. Eight long mournful tolls. I should be sitting down at my lab table in biology and crisscrossing my ankles and smiling jailbait-pretty at Dr. Farris in his horn-rimmed glasses.

I have to find Mack.

You and me, said Duncan. *We'd be power,* said Duncan. *You'd like it.*

Shut the bitch up, said Duncan. *God damn, she's feisty,* said Duncan. *You like it—*

I yank the doors open and rush out. I see white and dead kings. I see my good long knife turning red.

I need him dead.

I need to find Mack.

I'm almost running now—clattering over the wood and under the stone, running for the humanities hall, no plan and no control and I need it back but first—

I need Mack.

I wing around the corner and there he is, with a classroom door swinging shut behind him. Empty-handed and so full of pain and fury it stops me dead in my tracks because—

until he finds out who you really are, said Duncan—

But he grabs my arms and I grab his and we spin into the wall and stumble into a cobwebbed prayer niche with two tapers flickering and a cracked Bible gathering dust.

We fall onto a red velvet kneeling bench, clinging to each other.

Mack says, "Jade."

I breathe in.

His face flickers with something darker than I've ever seen in him. "I knew. I knew enough—"

I breathe out. The flames shiver.

He says, "Friday night—"

The walls crawl in close.

"Banks told me," says Mack, and I see him there at Duncan's house: Banks with the drink. Banks closing in. Banks washing out to a blank face and a dazzling smile and teeth I'll break like glass. "Because Connor's dead and I'm one of them now. I'm *one* of them—" And he shudders hard and deep. "He told me what they did. All of it."

His eyes search mine.

"You know," he says.

The scream in my throat finally dissolves. The velvet bristles under my skin and the cobwebs float weightless. My voice slides out smooth. "I know."

"I thought it was over—" His hands grip tighter. "Because Connor posted that picture. Because too many people know, and even Lilia's ready to tell. And because Connor's dead. Dunc killed him for it and I let him, I *let* him, because I thought then they'd have to stop. But Banks—my best damn friend, since we were *five,* and it's not like I didn't know the way he is when he's with Dunc and the boys—but when I told him, he laughed in my face. It's not over, it's never over, and now I'm one of them. I *killed* for them—"

My heartbeat is even. I won't lose myself again.

Mack still has his eyes on me, wild and betrayed. "You—" he says, like he's just now realizing how spinning-unwound I was when he found me and I found him. "What happened?"

I'm steel and control. I'm winged and ready.

I say, "Duncan—"

We'd be good together. You'd like it—

I weld his threat into what I need. Let it show just enough and just the right way.

I say, "He knows I know. Piper told me and he found out—"

Lies. But lies that tell the truth.

I say, "He was talking about Connor. He said—" And I take good-king Duncan's words back and hold them up to his neck, blade-first. "'Betrayal doesn't get you anywhere.'"

Mack's hands tighten to fists.

"He said he doesn't trust me," I whisper.

Our nook swallows the words up whole. The narrow flames stand broken-clock still.

"I know," I tell Mack. "And nobody who knows is safe."

He pulls me into his arms. He kisses me. Soft and plain, but with something running under it that shocks through me like lightning. His weakness is cracking away. What's left is loyal and ruthless.

He says, "I won't let him hurt you."

I say, "He'll get away with it."

Truth.

His eyes stay on mine. The flames glow bright.

He says, "He won't if we stop him."

LAIR

Mads—Madalena dos Santos, my best friend and my blood-sister and the hard heart of our coven—is on her front steps between the crowding palmetto branches when I pull in.

The house sprawls California classic, stucco and terra cotta, behind a gate vicious enough for a country where warlords set the rules. Her father makes deals with men in Lagos and Malibu; in São Paulo and Shanghai. Men who show up at this gate, wrecked and raging, when the land they sold for nothing sells again for everything.

The gate keeps them out but lets me in.

"Jade," says Mads when I get to the steps. The security cameras blink. She's in visor-heavy sunglasses and a dress the color of fire.

"It's done," I say, and we go inside. The housekeeper takes my blazer without a word and disappears down a corridor. "He'll kill them."

"You're sure?" Mads asks.

"Yes," I say.

She wraps me into a hug and we spin around and through the hall. "When?"

"This weekend."

"Does he know?"

Of course she asks, because she knows me better than anyone. Of course I answer, because she's her. "Almost," I say. "Soon. He'll do it and he'll think he chose it all on his own." We come back outside, along the courtyard and in the shade. "His parents are out of town this weekend. Duncan already told him to have a party on Friday."

I could have told her eight hours ago when Mack went from follower to king just for me. Instead I texted the coven one word, *Closer.* I'm not leaving a trail anyone can trace. Not when Duncan is watching me almost as close as I'm watching him.

"How's he going to get away with it?" Mads asks.

I open the door to the training room. "I'm going to make his watchdog take the fall."

"Duffy?"

"Porter," I say. The boy who stood at the door and asked Connor, *are you sure?* "He carries a knife. He's not smart enough to see anything coming and he's not smart enough for Duncan to think he's a threat."

She nods. We sit down along the wall. The training room echoes empty: her father's weights, her brothers' boxing ring, her fencing piste. Window-lined and sparkling clean.

We're safer here than anywhere else in the world. Here behind the humming fence in the house where almost everyone carries a gun and everyone knows how to use one.

No one is weak at Mads's house.

"Mack kills Duncan and Porter gets framed," says Mads. Her sunglasses are still in place. She stares straight ahead like she can see through walls and time and lies. "What happens to Porter?"

"Let him self-destruct."

"Too risky."

She doesn't know how weak Porter is. Hunching in front of the door. Panicking when Banks asked for his knife. Afraid enough to carry a weapon to a party where everyone is his friend. Where everyone has deadly secrets, and he knows every last one of them.

Afraid enough to snap. Everyone will believe it, just like everyone believed Connor couldn't keep his mouth shut.

"He'll defend himself," says Mads. "Even if everybody thinks he's lying, they'll start looking at the rest of you."

"Then I'll *make* him self-destruct," I say. "Make the guilt ruin him."

Mads cracks her knuckles, one at a time. "Guilt won't ruin boys like them."

"It already is," I say. "They let Duncan kill Connor. Banks is ready to kill somebody else. Duffy's so nervous it's embarrassing. The whole thing—" I wave one hand: the pack, the flock, the perfect untouchable crowd with their iron grip on St Andrew's. "The cracks are showing."

"It's not guilt," says Mads. "It's fear."

"Fucking cowards," I hiss. For one fleeting second I'm proud of every bruise and every scratch—

the dark handprints on my arms and my neck and my ribs—

my broken claws—

the slash across my cheek—

—because every mark they left, everything they did, didn't even get close to breaking me.

I'm ten times stronger than they'll ever be.

A thousand times more ruthless.

"Fear," says Mads again. "That's what's ruining them."

I nod. Slow, but then certain. She's right. It's fear that turned the pack against Connor and made Porter drop his knife. All the brash brave boys with their crosses and their secrets—

They're fucking terrified.

"They don't even know what fear is yet," I tell Mads. She pushes her sunglasses up. Underneath, her eyes gleam cold. "By Friday they'll be looking over their shoulders so hard they won't even see what's right in front of them. Porter's going to snap. I know it."

Mads doesn't answer.

"What?"

"You can't do it alone," she says. Almost what Jenny said yesterday.

"I can do anything." The words swish sabre-sharp.

She scoots closer until there's no space between us. Summer would say, *You don't have to, not without us.* Jenny would say, *Don't lie,* even though I'm not.

Mads says, "I know."

But then she says, "Remember when we learned to fight?"

Six years ago. Here, in this same room with the windows shadowed by palms and banana plants green through every drought. Mads and me running in together too fast for even Jenny and Summer to keep up. Matching bloody lips. The first day we knew we had wings.

The first day Mads's father let her be her real self at school.

We got ready together, in matching girl-uniforms, like it always should have been. We wore our gold Best Friends necklaces outside our white shirts instead of hidden underneath. She painted my lips and I painted hers with a shiny perfect tube I stole off my mother's vanity. Bright red, halfway between Mads's color and mine.

We walked into school with our hands clutched together like the twin-C logo on our stolen lipstick. Ready. Daring them to say anything.

They didn't. Not with all of us, Jenny and Summer and Mads and me, linked elbows and whispering—

laughing—

eyes quick and narrowing—

—so every girl in school knew we were the ones to watch and the ones to watch out for. The cool girls. The mean girls. We were middle school six months early, wearing our shiny new crowns before anyone else knew a monarchy was coming.

We were glossy red-lipped victory. The other girls didn't even dare.

Then the last bell rang and Mrs. Maddox called me up to her desk to ask me why Kimberly Kostos was crying after lunch and blaming me for her broken phone, screen shattered against a table corner when she stared too long at Mads. It took two minutes of big eyes and smiling to trick Mrs. Maddox into thinking Kimberly made the whole story up—

and when I got outside Jenny and Summer were scrambling and stuck at the edge of a half-circle of boys, and Mads was caught against the wall with two of them too close. Pulling at her skirt. Twisting her necklace.

She was stone-still with her head high. Fear and pride on her face.

And I was angrier than I'd been in my whole life. I shoved in but the circle crushed tighter together and I couldn't get to her—

I shouted her name, *Mads*—

One of the boys laughed mean and said her deadname instead, and the other one slashed his hand across her face and smeared lipstick and blood across her skin and stained his palm guilt-red. *Fake,* he said, *like you*—

She pushed him. He fell. But there were too many of them, and she was alone, and I hated them so much I could feel it in my teeth—

And I ran hard at the circle and smashed through and fell almost into the wall so it was two of us now. Mads and me, together.

She shouted loud and I screamed, *Get away get away get away.* They laughed. Far away Summer and Jenny shrieked. The boy with the red hand staggered back up and said *bitch* and swung and hit me in the mouth, the same as Mads, and my scream got louder and my words came back new: *You'll pay you'll pay you'll pay.*

Mads found my hand and pulled so I looked at her for just long enough to read her face, and then we were both screaming and rushing at the two of them. Hard enough that they stumbled back. Fierce enough that the circle broke for us before we could break it ourselves.

We ran—

fast and hard without stopping, without looking back—

until we weren't running at all—

—until we flew.

Back to Mads's house, through the gate and through the doors and straight to her father. Tall and never smiling and always in suits that shone like mirrors. There were three men with him, the same kind of men who were always coming and going in black-windowed cars when Mads and I were playing in the yard.

He sent them away. They didn't ask questions.

Then he took Mads and me outside and past the courtyard to the training room. In the farthest corner her two brothers were dancing angry graceful circles in the boxing ring. Their coach shouted. They hit harder.

Her father said, *You need to learn how to fight.*

Mads said, *Yes, sir.*

I said, *We're going to kill them.*

Her father went to the case on the wall. Needle-thin swords hung under the glass. Shining. Tempting.

He took out two of the blades. He said, *You have to be brilliant.*

I reached for one.

He said, *You have to be patient.*

I didn't reach again, but I didn't look away from the blades.

One came up and tapped under my chin. It wasn't sharp, but it felt like power.

He said, *Make your rage fight for you. It's your greatest gift.*

We learned to fight. With our sabres and our claws. With schemes and patience.

With rage.

"They're afraid of us," says Mads. The same girl she was then, standing in that circle with blood on her face but her chin up. "The Hillview boys. And the girls."

She's right. We made them afraid—

of Summer's daisy smile painted over her black-widow heart—

of Jenny's candy necklaces and fire-fast rumors—

of Mads's fists looped with gold rings and her eyes that watch close—

of my forever-long plots so good that by the end they'd be begging me to *get it over with, please, just get your revenge and let me sleep again*—

We never needed other friends. We never wanted other friends.

She reads my mind: "We made them afraid."

I say, "We made them ours."

She nods. Then she says, "Porter. Send him to me after."

I say, "Done."

We stand up together.

We go to the glass case and get out our weapons.

We'll fight with rage.

GHOSTS

At night I sit in my bed under the window in the almost-dark. My phone glows with texts from Mack—

Jade, it sounds crazy but I think we were meant to meet like this—

Meant to be together—

It always had to be us, to change everything—

Partners in greatness.

Every time his words flicker onto the screen they warm my hands.

We don't talk about Duncan or Connor or what we have to do. But it glistens underneath every text anyway. We know what we aren't saying.

We know it so well we don't have to say it.

When my phone stops lighting up I leave it next to me and unfold the page Summer printed. Search for the dazzle-smiled boy again. Knock all the matching faces against my memory to try to bring him back. It was Banks on the dance floor, Banks with the drink, Banks with the boldest best laugh—

—but I have to see his smile on the page. See it clear, right in front of me, so I can see it again when I watch the life drain out of him. It's missing still, no matter how hard I stare at his teeth. No matter how much I test the rest of them: gleaming Duncan and all his wolves. Little-boy Malcolm, tight-lipped, and his clambering second-rank. Duffy and Porter and even Mack.

Every boy but one.

On Monday night, after Connor fell, I took out the long silver knife and stabbed it through his picture. Ripped his smirking face out of the page.

Next to his torn-open space Duncan's silver eyes glitter even on paper. He matters the most. The order is cracking already, but once Duncan is gone, it will crumble.

The rest of them will be easy.

We just have to kill the king.

Something taps against my bedroom door but I don't look up. I stare hard at Duncan. Let my rage turn from a storm to a sabre. Hold myself patient and brilliant even when his paper eyes wink and I smell mint and aftershave and hear his voice so clear the skin on my neck pricks tight—

You like it—

My bedroom door swings open dream-silent. Light streams in.

There it is, he hisses, right here in my room—

Duncan.

I grab the knife off my nightstand. The blood rushes in my ears.

There it is—

I'll kill him right here. I will.

The light switches on and my knife-hand comes back and I breathe in sharp—

It's my father.

Not Duncan.

"Elle—" he says—

The air floods back out of my lungs, singing shrill, until I'm hollow. I bring the knife down.

"He was here," I say, and it's the truth even though it can't be.

"He wasn't," my father tells me. His voice makes my ribs ache.

I hate Summer for making me tell.

"He was," I whisper, truth and lies and exactly why I need to kill the real Duncan. "I heard him. He was here."

My father sits down in my desk chair. He looks exactly as perfect as he always does.

Except for his eyes.

"He will never be here," my father says. "Never."

I trust it even more than I trust the barbed wire and the high fence around Mads's house.

"We'll do anything," he says, unwavering. "Anything for you."

I run one finger along the sharp edge of the knife. "I'm fine," I say, and it stabs into me worse than any blade ever could, the way this hurts him.

"You don't have to be," says my father. "You can cry. You can talk. You can tell, if you want."

"No," I say with my eyes not meeting his.

My father's hand finds mine. Wraps around it so we both hold the knife, together.

I look at him, finally.

He says, "Anything you want is yours."

We sit in silence until I'm sure I won't hear Duncan again. Until I fold the paper and tuck it into my pillowcase. Text back to Mack's good night: *Dream about me*. Text the coven: *Tomorrow morning, Mads's car*.

Until I set the knife back on my nightstand.

My father doesn't try to take it away.

He kisses the top of my head the way he did when I was five years old with eyes too big for my face and tiny gold hoops in my ears. He turns off the light. He rolls the desk chair out behind him and pulls the door almost closed.

And he sits outside my room until dawn.

HIT LIST

Piper is the one who finds my coven's work.

It's lunchtime and we're sitting at the long table along the leaded glass. Midday sunlight shines down on Duncan and his wolves and Lilia and her starlings. We're all together still, but not for long. Not with the way Duncan never looks at his queen and Piper isn't next to Duffy and Banks's grin is hungrier than it should be.

Not with the way they all look at Mack and me, strong instead of breaking.

The doors on the far side of the room fling open so hard they crack against the stone like thunder.

Piper flies in clutching a paper close to her chest. Her sabre cuts her path straight to our table. She snaps the page taut between her hands.

It's Connor's team portrait, blown up so it fills almost the whole page. Where his eyes should be, there are two ragged roles. Where his name should be, thick red letters say

WHO'S NEXT?

Piper straightens up so everyone can lean in and see the page. Then she drops it. It slices a zigzag down to the table and slides up to rest against Duncan's drink.

They face off. Their eyes sling suspicion. Both of them measuring the other. Both of them without one bit of trust left even though both of them know the other one wouldn't be stupid enough to dig their own grave like this.

Duncan's eyes say, *Stay quiet*.

Piper's whole face says, *Fuck you*.

She says, loud, "Whoever did this, you better talk."

The silence ripples out so it isn't just Duncan's table; it's half-circles spreading wide away from the wall. Lilia's girls are frozen still.

I look up at Piper and smile. "Or what?" I murmur so quiet she'll be the only one who can know for sure that I said it at all. "We're next?"

She grabs the paper and rips it in half, straight down Connor's crooked face. "*Fuck* you, new girl. You should know better by now."

I say, "So should you."

She rips the portrait again. "*All* of you should know better." Her eyes skim from Lilia to the lowliest freshman flock-girl and back. "Don't you think so, Lili?"

Lilia looks past her. Her gaze doesn't find its focus. "Were you the only one?"

"What?"

"Were you the only one," Lilia says again, dragging each word out of her throat. She doesn't have the breath to turn it into a question. "Who got a note."

Piper flares. "How should I know? I didn't do a fuck-ing census." Duffy pulls at her hand so she'll sit down and shut up, but she shakes him off. "I saw this shit on my car and I ripped it off and came in here to see who felt like confessing—"

Duncan stands up. "That's enough," he says. Impossibly even. "Let's find out."

His wolves fall into formation: Duffy and Banks and Mack flanking him and the rest of them falling in behind. The girls flutter alongside. A few not-it girls from the next table try to slip in but Piper sends them a glare that knocks them back into their seats. It holds, but only barely.

Duncan leads the pack through the halls and out the front doors. He stops at the top of the steps, and everyone else stops with him, and everyone looks down together at the parking lot.

I already know where every note is. So I watch their faces and see it sink in—

to each of them on their own when they see they're on the list—

—and then to all of them, together, when they realize what it means.

Duncan.

Duffy.

Banks.

Malcolm, the boy who mixed the drink.

Porter, the boy who guarded the door.

Piper, the girl who knew and smirked and left.

And—

"Mack," says Porter, and he checks his pocket for his knife. "Why did you get one when you didn't—"

Banks claps a hard hand down on Porter's shoulder.

"Doesn't mean anything," he says. "None of it means anything."

Duncan spins and faces the crowd. "Go back inside," he says.

Some of them stir. Some of them stay.

"You heard him," says Banks. "Shitty prank anyway."

They go, finally, grumbling and staring too long.

"Probably those damn girls in the masks," Banks says when the doors slam.

Duffy sways, gray and anxious. "I thought you said Connor sent those girls."

"Connor didn't do this." Duncan's voice cuts deep. He turns to Duffy: "Take care of it."

Duffy hurries double-time down the stairs. He crosses the lane to the parking lot without looking.

"We don't talk about this," says Duncan. "Not until we're alone."

He looks at Mack—golden-boy Mack, noble Mack, one of them now but all mine.

"Tomorrow," says Duncan. "Mack's house. The party's still on. Nobody gets in unless I say they get in. Until then—"

He lets the space hang heavy.

He goes back inside and the rest of them follow. Glancing over their shoulders. Watching Duffy pull the last note out from against the last windshield.

Afraid.

"Jade," says Mack from the door, "are you coming?"

For a second Duffy flounders, all alone in the dead-still parking lot, staring down at Connor's empty eyes and the smearing red threat.

"Yes," I say. Another hiss even though I don't mean to. But I don't move until Duffy looks up and sees me watching.

I smile bright and fearless. He shudders hard enough that I can see it from the top of the stairs.

I text the coven: *Perfect.* I turn on my heel and let my skirt flip a little.

No one trusts anyone anymore.

TANGLED

We meet late, at Mads's house. We sit knee-to-knee in a circle on the fencing strip. When Summer comes in she tries to turn on a light but I don't let her.

We don't need light.

"Tomorrow," I say, the same as Duncan said, except he was circling his troops to weather the storm and I'm circling mine to bring it. "Duncan dies."

Shadows weave in through the branches outside. They don't ask me if Mack promised. They don't ask me how. They already know.

"I'll wait for Porter," says Mads.

"We'll wait for Mads," says Jenny.

"Jade," says Summer. "Are you sure?"

Jenny laughs her little-girl laugh. "Of course she's sure."

"I'm serious." Summer puts one hand on mine. "This is real. You can't take it back."

Mads says, "Neither can they."

"I know," says Summer. "But what if you get caught?"

"I won't," I say.

And Jenny says, "The shittiest defense attorney in LA could guarantee she'd walk."

"I *know*," says Summer again. Her eyes cut quick to Jenny. "But what if Mack gets caught?"

"Oh fucking well," says Jenny, and Summer's lips press together.

"We won't get caught," I say. "And I'm glad I can't take it back. I hope I dream about him dying every night for the rest of my life."

Jenny says what she said the first time I told them what I was going to do to the boys:

Fair is foul, and foul is fair

I take Summer's hand and Mads's. They take Jenny's. We sit still in the rolling shadows. The room whispers Jenny's words back to us. Outside, the leaves stir.

We're magic. I can feel it right now in the dark. We're invisible when we need to be and then so firework-bright no one can look away. We're patience and brilliance. We never forget.

We never forgive.

We walk out together. The security fence hums overhead, friendly and warning. The spotlights star our shadows on the lawn.

Jenny stares up at the clear night sky and says, "A storm is coming."

It's the last thing we say. We don't say good-bye—not tonight. Jenny drives out first, and then me, and then Summer. Mads watches from the steps.

Summer follows me home and parks in the street. When I walk down to meet her she's already out and leaning against the door, looking up into the jacaranda leaves.

"Don't do it," she says. The breeze stirs through her hair. She smells like myrrh.

"It's done," I say.

"I don't mean don't kill him." Her gaze comes down and locks on me. "I mean don't fall in love."

"I'm not one of those boys you throw away."

She takes my hand and swings it back-and-forth the way she did back in our cul-de-sac days when the nanny dropped her off to play with Jenny and Mads and me, before the nanny tried too hard to take Summer's first stepmother's place and got sent back to wherever she came from. "Neither is he," she says.

"He's nothing," I tell her. A lie, because anyone who kills for me stops being no one the second the knife falls—

a lie, because no one is nothing if he wants everything enough to twist guilt and fear into whatever he needs it to be so he can pretend he's noble instead of just ambitious—

—a lie, because my heartbeat shivers faster every time he looks at me with dark resolve hardening his face.

Summer swings our hands higher. "Kill the king," she says. "Kill his boys. But don't—"

"Like you have any room to talk." I shouldn't say it, but I do.

She sighs and I hear her whole heart in it. "Exactly."

I come closer. "You know she loves you, too."

"She doesn't. Not like I love her."

"It's just the way she acts. You know how she is."

Summer shakes her head. Her hair shimmers on her shoulders like wings. "Even if you're right—"

"I'm right."

"Of course you are," she says with a little laugh, but it isn't sharp the way Jenny would make it. Summer, the deadliest of all of us, and still the one whose heart beats closest to her skin. "But even if she loves me we could never be together. It would ruin the coven."

I don't tell her she's wrong. The breeze picks up again, warm and thick and wanting.

"Don't fall in love," Summer says. She lets go of my hands. "Not with him."

THE FORTRESS

Mack lives high in the hills, a long winding drive away from the heat and light of the city. Past Lilia's house and Duncan's. Up so many twists and turns that when I look back to where we came from, the skyscrapers are small enough to brush away with one hand.

"They're never home," says Mack when we pull up to his drive. There's a gate, but it isn't like the gate at Mads's house. It's a gate that asks you to stay out. At Mads's house, it's an order. "They're always away on business."

The gate slides open. Sturdy metal letters spell out INVERNESS along the top row of bars. "My dad used to be around. He'd take a whole week off and we'd take the yacht down to Mexico. Then he got his promotion, and you know . . ." He looks at me and shrugs. Behind him the lawn is green like his eyes. Green with promise.

"Ambition," I say.

That one word squares his shoulders. "Last summer I took it out myself. The boat, down to San Diego. They never knew. He called while I was out—like, 'Hey, it'll be another week, we're right on the edge of a deal that'll blow everybody away.'"

"You don't need him here," I say, and I kiss him. "More time for us."

His smile wavers more than it should.

"You'll be greater than he'll ever be."

His shoulders square again.

"Come on," I say. I bring one hand up to his face and make him look into my eyes. I kiss him again, hard and certain. He takes his hands off the wheel and kisses me back.

I don't pull away until I feel his fear fire into resolve. When I do, he doesn't settle back into his seat. He wants more. He wants me.

Not yet.

Not until I know he's worth me.

"Come on," I say again. "We have to get ready. We're not leaving anything to chance."

Mack pulls into the garage and taps the door shut behind us. For a second we're alone in the dark. I can feel it—

just a shifting hologram glimpse of it, but there—

—the future, right here in this instant. *Our* future.

I say, "Promise me you're not afraid."

He says, "I promise."

I say, "Promise me you won't be afraid tonight."

He says, "I promise."

But it isn't as deadbolt-strong as I want it to be.

I can't win him with fear—not tonight. I can't win him with guilt, either, until the knife is in his hands and we've come too far to go back.

So I say it, stupid and bold in one quick breath: "Promise me you love me."

He says, "I promise."

He says, "I've never loved anyone more."

And I feel my smile blooming bright across my face.

By the time Duncan's car starts its crawl up the hill to Inverness we're ready. The liquor decks every counter. Everything is top-shelf and brand-new, so strong Duncan and his wolves won't realize how drunk they are until the whole world blurs. The man at the store didn't even look twice when I handed him the license I stole out of my sister's purse at Christmas. When I need to be, I'm twenty-six, with tastes to match.

I've wound through every room. I've chosen where each of them will be. Duncan and Lilia are in the master suite, exactly like a king deserves. Tucked away on the very end of the house where no one will hear him if he screams.

If he can.

Mack and I are one door away, in his room, the last stop on the only hall that goes to Duncan's suite. Porter will sleep on the floor outside Duncan's door: Duncan ordered it, doubling down and paranoid enough to need a guard-dog, but it won't keep him safe. Duffy and Piper get the best guest room, downstairs and far away. Banks and Malcolm can fight over whatever rooms are left.

One hour past midnight, they'll all be happy-drunk and

dozing off. Forgetting Connor's eyeless soulless face staring them down from their windshields. Forgetting *that little whore with the jade-green eyes.*

Two hours past midnight, Duncan will be dead.

"He'll be here in five minutes," says Mack. We're on a balcony looking down to where the road curls out between the houses and turns back on itself to climb higher. Duncan takes the turns fast and smooth. "Banks is with him."

A shadow skims across the sun and a huge dark-winged bird glides down to the oleander tree just inside the gate. It's hideous and beautiful and I've never seen anything like it. It lands on an almost-bare branch and its talons wrap tight. The branch bows lower. The bird cries out, harsh and piercing. Duncan's car disappears behind another row of trees.

"When will they leave?" I ask Mack. Testing him, always, because I need to be sure.

"Tomorrow," he says. "In the morning. That's what Duncan said."

"Tomorrow. Of course." I keep my voice even. Practice, for Duncan and his boys. "Not that Duncan's going to be around to see the sunrise."

I watch Mack when I say it. The guilt writes itself across his face so clear anyone could read it.

"God, look at you," I say, and I trace my index fingers from his temples down along his jaw. "You're so obvious, golden boy."

"How do you do it?" He traces my face, too. "How do you hide it when you're with him?"

I shrug like I've never thought about it. Like I've never had to fold up my wings and think *innocent, innocent, innocent.* "It's a party," I say, and my smile flashes as bold as it did last week when we spun through the doors into Duncan's house with the shimmering music and the lights and the wolves. "We're drinking. We're celebrating. We're saying, fuck whoever left those pictures, fuck everyone in the world who isn't us. So look like it."

He unburies a smile, but it crawls with secrets.

"Don't think about anything that comes later," I tell him. "He trusts you. You're one of them."

His smile fades back to guilt.

"No." I wrap my arms around him and turn so my back presses against the railing and I stand between him and the boy he'll kill tonight. "When they come in, you'll take care of them. Give them drinks. Talk about how great Banks was at practice and how impressive it is that Duncan's going to Dartmouth and how Piper needs to learn how to shut up."

"It's a party," he says. He stares so deep into my eyes I almost think he can see who I really am.

Almost. Not quite.

I give him my very best St Andrew's smile like the good girl the teachers think I am. Like the bleeding-bright flowers creeping up the stone walls, hiding the cracks and the secrets.

"Look like the innocent flower," I say, and I kiss him—

so virgin-pure he wouldn't even know it was me if he closed his eyes—

but then I turn it deep and cruel, and he feels it and he kisses back just as hungry—

—and I catch his lip between my teeth, but he doesn't pull away.

I let him go. I say, "But be the serpent under it."

Downstairs, a bell rings. Duncan's car waits at the gate.

I breathe out my last line: *Leave all the rest to me.*

TRUTH OR DARE

Midnight comes blindingly fast. The grandfather clock on the landing clangs loud and out of tune. Drowning out Banks's rap so only the blown-out bass comes through.

When the last chime tolls, all of us—the best and the brightest St Andrew's has ever had—cheer. A wild loud shout. Raising our glasses: the most expensive crystal in the cabinet, not one red plastic cup in sight, because tonight we're drinking for the king.

"To Duncan!" I shout when the cheer ends.

"To Duncan!" the rest of them yell.

And I weave in with vodka in one hand and tequila in the other and pour too much and they drink it anyway.

Tonight, I decide how it ends.

"Maybe you don't suck," says Piper, too drunk already, when I get to her. "Maybe you'll be me when I'm Lilia."

I fill her glass. "I doubt it."

She raises it. "Maybe. And we'll make sure shit like that doesn't happen." She nods at the sofa across from us. Three flock-girls and two of Malcolm's second-rank boys tangle together and laugh. Malcolm brought the boys and Porter brought the girls, stumbling in wide-eyed with his hand hovering over his knife. Duncan didn't send them home. Instead he looked at Banks and said, *Watch them,* and looked at Porter and said, *We'll talk Monday.*

They won't.

"I mean, God, we still don't know who left those notes." Her words are liquor-loose. "Somebody fucking threatens us, and Malcolm shows up with half the school. He's fucked if someone tries to push *me* off a damn roof."

"Fuck their threats," I say. "We're untouchable."

She narrows her eyes at me over her glass. She says, "You're too fucking fearless for your own good." Then she laughs loud and the sound scatters up to the high ceiling.

But she doesn't feel the threat tonight. Not with every drink I've poured for her. Not with scared-stupid Duffy even drunker than she is, clumsy and eager with his hands roaming every inch of her. They're not thinking about why we're here anymore. They're not worrying that one of us talked, one of us told—

—one of us meant it when we asked who was next.

When the clock strikes one, one cold clang ringing out from above us, they're already fading. Lilia is upstairs. Duncan had Banks carry her up while her eyelids dragged shut and she slurred about one more drink. Malcolm and his boys are passed out in the game room with the flock-girls curled next to them and the screen blinking GAME OVER. Porter slouches twitching at the front door with his eyes on the night.

I've turned the lights out, one by one. An hour ago the house blazed fire-bright. Now it glows dim.

No one has noticed the darkness creeping in.

We sit at the long dining room table under a half-lit chandelier. The lights hang through a cluster of bleached-white antlers that aim sharp points to the darkest corners of the room. Duffy and Banks share a joint and the smoke hazes the air. The music stopped half an hour ago.

"Truth or dare," says Piper. Her voice sticks to itself. Duffy's face is lost against her neck.

Banks laughs and blows smoke. "Girls," he says. "Damn."

"Truth," says Duncan from the head of the table.

Piper is bird-eyes and sharp words. Her hand digs into Duffy's hair. She says, "Who's next?"

Duncan's teeth glitter in the low light. "That's the question, isn't it?"

"You have to answer."

He drinks. "Whoever made those signs is who's next. Whoever ran their mouth."

"Is that a promise?" Piper asks. Duffy's lips move lower, to her collarbone, and her chin tips back.

Duncan sets down his glass. "You only get one question. My turn now."

"Truth," says Piper.

"Who did you tell?"

"Fuck you."

Duncan doesn't move. "Who did you tell?"

"Nobody."

"Jesus," says Banks. He takes another hit. "If you're that fucked about it, go wake everybody up and walk them out on the roof and make them talk. God, you know how to kill a buzz."

"Seconded," I say, and I raise my glass.

"It's not even your business," says Piper. "You didn't get a note. You weren't at Dunc's last week."

"Piper." Duncan's eyes cut to me and back. "Don't."

"Like she doesn't already know." Piper pushes Duffy away. He blinks bleary-eyed and wipes his hand across his mouth.

Duncan's face smooths over. "She's drunk," he tells Duffy. "Take her to bed."

The room is already silent, but it goes quieter somehow. Piper laughs into the void. "I'm not one of your damn victims," she spits.

Banks shifts forward in his seat. The wood creaks and the muscles in his arms shiver. Duncan glances at him, quick: *Not yet.*

"Truth or dare," says Mack, finally not-mute. I can feel the nerves strung tight under the words, but his face doesn't give anything away.

"Fuck," says Banks. "Thank you. Dare."

"Finish the bottle." Mack pushes the tequila across the table.

"Fuck," says Banks again. "Gladly. Here's to forgetting this bitch of a game ever happened." He knocks back the last inch of liquor. When he's done he whoops and slams the bottle down and the crack splits the dark like lightning. "Who's next?"

Duncan measures out a long look. "Careful," he says. He catches me watching.

I don't look away.

He tilts his chin again, the way he did when he had me cornered in the chapel and I still pushed back.

Banks laughs. "Mack's the one who better be careful. Right, Dunc?"

Duncan's eyes drop colder. He's drunk enough that his polish is starting to chip away just enough to show who he is under it—

the boy he was one week ago when the door swung shut—

—the boy who gave the orders in the first place.

"Dare," he says to Banks.

Banks knows what he really means. He laughs again anyway: almost bold enough to dazzle. "Drink up, captain," he says, and he slides the vodka to Duncan.

Duncan grabs the bottle with one hand. Five long seconds tick out so loud I can hear them hanging over us. "Is that all you've got?"

"For now," says Banks. He wants to fight, but he won't. Not tonight.

"I thought you had more in you." Duncan's words sing against each other, metal on metal. He looks at me again. I sink back against Mack's chest and run my hand down his arm until our fingers fold together.

Duncan drinks. When the bottle is empty, he holds it in front of him and spins it. The glass twinkles like charm and candlelight. He flips the bottle and catches the neck in one hand. For a second he's a portrait of his good-king self, lit soft and raising his scepter.

He cracks the bottle down against the edge of the table. The glass explodes—

—ice and knives and dying-bright light.

"Fuck!" Banks shouts. He leaps up and swats the shards away. Two rooms over Porter yelps like a dog with his tail caught underfoot. Piper starts to whine and Duffy squeezes his hand against her arm so tight her whine turns into a pain-sharp cry.

Mack doesn't move. Neither do I.

Duncan raises his scepter again. The broken edges gleam like teeth. "Who's next?"

He said, *Shut the bitch up.* He said, *We'd be power.* He said, *I'm sure.*

But the clock ticking over his head is running down to zero. He's dead already.

"Dare," I say to Duncan.

His polish flakes away again. He's too drunk to do anything about it. He's the wolf from the white-sheets room and the rooftop.

He says, "Kiss me."

"Fuck you, Dunc," says Mack, sudden and angry. Banks laughs and flicks a sliver of glass across the table.

"Jade?" says Duncan. He's a strange sideways version of his St Andrew's self. Still all assurance and expectation, but bleeding thick truth from the cracks the liquor made.

"She won't," says Mack.

"She will," says Duncan.

They watch, Mack and his king and the rest of them, hanging tight to every breath.

You'd like it, said Duncan, *You like it—*

I stand up. The room spins fast. Deadlocked antlers and broken glass. Liquor and weed and lust and hate. Mack says *Jade, don't,* and Piper's nervous starling laugh shatters like the bottle. Mack says it again—

Jade, don't—

—but tonight I decide.

I take Duncan's hand in mine. Coil my fingers around the cold glass and his kill-tight grip. He stands up. Taller than me and stronger and balancing on the knife-thin edge of control. Glinting greed and power.

"Look at you," he murmurs. His mint-and-aftershave smell rolls over me, and vodka drips off his breath, and the blood rises in my throat. He'll taste it when he kisses me. "You wanted this, didn't you?"

He presses hard against me and I swallow down the blood. His smile etches deeper. His hand slips off the broken bottle and onto my back—under the waistband of my skirt—onto my skin—

—but the knife-sharp glass is in my hand now.

He cages me against him. One hand on my ass and the other on my neck, three fingers pressing up under my skull.

He kisses me.

Everything goes wreckingly white and the scream that lives in my lungs cracks every rib and poisons all of me. And there's nothing except dead white and his mouth suffocating mine and his hands burning into the bruises he left last week—

—but I kiss him back, exactly like he wants. Exactly like he would have felt anyway no matter what I did. Fangs grazing his lips. Claws finding his skin. Broken bottle sliding up his throat.

He lets me go.

Three tiny cuts under his jaw bloom red. I can still taste his tongue. He slips his hand back out of my skirt and I bring the bottle down. Slow and deliberate, so I don't lose myself and bury it in his neck in front of all of them.

"Damn," says Duncan, drunker than before.

I am deadly. I'm a poisoned blade. I'm all the power he thinks he has and more.

I say, smoke and dusk, "Truth or dare."

He says, starving, "Truth."

I say, "Do you believe in fate?"

He says, "No."

I say, "You should."

Before he can ask me what I mean Porter yelps again from the door. Around the table everyone comes back to life. Banks picks up the last scrap of the joint. Mack sweeps his hands

across the shining wood and gathers the shards of glass together. He doesn't look at Duncan or at me. Duffy whispers
into Piper's ear and she pulls away.

"Mack," Porter calls. His voice wavers and echoes. "Mack.
Come here."

Mack sweeps up another handful of glass.

I walk out on them.

Porter cowers in the front hall. He has his knife out and
his face pressed to the window. Outside, the lights on the gate
beam bright and the spotlights buried along the edge of the
house leave us blind.

"Out there," says Porter. He reaches behind him with
the hand that isn't on the knife. His hand finds his glass on
the side table and he drinks deep. He's so scared I can smell
it on his skin. He taps the glass with his knife and the blade
shivers.

Beside the gate, in the oleander tree, the huge dark bird
is still waiting. Watching. Its belly and its eyes gleam in the
steady light.

"What *is* it?" Porter asks, all wonder and fear.

I think of Mads in her car in the dark. Jenny and Summer
far down below, where the road makes a breathless tight turn
into traffic that speeds too fast. The good long knife from my
sister's wedding silver. My own black wings wrapping Inverness in a darkness so heavy not even the stars shine through.

I say, "There's nothing there."

OATH

When I get back to the dining room Mack is gone. Banks stares out the window at the lights in the valley. Duncan is back in his seat, elbows balanced on the armrests, fingers tented together. Duffy leans against the wall next to Piper's chair and pulls at her arm. The broken glass is a glittering pyramid in the center of the table.

"Where's Mack?" I ask.

"Upstairs," says Banks without moving.

I turn to leave again.

"Stay with us," says Duncan.

Piper stands up and pushes Duffy away. "You're drunk," she says. "And you're drunk, and you're drunk. You're all drunk. Good night." She brushes past me and stalks into the shadows. Duffy trails after her, stumbling.

"I need to talk to Mack," says Duncan.

Banks pulls a clip out of his pocket and lights another joint. "He's not going to give her up," he says.

"Leave us alone, Banks," says Duncan. Outside, past the faraway lights, a tiny white flashbulb burst burns itself out.

"I'll find him," I tell Duncan before the flickering white can come closer.

The stairway is wide and waiting. It shifts under my feet, but only a little. It's with me—the hidden turns and the dark corners and the huge black bird outside. Loyal. Lined up to make the night unfold exactly the way I want it to.

I find one more switch at the top of the stairs and plunge

the landing from dim to pitch. I don't need light to find my way down the hall to Mack's room. I hear him—his footsteps pacing, his voice rising and falling, his heartbeat matched with mine.

"Mack?" I call, quiet. I open the door.

The night breeze rushes up to meet me. Mack is on the balcony, turning back toward the house. His room is dark.

"Jade," he says. And then the words tumble out: "What we have to do—we have to do it now. So it's done. So we're done." He takes a quick step toward me. The guilt glows on his face. "If this ends it. Just Duncan. No one else."

"Just Duncan." I close the distance between us.

It's a lie. But he'll forget once he's killed Duncan. Once he knows what he can do, he won't ever be afraid again. He'll beg me to let him kill the rest of them.

"Everything there is says I shouldn't do it," he says. "We're brothers, the whole team—like soldiers are, you know? Duncan and us."

"Connor was one of you," I say. "Duncan will turn on you the same way he turned on him."

"I should be the one fighting off whoever left those notes. Not the one holding the knife."

I take his hands. "It was Dunc. He knows someone else is going to talk. You know what he's willing to do. He'll kill you like he killed Connor if he decides he doesn't trust you. And he'll—"

I look away. For him, so he'll see what he needs to say. And because behind him the sky is fluttering white again.

I say, low, "You saw how he looked at me. You know what he wants."

His breath catches between his teeth. "You shouldn't have let him kiss you."

A biting bitter laugh slips out before I can stop it. "He would've even if I didn't let him. That's what he does. Don't you get it? He's not all great and virtuous. He—"

"I know he's not," says Mack. He takes me into his arms. Not like Duncan did—not like I'm something he owns. Like I'm something he treasures. "He won't touch you again."

"He won't touch anyone again."

"This is the only way," he says. But he's asking me, not telling me.

"You know it is."

"The only way to end it all."

I nod. "You're the one St Andrew's needs. You'll change everything." I let the words sink all the way down into his bones. "You deserve it. Just like Duncan deserves to die."

He breathes out again, slower. Steady. "St Andrew's will be ours," he says.

"The whole fucking world will be ours."

He's still afraid. I can see it on his face and feel it in his heartbeat. But bravery isn't being fearless—

—it's swallowing the fear and spitting it back out.

"Just—what if—"

I pull away from him. Find my good long knife. I hold it between us, so when I look at him I see the blade across his face and my eyes, mirrored back, instead of his.

"What if," says Mack, "doing this makes me the same as them?"

"You could never be anything like them."

"What if I can't do it?"

I hold the knife to Mack's throat. "You're a coward."

He presses closer against the blade. "I'm not."

"You're a fucking coward." I won't give him the blindfold he wants—the one he's hiding behind every time he doesn't say what he means. Doesn't say *kill the king*. "You said you'd kill him. You do what you swear you'll do." I press the knife tighter. "If I promised I'd kill Duncan I'd kill him. If I promised I'd kill you—"

I come so close that if either of us slipped his throat would split open.

"—I'd kill you right here," I hiss.

I drop the knife. It falls between our feet. The room shines white and outside, below us, a low warning rumble snakes up from the valley.

"I'm not a coward," he says. There's a red line against his throat where the blade marked him mine. "I'll do it."

"You will," I tell him. "And it's going to make you. Being great is being more than what you were. Tonight you'll be more."

Mack picks up the knife and holds it, blade up, in both hands. "And if we fail?"

I wrap my hands around his. "Take your courage and nail it down. Nail it to your heart. We won't fail."

The starlight sparks off the knife and paints his face darker than I've ever seen it.

I speak faster now. An incantation. "As soon as they're sleeping I'll take Porter's knife. You'll do what you promised. They're drunk enough that they'll sleep harder than dead boys sleep. There's nothing we can't do."

He looks at me like the world is only this room. Only the two of us with our hands locked around the knife.

We draw together like something outside of us is guiding us to each other. Our lips meet with the knife between our hearts. We kiss. It's an oath.

"You're sure they'll believe it was Porter?" he murmurs against me.

"They couldn't think anything else."

"Then it's settled," he says. Deadly and resolved.

Outside the sky flashes its brightest yet—

and it's lightning, real now because I made it real—

and the thunder claps hard and trembling—

—and the rain pours down.

DEFENSELESS

Mack takes the stairs so stalking-silent I feel my chest fill up with pride. He's the warrior king and I'm his queen and together, we are fate.

I stand on the landing in front of the grandfather clock. My wings loom wide. The shadows bury me. The rain rushes and the thunder cracks—the storm only Jenny knew was coming.

Downstairs in the living room, Banks says, "Who's there?"

And Mack says, "Just me."

Smoke rises up to where I stand. "God, I'm tired," says Banks.

"Drunk," says Mack, and they both laugh.

"That, too," says Banks. Thunder cracks again. "Why are you still up? Even Dunc's in bed now."

My claws dig into the railing.

"Your girl made his night. What did he call her—" His sneer turns it bright. "'A girl to end them all.' I think that was it. You know drunk Dunc."

Mack doesn't answer.

"Got him in a good mood, anyway. Maybe he'll be off the martial law tomorrow. You know he's got Porter outside his door? With his damn knife. This week is fucked."

Finally Mack says, "So was last week."

Banks makes a low sound deep in his throat. For a long slow moment they're both silent. Behind me the clock ticks louder. The metal inside it groans and clanks.

Banks says, "I dreamed about those girls last night." His voice edges darker. "Turns out they told you the truth. At least part of it. Right, golden boy?"

I think, *All of it.*

"'Connor will fall,'" says Banks. "Have to wonder what they know. Have to wonder—"

I send my words to Mack without speaking: *Let him say it. Let him believe it.*

"Have to wonder if it was Dunc all along." Banks is slurring deeper now. He'll fight sleep—tonight and the night it's his turn for the dagger—but he'll fail. "And the posters. If he's just trying to keep us under him."

Mack waits. The clock creaks again. "If you're right," he says, careful but with meaning clinging to it, "can I count on you to stick with me when the time comes?"

The silence sags with everything they haven't said.

And Banks says, "If that's what it comes to."

Their handshake claps together.

I slip away down the hall to the very end. Porter sprawls outside of Duncan's suite, his mouth hanging wide and his head heavy against the wall. Behind him, the door is cracked just enough for the spirit-stillness to leak out.

It's a dream, all of it, almost. I'm a wraith floating close and kneeling down. I'm a guardian angel who fell from heaven before I ever got inside the gates. He's a stupid child with drool on his face and his knife sliding out of his hand.

He doesn't stir when my thumb grazes across his eyelids like he's the corpse and I'm the coroner. Or when I pick up his knife and tuck it into the back of my waistband, exactly where Duncan slipped his hand onto my skin.

Or when I pluck his phone out of his pocket and press his finger against it until it blinks unlocked.

I find Duffy's name. Dead-drunk dead-asleep Duffy, who won't look until the morning rips all of them apart.

I text him—Porter texts him, *im scared. im seeing things. he said whos next—*

Porter texts him, *i think its me, i think hell kill me—*

Porter texts him, *i dont know what to do. its already too late.*

I wipe my fingerprints away. I take Porter's blue-webbed hand in mine and press it around the phone and slide it back into his pocket.

Poor Porter. Too drunk to remember. Too drunk to be trusted with the truth once the sun comes up.

It's his fault.

I leave him where he lies. Lightning hits, and thunder, exactly at once. Singing along the knife-blade.

In Duncan's room Lilia sleeps on the window seat with her breath so shallow I could think she was already dead. Her king splays out across knotted sheets. Strong arms limp. Bruising hands trailing harmless.

My hand finds Porter's knife. I close in on him. I block out the door.

I look down at my prey and I say, *You'll like it.*

My knife comes up. I'll kill him here in his bed where he can't fight back.

There's a flicker of light. In my head and outside and all around. I blink it away and instead of Duncan I see my father when he found me holding my silver knife and looking for a boy to kill. Then it's dark again and Duncan is back but my hand drops.

Mack will kill him. He's sworn it.

He'll be the guilty one.

He'll do it if he loves me. And if he does it, I'll love him, too.

MORTAL THOUGHTS

I put the knife at the foot of Mack's bed. When it leaves my hand all the energy pours out of my fingertips with it.

I'm shaking.

I lock myself in the bathroom. A light from outside shines in and turns the wide mirror to a movie screen.

The stage is mine. *Vengeance Paid*, starring Jade Khanjara—

last week *Elle, pretty name, but not as pretty as you*, platinum blond and dressed in white—

last week *that little whore with the jade-green eyes*, caught and clawing—

this week *new girl, twisted bitch, we'd be power*, revenge-black hair and a rosy pink flock-girl shirt and a skirt too short for Duncan to ignore—

this week *partners in greatness, I've never loved anyone more*, with a boy strung so tight around my fingers and my heart that he'll kill for me.

Kill for *her*.

I'm not *just a girl* anymore. Tonight I'm only cruelty. No pity. No mercy. No fear of what comes next.

I bring the darkness close. It sifts smoky around me and clings to my skin. No one living and no one dead will find my heart tonight.

No one will see where the dagger finds its wound.

Not until it's done.

Outside the door Mack paces. He whispers thoughts he shouldn't speak—

thoughts I'd hear even if he didn't say them out loud at all—

whispers, *Is that the knife?*

I say, *yes.*

He says, *I see his blood.*

I say, *you will.*

He says, *The whole world's asleep.*

I say, *The whole world is dead.*

He says, *I hear him breathing.*
I say, *His time is up.*
The clock chimes out its death-knell. Two long cold clangs.
He says, *I'm going now. It's done.*

REGICIDE

The liquor that made them drunk made me bold.

The night that left them full and sleeping has me lit on fire. I can feel it burning cold along my wings.

It's happening, right now. The most beautiful moment I've ever felt.

I sit on the end of Mack's bed, exactly where I left the knife for him. Ankles crossed and claws buried in the duvet.

Outside an owl cries. It's so close I can feel its call in my teeth and hear the breeze shift when its wings brush down. The rain is over as strange and sudden as it started.

Then—

"Who's there?"

I leap up. If it's Porter—

The door swings open and Mack staggers in. The knife shakes in his grip. His hands are red with blood.

"Mack!" I cry out sharper than I should but I don't care—

I don't care who hears or what happens in the morning—

—because his hands are bloody and Duncan is dead.

"I did it," he says, breathless.

I take his hands in mine. "I knew you would." I try to kiss him but he pulls away.

"Lilia," he says. "She was with him."

I push him back against the door. Shut the world out. I don't want his frantic grasping questions. I want his victory and his blood-sworn devotion. "Asleep. Half dead."

His eyes fix on our hands. Bloody and bound together. "God," he breathes out. Praying. "This is hell. We're ruined."

"Don't be stupid," I say, and finally he lets me kiss him. His lips are prison-cold.

"She laughed." He almost gags on the words. "Lilia laughed."

"No, she didn't."

"She did."

"It's nothing." I pull at his knife-hand. Try to pry his fingers away from the handle. "She was asleep."

"What if she wasn't?" His voice is rising and curling into itself. "What if she saw?"

I get my hand onto the knife, under two of his fingers. He still holds tight. "She didn't."

"What if she knows? And Porter—"

"Mack!" I push him hard against the wall. "Stop it. It's *done*. Give me the knife."

He lets go. His arms drop down to his sides and his eyes fall hollow on mine.

"Wash your hands," I say. "Drink something. Don't leave this room until I get back."

When I step back he slides down the wall and sits staring at his hands. "I'm afraid," he whispers. "I can't go back in there."

"Good," I say, and I hate him for his fear, even now. "Don't."

"Jade—" he starts, but I step over him and pull the door shut behind me. I stand in the hall, in the dark, holding the dagger.

Smiling so hard my face sparks with pain.

Porter is still asleep. Crooked against the wall exactly the way he was when I left him. I crouch down with the knife and reach for his hand—

A choking rasping gasp tears through the silence.

Adrenaline spikes through me. More than I already felt and more than I knew I could feel. I should wait. I should leave the knife and warn Mack—

But instead I stand. My claws tap down on the door and nudge it just far enough open that I can slip into the room.

The light shining in through the windows is a pale sickly green. The room floats. Lilia is still rag-doll dead on the window seat with her skin blue-white.

But the bed is bleeding a dark red circle into the sheets. A circle that blooms out from good-king Duncan's chest.

He gasps again. The sound shatters out of him.

I take three steps closer. The souring light finds my face in the shadows.

He sees me.

He struggles harder. Pulling at the air and pushing against the sheets. Dragging his other hand to the dark place below his heart where his blood drains out.

I come closer. To the very edge of the bed. His eyes are ripped wide open. He's terror but still arrogance.

He doesn't believe that he's going to die. Not like this.

He gulps at the air. The wound on his chest whines and

gurgles. He chokes out, "Jade—" and thin blood trickles out between his lips.

"Duncan," I say. My lungs are full of life and my veins are full of blood.

"Call—" he rasps, "call—"

The word bubbles wet. His eyes flash fear and he chokes and chokes.

I sit down on the bed. The silk-white sheets are soaked through. I bring my legs under me and kneel low next to him.

"Jade—" He starts to choke again.

I put one finger on his lips. His blood stains it. I hiss, "Shh."

His face changes even under the agony. He sees it now—not all of it yet, but some of it. Enough to know something isn't right.

He's afraid.

He tries to speak again but his lungs fight him and win. He grabs my hand instead—the hand on the bed. I break out of his grip without even trying—

hold my hand up to the light—

—show him the knife, dirty and dripping.

He gasps sharper than before. His lungs wrack but he gasps again. Not to speak. To live.

I bring the knife down torture-slow. Touch it down on his high proud cheekbone. Trace it to his jaw. Hold it against his throat exactly where I held the broken bottle.

I smell mint and aftershave and hot blood.

He chokes on one more word. A weak drowning mew: *No.*

I laugh. It ripples out of me like I'm a tiny joyful child again. Like nothing in the world could ever go wrong.

I slide my knife-hand down and lock it around his arm.

Shut the bitch up, said good-king Duncan one week ago. Cold eyes. Commands his whole pack followed.

And Banks said, *Fuck, Dunc, you know how to pick them*—

Duncan's eyes hold onto mine now the way they did last week, when I danced and spun in the glossy St Andrew's crowd with my long hair flying and my eyes shimmering drunk and green.

He chose me. Chose who made the drink and who caught me by the statues. Chose who dragged me down the hall and who guarded the door. Chose who came with him into the white-sheets room.

Chose what happened to *that little whore with the jade-green eyes*.

Tonight, I choose what happens to him.

I pull his other hand away from the wound between his ribs. Weave our fingers together and press his palm to his lips. He thrashes weak and desperate.

I bring my lips to his ear. His pulse rushes shallow at his temples.

I whisper, sweet: "You picked the wrong girl."

He goes frozen.

I pull back so he can look into my eyes. He stays as still as his dead-king statues for five tripping heartbeats and then I know—

—he knows I'm her.

He knows I'll kill him.

Now he fights. Hard, with everything he still has. His blood pours out faster. His lungs moan and cry.

He knows who I am and he knows why he'll die here to-night.

I lean close again. I press his hand down against his mouth, against his nose, against the tide of blood that seeps between our woven-tight fingers. He fights. I fight back.

He won't win.

His pulse climbs faster. Spinning white firecrackers pop all around us and last week and this week melt together but his blood washes everything else away.

I press his hand down.

His lungs rattle out a sound so twisted and broken I know it's his last.

He goes still. His silver eyes are dull and fixed.

He knows.

I pull my hand free. His falls limp against the pillows.

I kiss him on the lips.

I say, "Sleep well."

CLEAN

I walk dizzy out of Duncan's room. There's a spinning hum in my ears and the halls shift and breathe.

Duncan is dead.

I pull his door almost-shut. I kneel next to Porter and wipe the handle of his knife against my shirt. I wrap Porter's hand back around his knife. My fingers linger on his—let Duncan's blood paint guilt on his hands. When I step back he's a ruined traitor slumped in the shadows. Broken under his fear.

They've fallen apart. The whole glorious ravaging pack.

Something creaks downstairs. I turn toward the sound: waiting, ready, listening with ears that can hear ten times better than they ever did before tonight.

Nothing else moves. Inverness is as quiet as a crypt.

"Who's there?" Mack calls, a tremor in his voice.

I leave dead Duncan and dead-asleep Porter. I tap at Mack's door and he calls out again—*Who's there?*

I slip in and lock the door behind me.

Mack sits exactly where I left him. Folded against the wall. Shaking. "Every sound—" he says, and his eyes don't waver away from the blood on his hands, and he doesn't blink. "I think they're coming. They know. God—"

And his whole body shudders.

My heart is still pounding, flying, soaring. I can still feel Duncan rigid and terrified and then limp. Still see the sharp silver light in his eyes going out. Still taste his fear when he knew *that little whore with the jade-green eyes* was the very last thing he'd ever see. That all his power was gone. That all his power was mine.

I don't have time for Mack's stupid weak doubts. I want to grab him off the floor and kiss him and shriek triumph into the starless sky with him.

I reach out. "Mack. Get up. Go wash your hands."

His eyes shift to my hand and he shudders again. "The whole ocean couldn't wash this blood away," he whispers.

"*Mack,*" I say, and it's harsh and biting but I don't care. I don't regret one single second of this and neither should he.

Kings don't flinch at the kill.

"Look," I say, and a drop of blood drips off my hand and onto his. "My hands are just as red as yours. And I'm glad."

Something stirs downstairs. I feel it more than see it, shivering up my wings.

Mack feels it, too. His eyes snap up. They're wide with fear. "Who is it?" he whispers.

"I don't know." I pull at him until finally he stumbles to his feet. "But you need to get the blood off your hands before they come upstairs."

The fear pushes him in front of me and into the bathroom. He reaches for the switch but I knock his hand away. "No light," I say.

Together we walk to the wide sink in front of the mirror. We stand far apart but holding hands. Sealed together with Duncan's blood.

"How can you smile?" His voice is doubt and horror.

"Because it's done," I say. "Because he deserved it." I turn on the water and the handle chirps out a giddy cry. "Come on. We'll wash it all away."

The water is cold as ice and steady. It turns red under our hands and swirls in dizzy circles around the drain.

It's beautiful. We're beautiful. This night, dark and deadly and stained with blood, is a masterpiece too perfect for any museum in the whole world.

I bring Mack's hands back out of the water. "See how easy it is?"

"No," he says. "Look at us." In one rushing burst he pulls his shirt over his head and holds it up. "Blood. There's always blood. We have to burn it. Take it out to the balcony—" And he's starting on his thoughtless stupid plan already. Ducking for the metal bin next the counter and sending it scraping across the tile.

I grab his hand again. "It's nothing," I say, and I drop his shirt into the sink. "You ran out before he even started bleeding."

"But look at *you*." He's staring at me in the mirror. "God, Jade, you're—"

"I'm fine," I say. And now I'm the one who can't look away. The version of me in the mirror is every inch of the sharp-clawed ruinous creature I wanted—

begged for—

begged to *be* one week ago. There's no guilt in my eyes. Only cold pride at the dark stains on my shirt and my skirt and my skin.

I am the broad-winged angel blotting out the blinding white of that room. The reaper who deals out the fates boys like Duncan deserve. I'm death and retribution.

I murder and save.

"Jade," Mack whispers. Weighted down with concrete dread. "Are we the villains?"

"No," I say. "We're fate."

There's something in his eyes swimming deep down. Something that agrees with me.

"You did what you had to do," I tell him. "St Andrew's is yours now. He'll never hurt anyone again."

The darkness in his face curls deeper. Stronger.

"You're the king now," I say.

He says, "And you're the queen."

I nod. "Partners in greatness."

I turn back to the mirror. I slip my shirt over my head and drop it in the sink. I unhook my skirt and let it fall around my feet. Under the black lace my skin is shadowed in purple-blue bruises, but in the dark they're almost invisible. Mack won't see the dead boys' handprints. He'll see what I want him to see.

He'll see the girl he loves more than he's ever loved anyone.

Tonight, I decide.

I turn my back to the mirror and pull Mack close to me, swift and sure. Bring my lips to his. I taste Duncan's blood between us and I know it—

He's worthy.

I whisper, "I love you."

We stumble back together from darkness to darkness. The water rushes loud.

His lips are on mine and his hands are on my skin. We fall onto his bed and my long silver knife winks and gleams from across the room. Outside thunder shakes Inverness to its foundation and in the next room Duncan sleeps forever.

Mack says, "Are you sure?"

I say, "Yes."

He is mine.

MORNING

Mack sleeps, but I don't.

We lie wrapped together, skin against skin under dark silk sheets. I watch him spent and dreamless in my arms as the night burns through into cool still dawn. The sky fades brighter so slow it takes hours more than it should. So slow I wonder if day will come at all.

Mack doesn't stir when the little birds outside sing broken morning-songs. Doesn't stir when I steal away to unlock the door and stop the water and throw our clothes, scrubbed clean, out onto the balcony by the shining puddles from last night's storm. Forgotten and accidental.

I wash the last of the blood off my lips and I curl back into our nest.

Mack sighs in his sleep.

Dawn casts the whole room in rose-gold. All the lights in the hills drown in daybreak. A shadow sings across the window and circles once over the balcony—

huge dark wings, dipping down in reverence—

—and then the bird glides away from Inverness and disappears into the valley.

The night is over.

The house creaks awake. Someone is on the stairs. Climbing hangover-slow and heavy with last night's shame. A shiver traces fast and thrilled down my spine.

The new world is about to start. The world I made.

"Hey," says Duffy, thick-tongued, on the other side of the door. The weakest of all of them. The one Porter texted last night before his guilt took him over and he buried his knife in Duncan's side.

"Hey," says Duffy again. "Porter. Get up. We have to talk."

There are no windows in the hall and I pulled Duncan's door almost-shut, so just the slimmest trace of truth could ease through. The only light in Duffy's sleep-blurred eyes is from far down the hall, slanting through the windows on the landing.

He can't see the blood on Porter's shirt or the knife in his hand.

"Porter," says Duffy, loud and rude. "God, that vodka laid you out." His foot scuffs against the floor and Porter groans. "How late were you up?"

"Hell if I know." Porter is still half-dead. "Fuck, my head hurts."

Next to me, Mack stirs awake. He starts to sit up, but I pull him back into my arms. He smiles before he remembers.

Then it comes back and I see it all in his eyes—

guilt and fear and pride—

—and I whisper into his ear, "Don't go until they call you."

He nods. He swallows hard.

"You only did what you had to do," I say.

He nods again.

"I love you," I say, and his arms circle me closer to him.

I let my eyes flutter closed.

"We have to talk," says Duffy outside the door. Urgent and nervous. "Before Dunc's up. Is he up?"

Porter groans again. "Don't know."

"You texted me."

"Don't remember." Porter huffs out a laugh. "Don't remember much."

"You have to rein it in, man. Dunc's going to be pissed. He won't let it go like he did when he was drinking and crawling all over the new girl."

Porter shifts and his head thumps against the wall. "Twisted bitch. She scares me."

"Everything scares you." Duffy scoffs like he isn't every bit as worrying and wondering as Porter is. Like it isn't just the way he's more afraid of Duncan than anything that makes him do the things Porter is afraid to do. "But Dunc likes her. She's our shot, okay? We get her on our side, we get her to play nice with Dunc, and things will be fine."

"Things are never going to be fine."

"Fuck," says Duffy. "That's exactly what I mean. Don't try that shit with Duncan. Play by the rules or—"

"Or I'm next?"

"*Fuck*, man. I give up."

Then there's a knock at the door. Three quick raps.

Mack shifts next to me, but I hold him back.

Duffy knocks again. "Mack. We need you."

The door swings open. A creeping bold bolt of last night's adrenaline slices up my veins but I keep my eyes almost-shut. I watch Duffy through eyelash-webbed slivers. His hair is tossed with sleep and his face is tired. When he sees us a smirk plays over his lips.

My hand loosens on Mack's arm. He sits up as slow as he should. "What is it?"

"Damn. You got her before Duncan did," says Duffy, and my hate wakes me with a welcome little blade-twist. I want him to be next. Right on the heels of his precious king, just the way he does everything.

"What do you want?" Mack asks. The way he says it makes Duffy take a step back.

"Dunc wanted me to wake him up early," says Duffy. Eager and shameless. "We need to get on the same page first."

Mack pulls the sheets around me to keep Duffy's eyes off. "Why? I didn't piss him off last night."

"Exactly. You've been his favorite ever since Connor fucked things up."

"It wasn't just Connor."

Duffy smiles, bitter. "Don't. None of that was my fault. I do what Dunc says. You know that. You're as guilty as me."

That brings Mack up and out of bed. "Careful. You came in here for help, didn't you?"

I'm proud enough that they'd see it on my face if they were looking.

"Fine," says Duffy, both hands up. "I know you've got a thing with the new girl—"

"Jade."

"—but Dunc wants her. You're not going to stay his golden boy if you stay with her."

"Jade," Mack says again, half-turning toward me. "Her name is Jade."

"Jade," says Duffy. It catches in his throat: half in scorn and half in fear.

"She's not a damn prize. She chose me."

Duffy shrugs. "I'm just telling you, you're the only one who can smooth it over when Dunc decides what to do about this shit."

"It's not my shit," says Mack. He's next to Duffy now, taller and stronger and holding the cards. "You and Piper are going to have to find your own way out." He rests one hand high up on the door until Duffy drops his head and ducks back out.

Mack shifts into the hallway. "Get it over with. The worst he can do is tell you you're next." It's dark and mocking and I love him for it.

Duffy mutters something and shuffles down the hall. He knocks at Duncan's door. My eyes open wide and soak in the brilliant blazing morning. The breeze curls in through the balcony door. Inverness is all mine.

"Rough night?" Mack says to Porter.

"Fuck," says Porter. "That storm freaked me the hell out. I was seeing shit."

Duffy knocks again. "Dunc," he calls, tentative. "Dunc, you up?"

"There was this bird—" Porter is almost laughing. Even in the morning light he's balancing on the edge of here and gone. Hammering the nails into his own coffin with every word he says. "Outside, by the gate. Jade didn't see it, but damn, I swear I heard that thing cawing all night—swear it was in here standing over me—"

"Duncan," says Duffy. Clearing his throat. "I'm coming in."

"Just," says Porter with a strange rueful laugh, "fuck that storm."

There's a pause so breathless and full of knowing that I sit up tall in Mack's bed. Hold the sheets close. Feel Inverness hold itself still with me.

"Jesus!" Duffy is shrill and crashing. "Jesus. *Fuck*, Dunc, get up!"

"What is it?" says Mack.

"*Fuck*, Dunc! Mack, get in here!"

And then Lilia screams high and awful and loud enough to wake the dead.

"Don't look," Duffy says, "Call somebody, get somebody—"

Lilia's shriek turns to a wail. A wounded wounding cry shattering open the doors to heaven and hell.

"Get Banks," Duffy shouts. "Get Malcolm." And it's all a jumble, and Mack talks over him and through him and then his footsteps fly past the door. Lilia still screams and Porter mumbles *what is it*. It's chaos. It's destruction.

I've torn their tower down.

I should wait until Mack comes back with Banks and they find Porter with the knife. Until their whole tragic mess has played itself out and they've sewn all the pieces together without even remembering Mack's girl sleeping innocent in the next room.

But this is my moment. It's been nipping at my neck since the slanting second when Connor fell. Since the night I lay twisted in the white-sheets room where Duncan and Duffy and Connor and Banks left me.

I draw the sheets around my shoulders. I stand up regal and ready. I go to the door and pull it open. The balcony light floods into the hallway all around me. Gleaming off my silk robe and my revenge-black hair. Turning me into a dark shining silhouette.

My best entrance yet.

"What is it?" I say. White lilies blossom thick under my words. A snake weaves through their stems, but no one will see it until it's wrapped itself around them and choked their breath away.

Duffy leans against the dead king's door, doubled over

with one hand clutched to his mouth. His neck cranes up. He says, "No—don't—it's horrible—it'd kill you—"

"What?" Flock-girl Jade is all sleepy delight. The sheet slips off my shoulder and I pretend I don't notice. Pretend I don't see Duffy retch yellow. Keep my eyes from lingering on Porter with his face as horror-bent as Duffy's and his eyes on the knife in his hand.

"Just—don't, don't, it's nothing," Duffy babbles. In Duncan's room, Lilia's cry snuffs out to tiny wobbling gasps. Voices clamor downstairs and footsteps trample up to the landing.

Then Banks is rushing past me with Mack behind him. "God damn, Duff, move!" Banks shouts, and he sends Duncan's little dog reeling into the hall.

The instant stretches tight enough to break. Duffy's eyes are locked on mine.

Then Banks and Mack burst back through the door. They don't speak. Their faces almost match.

"Banks," says Duffy, and he breathes hard and spits bile. "He's dead. He's murdered."

I give them my line: "What?"

They look at me. All of them. Porter panicking on the floor and Duffy with his shoulders sagging and Banks and Mack guarding the king's doorway too late. I'm *just a girl* to them. *Never a St Andrew's girl*, not half shiny-hard enough to take the news that poor dead Duncan met his end one door down.

"No," I breathe out. I read it on their faces. Write it on mine. "*No*," I say again, sharper.

Banks nods. I let my hand come up shaking in front of my mouth.

"Somebody has to tell Malcolm," says Duffy, still babbling.

"Tell everyone," Mack says. His words toll heavy. "Duncan is dead."

It sinks in for the rest of them when he says it. Lands soft like the bird that guarded Inverness from the oleander tree.

Someone killed their king while they slept.

Someone here in this house.

Then Mack is diving for the floor. "Porter!" he shouts, and Porter howls like he's already seeing himself strung up by the neck. Duffy scrambles for the lights and then the hall shines bright. Mack is on top of Porter grabbing for his knife. Shouting, "It was you!"

Banks and Duffy spring to the ready. They know it's true: it was Porter with his drunk fraying texts and his knife drawn all night. Porter who knew too much.

"Say it!" Mack shouts, and his hand is on Porter's throat and Porter squeals and they struggle for the knife—

"Mack!" I cry with all the desperate dread I can wring out. "No!"

He stops. He turns with his hand over Porter's on the knife.

I let my legs go weak. Grab for the door and try hard to stay standing—

poor brave new girl, drowning in the knotted St Andrew's secrets—

—and I whisper, "Mack—" and I crumple to the floor. My eyes fade closed.

"Help her," says Banks. "Leave Porter. We'll deal with him later."

"I didn't—" Porter gasps.

"You killed him in cold blood." Mack is next to me now.

Tucking the sheet closer around me. Brushing my hair out of my face.

"I didn't!" Porter says again.

No one believes him.

There's noise from the stairs. I raise a weak hand and find Mack's face. Open my eyes. Stay where I am, the perfect portrait of shock, so when Piper and Malcolm and the rest of them crowd into the hall I'm just last night's conquest on Mack's arm. Not even worth a second glance.

"What is it?" Malcolm stands in front of his worried little pack. He's barely a wolf this morning. He already knows what he's almost too afraid to ask.

Their eyes meet. Duffy and Banks and Mack.

I blurt it out. "It's Duncan. He's dead. Porter—" I bring one hand up and point. Shaking so hard Mack wraps his arms around me and draws me in. Our hands stay folded together over my skipping-fast heartbeat.

The color drains out of Malcolm's face until he's as bloodless as his brother. "No," he says. "No." He pushes toward the door but Banks and Duffy block his way.

"Malcolm," says Mack. "Don't. You don't want to remember him like this." He squeezes my hand tight and then he lets me go. Then he's next to Malcolm, one hand on his arm, captain to soldier. The second-string boys and the flock-girls shift a little and I know they feel the way everything has changed—

—the way Mack is king now.

"Go with Jade," says Mack. "Take her downstairs. The rest of them, too." He turns to Duffy and Banks guarding the tomb with Lilia still sealed inside. "We'll talk," he says, as heavy with meaning as anything Duncan ever said before I cracked his kingdom apart.

Little-boy Malcolm, baby-wolf Malcolm, crouches down next to me and helps me stand. He's trembling. He's ruined. But I'm glad, because baby-wolf Malcolm is still the boy who mixed the drink and sneered wide in the doorway and said, *you know I trust my dealer,* and waited for me to go still.

"Mack—" I say before Malcolm can lead me away from the horror I made. "Don't leave me." Still playing the flock-girl, but under it I'm twitching tight. He's different this morning, the boy I've turned him into, and I'm glad. He'll kill the rest of them when it's time. He'll even like it the way I do.

But if I hadn't stopped him when he had one hand on Porter's throat and the other on his knife—

I need him close to my promises and my lips. Where I can keep him from ruining the careful plot I've built.

"I'll be downstairs soon," he says, and then he and Duffy and Banks slip through the doorway into Duncan's room.

I steal a glance at Porter. He's clutching his knife close. His eyes dart from the pack at Duncan's door to the rust-red blade in his hands.

He knows he's finished.

"Malcolm—" I stop. "Wait. I'm dizzy—" And I stumble another step out to where the hall widens onto the landing. I steady myself on the wall and lean my head on Malcolm's shoulder. Keep him there with me, caught, and let my eyelids droop heavy for just long enough that everyone ahead of us troops the rest of the way down the stairs.

I lift my head and look over Malcolm's shoulder. The lights gleam brighter than the sun outside. Sweat beads up on Porter's lip and his hands tremble. I lock my eyes to his until his shivering stops. He's desperate. He'll do anything to get away from the pack that's turned against him.

I cut my gaze hard toward the stairs and back. My lips make one word, murder-silent: *Run*.

Then I let my head fall back onto Malcolm's shoulder. I whisper into his ear, "You can't trust them."

He goes still. There's something aching about him, something that feels different when his brother isn't watching. Like he's almost a boy who would never do the things his brother made him do. Almost a boy I could see and touch and trust.

Almost. Not quite.

"You'll be next," I say. Hushed and scared. "I heard them talking—" The words float up higher and higher toward the skylights, toward heaven—

and I collapse with my arms wrapped tight around Malcolm's neck—

—and he falls with me.

Almost before we land Porter springs up and dashes past us. His heels are on fire and he swings the knife unsheathed and aimless. Flying breakneck fast down the stairs and into the hall and out the door before anyone can think to leap up and stop him.

"Get him!" Malcolm yells and flings me away. He runs for the stairs.

But outside a door slams and an engine roars.

He's gone.

I stay where I am. Distraught and trembling. Staring between the polished metal bars of the landing and down to the front hall. Out the gaping space where the door still swings to the gate Porter leaped.

He's gone, flying a hundred miles an hour down a road that twists tight enough to break spines.

Mads is behind him. Sharper than the blade that killed the king.

She'll follow him to where Jenny and Summer wait.

Until they catch him and make him choose life or death— prison or his pack—

confess to his father's lawyers, or go back to the boys who want him dead—

—and he already knows he's guilty. He saw it in the texts he sent Duffy. He saw it in the bloody knife. He saw it in the fear on my face when I told him, *Run*.

Duncan is dead. Porter killed him.

Mack is king.

AFTERMATH

Everyone tells the same story.

Lilia, shattered, standing in sunlight that burns through her skin—

Duffy and Piper, together again and arm in arm, her finishing his sentences when his face goes sick—

Banks with his eyes pinning a target to anyone who crosses his path—

Malcolm, eyes hard, hands digging against his thighs—

the second-rank boys and the flock-girls, even though they don't matter enough to separate one from the other—

Mack, taller and broader-shouldered every minute and holding me close, swearing vivid earnest fury at Porter—

and me, trembling bravery, wrapped in silk.

We tell it to each other, anyway. By the time the whining sirens wind up the hill we've all gone silent. Their questions stack high and empty: *who found him first, who saw him last, is there anyone with a reason to want him dead?* We shut them down with thousand-dollar smiles and attorneys' names. No one answers anything. No one except Piper, who slivers her eyes and says it was Porter and that when they find him they'll find the murder weapon in his pocket and his motive on his phone.

The wolves and the starlings leave one by one. Washed out and dim-eyed in the close morning light. Thinking, *who's next?*

I stay with Mack while dark unmarked cars pull through the iron gates to Inverness. The men cluster outside with one baby-faced baby-cop standing guard at the door to the master suite. I ask, shy and shivering, if I can just get my clothes from Mack's room. He glances toward the landing and then back at me in my sheets and he nods.

He says, "Be quick."

I lock myself in. The balcony door hangs open with the morning creeping close and I go out and stand in the sun. It's Saturday and my week-old nails are still perfect. Sharper than they were. I stand so tall that anyone who looked, even all the way from the valley, would know I'm queen.

I call Mads.

She says, "Did they tell you?"

I say, "Who?"

She says, "The cops." A careful pause. "He's dead."

"I *know.*"

"Porter," she says.

My lungs pull in a sharp gasp of air so quick it stabs against my ribs exactly where Porter's knife stabbed Duncan.

"He was flying," says Mads. "He almost ran off the road. Jenny and Summer were waiting for him—"

A breeze swirls up and breathes itself into my wings.

"They cut him off," she says. "The blind corner before the freeway, like you said. He barely stopped in time. We had our masks on."

It won't take much, I told them when we planned it. *The boys will want him dead. A weak scared boy like Porter—if you tell him he can live if he just confesses—*

they'd hold out a phone, dial 911, let it ring—

let it say *what is the nature of your emergency—*

watch him collapse and lie and say he did it, all tears and relief, because a weak scared boy like Porter would rather hide in prison for the rest of his worthless life than see the wolves circling him the way they circled Connor on the roof—

"But he was already dead," says Mads. "I could see it in his eyes. He backed up and gunned it so hard Summer barely cleared out of the way and he went around that curve straight onto the freeway and—"

She doesn't need to finish.

"Jenny and Summer left. I parked higher up and waited until they cleared off the road. They took the truck driver out in an ambulance. Porter's dead."

The little knife of air spins back out of my lungs.

Porter is dead.

I'm almost disappointed. I knew he'd never dare crawl

back to the pack that was ready to let Mack dole out justice with a dirty knife. He'd cave. He'd take the phone and tell the police he killed Duncan all on his own. Plead insanity. Believe it. Wonder about texts he didn't remember and birds I couldn't see. Remember Connor's empty eyes and the rough red letters: *Who's next?*

Remember that he knew too much.

Remember the guilt.

Remember the fear.

He'd confess so well he'd make the tabloids. Hide behind iron bars, safe from the pack and from himself if he did do it—

—and from whoever really did it if he didn't.

Dead someday. Probably not soon enough, but soon. And tortured until then.

But I never thought he'd die today, without confessing.

It leaves me feeling nothing at all.

Mads says, "That's it."

I say, "Good."

We hang up. I pick up my clothes. They're almost dry and absolutely clean.

I dress in the bathroom where Mack and I stood together covered in Duncan's blood. Smooth my hair and put on enough makeup to look as innocence-pretty as I need to look, but not so much that they'll think I look too perfect for the sort of lip-bitingly brave girl who wakes up in a house from a horror film. Trail through the room, looking for anything out of place. Leave the bed unmade and slept-in. Wipe the dried blood off the sink. Slide the bookcase over the stained-dark spot where Mack sat trembling.

When everything is spotless I slip back out. The baby-faced

cop nods, sicker than before. Duncan's door is open now, leaking shadows—

—and a man in worn gray steps out.

He says, eyes on me, "What's she doing up here?"

The baby-faced cop stammers and the man in gray waves him away. The detective, the one who stood at the back of the chapel for Connor's service and shook dead Duncan's hand. "Your name?" he asks. His voice sheds gravel and blame.

"Jade Khanjara." I give him the same drawn smile I gave the rest of them downstairs. "If you have any questions, you'll need to speak with my attorney. Ji-Hwan Kim."

The detective's eyes fade grayer when I say Jenny's father's name. He hates me the way he hates all of them: haughty rich boys and their numb mindless girls, untouchable behind defense teams only the guilty can afford. "Jade Khanjara," he says. "Good lawyer your parents have."

"My parents would do anything to keep me safe," I say with a quaver that matches the girl he thinks I am. A girl like Lilia, ghostly and gone.

He nods. Hating me still, but toothless, because I'm *just a girl*.

"I'll go," I say, and I smile innocent again, and I pull the door shut—

—and his eyes lock onto the space just above my hand.

I shouldn't look, but I do.

There on Mack's door is a streak of dried blood, grasping toward the handle, one long drip trailing down to the floor.

I look up again and his eyes are back on mine. Hungrier now. "Miss Khanjara," he says. "Who slept in that room last night?"

"I did," I tell him, and my gaze darts away on purpose. Behind him, the baby-faced baby-cop shifts another step away from Duncan's door. The smell of blood floats out so strong it almost makes me dizzy.

"Only you?" asks the man in gray.

Duncan is dead and his blood is in my lungs and I want to stay here and savor it until he rots to bone.

"Miss Khanjara," the detective says. "Was there anyone with you last night?"

My lips pull at a smile. I hide it with a shuddering breath and one hand brushing at the corner of my eyes. "Just—a boy."

"Name?"

I shudder-breathe again. "He didn't do anything. He was with me."

He says, "His name, Miss Khanjara."

Duncan's blood curls against my skin and my hair and my teeth. I see Mack with his knife, killing for me—

Mack in his bed, mine—

Mack in the dark, whispering betrayal: *You shouldn't have let him kiss you.*

I smile sweet and fragile. I say, "Andrew Mack."

SUNSET

We meet at Mads's on Saturday afternoon. Jenny and Summer and Mads and me.

I still haven't slept.

They're waiting for me when I drive through the gate.

Standing in line in front of the door. My shoes are black arrows on the short bright grass, pointing the way to where we'll breathe our secrets to life.

We go to the training room like always. Everything shines lemon-fresh.

Jenny swings herself up into the boxing ring and ducks under the ropes. She grabs Mads's brother's gloves and hides her hands inside. "Damn, it's dark," she says, and she shadowboxes the ghost blocking the light from the windows.

"You said it would storm," says Summer, watching Jenny with enough longing in her eyes that it almost makes up for the strange heavy clouds blotting out the sun.

Jenny grins and throws three more punches: right-left-right.

"That's not a storm now," says Mads. She's right. Last night was thunder and lightning and rain. Today the clouds are still and sagging. Hanging like the stinging haze in August the year the wildfires burned so close to the city that men stood on Mads's roof three hours past midnight drowning it with water. "That's smoke."

"There's no fire," says Summer. She jumps up to join Jenny, clawed grace.

I say, "There is."

"God, so dramatic," says Jenny. "SoCal girls. It rains once and you think it's the fucking apocalypse." She swings at Summer but Summer slips past her, dancer-light. Her dress flares out and her necklace catches the only sunbeam in the room and throws it onto the wall. She hooks one arm around Jenny's neck, but Jenny twists fast and suddenly they're face-to-face.

They stay frozen for just long enough that it means what Summer wants it to mean—

—but then they spin away, exactly at the same time, and drop against the ropes on opposite sides of the ring. Mads and I climb up, too. We sit so each of us takes one side of the ring around the dim square of light in the middle.

"So," says Summer, still breathing quick. "Murderess."

I bow my head, but I can't keep the smile from playing along my lips.

"Look at you," says Jenny. She's all shining ecstasy. "You love it. You fucking psychopath."

I raise my eyes to meet hers. "I know what I'm doing."

And Mads crosses her arms and says, "No one fucks with our coven."

Jenny raises one boxing-gloved fist. "No one fucks with our coven." Then she casts a sly little look my way and says, "But I've got you figured out."

I wait.

"You don't love him after all. You're too *us* for love. You're the most us of all of us."

Summer shifts and bites her lip.

"You're playing him worse than any of them. I mean, you're destroying him, right? That's the endgame. Soon they'll all be dead and it will just be your golden boy all alone. Guilty and damned."

"Not guilty," I say, and it's not even a lie. "Great."

"All great men kill kings," says Mads. Half soothsayer and half mockingbird.

Summer laughs a shivering-gold laugh. "You'd be sweeter to kill him. It'd be fair."

I let my head fall back against the rope and stare up at the lush layered branches outside.

Jenny's hand flashes out and a perfume vial lands in my lap. White powder gleams inside. "For when you're done with him," she says.

"You fucking didn't," says Mads, but she's barely more than bored.

"Right. Summer did."

Mads unfolds lithe and grabs the vial. "You made Summer break into the secret room again?"

"Not very secret," Summer says, too pure. And it's true: the secret room has been ours for as long as we've been us. The room off along a back hall, with bulletproof walls and bank-safe doors. With a portrait on the wall, Mads and her brothers, on hinges that swing back to a cabinet of pills and poison: *better safe than helpless*.

"Which one is it?"

Summer shrugs. "I don't remember. The one with the prettiest name. Arsenic, or cyanide—" And her laugh sings out. "Something that works."

"Let me see," I say, and Mads tosses it back.

Jenny smirks across the ring. "Told you she'd want it."

We stole the vial from the woman who smiled too much at Jenny's father in the front-page photos four winters ago. We poured her perfume out. A defendant's wife, the one who called Jenny a *little creeping bastard brat*. The one who spent nights when Jenny's mother was away and left lipstick-stained coffee cups exactly where Jenny's mother would find them, except we always found them first.

The one who called Jenny a *little creeping bastard brat* for the very last time the night I had Mads let us into the room with the bulletproof walls and the bottles full of poison. I measured out the one I wanted: not enough to kill, but almost.

When the ambulance left I stole back her last lipstick-stained coffee cup and breathed in the burnt-sweet smell of bitter almonds.

I send the vial spinning back to Jenny. "Not yet."

"But soon," she says. "For Mack."

I glare.

"What did he do?" Jenny asks. No cherub-voice. All focus.

"Nothing," I say.

"Bullshit. You chose him to take the fall. What did he *do*?"

"Nothing," I say again. "That's the point. He's the noble one. The one they'd never suspect."

"Fine. Whatever." Jenny punches the sunbeam. "Can't wait for the day you stop lying, by the way."

"I'm not lying."

"I'm just saying, we're killing for you."

"You know that's what we do," says Summer, slithering sweet. "You know what Jade's done for you—"

"For me, or for her?" Jenny bites down on the smoke-still air.

"For us," I say. My hand goes to the crucifix my coven left for me. I spin it between my fingers and my skin catches on a rough place. I scrape it with a nail and dull dark red flakes down onto my lap.

Mads sits up straighter. She's taller than all of us. Anchored deeper and iron-steady, even when her temper fires bright. "Duncan is dead," she says. "They blame Porter. What happens next?"

They all look to me. Loyal even when we have our clipping little spats.

"We use their fear," I say. "Split each one of them off so there's no one they can trust. So it's every boy for himself."

They nod.

"They're ready to believe anything," I say. "You saw Porter. He almost thought he'd really put that knife in Duncan's heart. Now we make the rest of them think maybe it wasn't him. Maybe—anything."

They're leaning closer. My whole heart swells for them. My beautiful coven. My flock, but instead of starlings they're falcons with wings that turn the whole sky dark. Summer's doubts and Jenny's sass. Mads knowing all my lies.

"We need a phone no one can trace," I say. "We'll tell them things they're afraid to tell themselves. We'll turn them against each other."

Outside, the sky goes even darker. Like the night is stronger than the day. Like the day is afraid to show its face even when it should.

I say, "We'll be the witches they don't believe in until it's too late."

HUNGER

We eat dinner together for the first time in a month. My father and my mother and me, sitting far apart at the long wide table in the sunroom. It's eight o'clock. They've seen the news. I haven't, but the messages shooting from flock-girl to wolf leave a trail of sparks hot enough to start fires worth the clouds still fouling the sky.

Porter's dead, said Lilia. To Mack and me, to Duffy and Piper, to Banks.

And Banks said, *Had it coming.*

The rumors pitch and heel: *Malcolm's gone,* they say. *He's afraid he's next.* No one argues back that Porter's dead. They know it wasn't Porter who left the dead-eyed signs in the parking lot and turned us afraid of each other.

Porter held the knife, but fear drove it between Duncan's ribs, the same way fear shoved Connor off the roof. And if stammering-scared Porter could kill the king—

well—

—*who's next?*

So by dinnertime I know everything I need to know.

My father says, when our plates are empty and our forks and knives rest against the china, "The boy. The one who died last night. You knew him?"

I say, "Yes."

He says, "What sort of boy was he?"

I say, "The sort of boy with daggers in his smile."

They watch me. Both of them. Their faces give nothing away.

I say, "The sort of boy who needed a dagger in his ribs to match."

My mother says, "And the boy who killed him?"

I say, "He knew too much."

My father straightens the napkin tucked into his collar.

My mother says, "There was no mercy last night."

I say, "There's no mercy left."

When night comes they sit together outside my door

until my breath comes deep and even. After a long time, my mother murmurs, "Then it's done?"

I know my father nods yes.

Their shadows move away together and the lights go out.

REFLECTION

The fire-clouds are gone on Sunday. Time stretches long and strange. The morning shines too clear and waits too quiet.

I run. I plan. I turn through the scenes from Inverness, all filtered and fogged like Piper's pictures:

the huge dark bird looms watchful on the oleander—

the metal gate, INVERNESS, catches the lightning and shocks bright against the dark—

Duncan brings the empty bottle down and it shatters spectacular—

his fingers dig at my skin—

the sheets bleed—

the water turns red—

Mack swears himself to me.

The whole night haunts me in the most perfect way anything could. It grows viney around my ankles and snakes up my legs and through my ribs. Blooms over the bruises and the scaling scabs.

Creeps over the broken static from the party at Duncan's house.

When I closed my eyes last night sleep hardly came. Instead I saw white—only white. At first my eyes snapped open to bring in the dark. To fix on my knife and skim across the black-framed pictures on my desk—

my coven and me, last homecoming, in dresses all the same shade of red—

my coven and me, middle-school cruel at Holi, painted bright and brilliant—

my coven and me, New Year's Eve in satin masks and lipstick smiles and fangs—

my coven and me, skinned knees and eight years old but already fierce and fearsome—

—until my breath hissed back out and I could close my eyes again.

But then the hours slowed their crawl so drought-dead that I let my eyes stay closed. The white came back again. I let it. I waited.

Then it bled to red.

I slept, finally, wrapped safe in the storm I brought down on Inverness.

But today my hands are too clean. I want my heart in my throat again. I want the moment that drowned everything away—all of it—so there was no past and no world outside. Only me with fate and a knife and the future in my hands.

Finally Mack texts me, *I need you,* after a too-long silence that chewed at my fingertips every time my phone buzzed with Piper's dried-up gossip.

I say, *I need you, too.* It's a lie.

I think it's a lie.

He says, *Come to the marina.*

He sends the address and I drive fast with the wind in my

hair. The whole huge sky over me shifts in sleepless blurs. I park close to the boats and even my darkest sunglasses can't keep the water from searing golden gashes into my eyes. I wear a green dress that glows jewel-rich.

Green is our color. Green like his eyes. Like my name.

Mack stands on the upper deck of a blindingly blue-white boat, waiting for me, watching me walk out with my dress fluttering. He meets me on the narrow metal gangway that hangs us over the water. We kiss and everything between us brings us closer than anyone else could know.

"You're here," he whispers.

"I'm here," I reply.

He leads me through the tight neat halls. The boat shines like new: the bar and the bedrooms and the sleek-windowed room where the captain stands.

"Let's go out," I say.

"We shouldn't go alone," he tells me.

I laugh at him. He laughs back, a little haunted but a little more mine.

He takes us out to where the water is all around us and the shore is just a paper strand in the distance. Then we idle where we are and climb the thin stairs to the roof. We lie in the sun, Mack and me: partners in crime, partners in greatness. I think of what Jenny said—

you're destroying him, right?—

—and in the fever-hot sunlight all alone between the empty sky and the empty ocean I think, *we'd be power.* It's all that feels true. I don't need to know any more than that.

Mack says, soft enough to be dreaming, "They aren't coming back."

I say, "Good."

He says, "I mean my parents. He's in Tokyo. She's in Doha."

I say, "You don't need them."

He rolls onto his back. His shirt is off and the sun warms his skin. "The police told them what happened. That we can't be at home until they've finished with everything—"

His breath catches.

"It was Porter," I tell him. "Everyone knows it was Porter."

He squints. He never wears sunglasses. Never hides his eyes. "The attorneys are handling all of it. They told me I'd be fine on the boat until the police are done. They said, 'We'll be home when we're home.'"

"We needed a change of scenery anyway," I say. I tip my sunglasses up and let him look into my eyes until his face says what it should. "You don't need them."

"But you know how crazy that is? I kill someone in our house and they still don't come home. I can see it, you know—why Banks stopped giving a fuck. When he got so tight with Duncan and the boys. He said, 'Mack, come on, they're never going to see us anyway, the world's ours.'"

"It is," I say, and I sit up so he has to shield his eyes to see me in the sun. "It's yours whether they see you or not. Yours to say, fuck them, and be great. Be the greatest. You don't need them."

He says, plain, "It's lonely as hell."

I lean down over him. Slide my hands under his shoulders and kiss him. "You're not alone anymore," I whisper when we breathe again.

His eyes close and he stays still for a long moment. He says, "They took me in. For questioning."

"What did you say?"

"Nothing." The word is a dark star against the blinding

daylight. "My lawyer—he said, 'Don't say a damn word.' And I didn't."

"Good."

"They know something," he says, eyes still closed but flickering uncertain anyway. "They asked all about Dunc—and about Lilia's house, and Connor, and if Porter knew things about Dunc worth—worth killing for."

I wait.

His eyes open. "They asked about you."

I smile at him: certain, knowing, the girl he trusts too much. "What did they say?"

"They asked if you were in my room all night. And then the same questions they asked about everybody—if Dunc ever did anything to you, if you'd want to hurt him—"

Far off the words glitter: *God damn, she's feisty*—

—but they're only a whisper now, blotted out with his blood.

"They asked where you were before St Andrew's." He looks deep into my eyes. "Where were you?"

I draw my hands across his chest. Over his heart. "It doesn't matter," I say. "I'm here now."

Under my fingers, his heartbeat climbs faster. "They kept me longer than anybody else," he says. "Duffy was out in ten minutes."

"Because even that detective can tell Duffy's too weak to kill anyone."

"But what if they have something on us?"

I kiss him again. Murmur close against his lips: "They'll never catch us."

We lie still again under the scorching sun, burned clean.

Finally he says, "I can't sleep. All I see is Duncan—"

"It's done."

"Is it really?" he asks. "The guilt, Jade—it's so much—it's like there's this debt I'll never pay back—"

I bring my sunglasses back across my eyes because no matter how much I hide, I can't hide all of it. Not in light this bright with the sleepless hours stacking up and up. "You did the world a favor," I say. I keep it as even as I can, but the boat still shifts on the waves.

"I killed him. It's unforgivable."

I stand up all at once. Stand close to the edge, so my toes curl over it. I won't fall. "He's the one that's unforgivable. All of them. You're paying their debts."

Then I hear the way I said it: *paying*, not *paid*.

"No," says Mack, hearing it, too. "I can't."

I say, "We already are."

He breathes out so much guilt I can see it hazing the air. "I won't kill again," he says.

I reach out my hands—my spotless too-clean hands—and take his. He stands with me. We tower over the ocean. Everything looks flat and imaginary.

I say, "St Andrew's is yours now."

He says, "I know."

I say, "Would you let boys like them take it back again?"

"No," he says. Not even a heartbeat of hesitation.

"Would you let them do what they did to that girl?"

"No," he says. "But killing—"

"Mack!" I grab his hands and make him look at me. Everything is tangled: I hate him and I love him. He's noble and he's ruthless. He's brave and weak. "They deserve it. Duncan and Duffy and Connor and Banks. Their time is up."

His face goes almost still. "They said that," he murmurs.

"Who?"

"The girls in the masks. They said, 'Their time is up. Your time is here.'"

"It is," I say, coaxing and final. "We're killing them because they need to be killed. It isn't over until they're dead."

He breathes in deep and sighs. "Sometimes it feels like . . ."

He pauses. The wind whips up and lashes my dress close around my legs.

He says, "Like everything's already been decided."

I wrap my arms around him. "Maybe it has."

He says, "Like it had to be me all along."

I say, "It could never be anyone else."

The wind rushes the words fast out to sea, but I know he hears them anyway.

SUCCESSION

St Andrew's is ours now. I know it before I even walk through the door. The air feels different. The parking lot stretches broader and the school's shadow clings deeper. The flowers I hate shrink into themselves more than they did a week ago. Drooping guilty away from the stone.

I pull into my spot and cross the lane to the sidewalk, past a police car idling too close. The shadows shift and I look up—

—and birds bury the roof, all across every span. Little dark birds, lined up and looking down at all the beautiful vain St Andrew's Preppers pulling into the lot.

Waiting. Chirping secrets back and forth. Watching with bead-shiny eyes.

"It's like—it's not natural," Lilia says. I look away from the birds and see her right in front of me, leaning weak against the wall.

"It's just birds," I say.

"It's too much," she says. She wears a long dress that hangs from her shoulders. Shapeless and colorless.

She brings one hand to her mouth and lights a Parliament. She says, "I'm leaving."

Above us the roof rubs its thousand wings together.

Lilia says, "Rehab."

It's a lie. Not quite a lie, because she'll go.

But it's not why she's leaving. She's leaving because she can. Because she's free to melt away, now that Duncan is dead.

I say, "For what?"

She blinks like she's never thought about it. "Oh," she says. "You know."

We watch each other for a rustling feathered moment. The old queen and the new.

Then she darts forward and locks me into a strange sharp hug. She is bones and smoke. She is lighter than air. She won't come back to St Andrew's.

I pull away.

But just before I do, she breathes two words into my ear, whispered-nothing but bursting with all the ruffling conquest of the birds looking down at us—

thank you.

MARKED

Duncan was never king at all.

St Andrew's has swallowed him down into the crypt they'd find if they dug up the dark wood floors. James Duncan, last week the boasting pride of the school, king and captain, Dartmouth-bound, leading his pack through halls that parted for him—

—this week a ruin. The rumors swirl around the empty space where he used to stand and reign. No one says it out loud, but everyone whispers it: the jealous greasy-haired boys who hover at the edge of the commons, the mousy girls who couldn't look him in the eye, the baby-bird freshmen who couldn't look away.

Last week was silence. This week the truth seeps out in whispers.

Next week will be a scream, gutted and gutting.

I stand in Lilia's place in front of the Virgin Mary. When Piper comes in and sees me her sword-hand slides to the ready.

I smile.

My hand comes up the way it did last week when they walked in and found me standing exactly in this spot and Piper said—

who the fuck is that, and who does she think she is?—

—and the same as last week, I spin my crucifix.

Piper nods her fencer's nod. I've won this bout and she knows it.

She stands right-hand ready the same way she did for Lilia. She'll play friendly for now. Keep her friends close, if she had any, and her enemies closer, and her rivals where she can see them every second.

Today there are three boys instead of four. Duffy and Banks and Mack. They walk in together. I can almost see the blood flung across them and hear the weight of these ten days dragging behind. Scraping and clanging against the floor so loud that every single St Andrew's Prepper turns and stares.

They're marked. The hunters and the hunted. Culled down already and everyone knows they're not safe. Everyone's eyes say it, even if their lips don't: *who's next?*

I can feel the whole building sighing wicked and content. The buried secrets are spilling up at last. This has always been a place for knives sheathed in flesh and bone—

a place for traitors and killers—

a place for tyranny and anarchy—

—and now, finally, its true colors are bleeding through the sky-blue flags with their white-X badges.

The golden fuckboys on the walls smile harder. The sepia prints behind the glass sweat poison.

I love it. I rule it.

At lunch Mack sits in the king's place. It's never been anyone's other than his. I sit next to him and my heart almost bursts with pride for him—for *us*. He reaches for my hand at exactly the instant I reach for his. The rest of them lock into place around us, circled tight against the stares and the whispers. Circled tight against *who's next*.

But carefully apart because most of all, we're scared of the rest of us.

No one speaks louder than a secret-strained murmur. Everyone glances furtive over their shoulders. We're quiet terror. Waiting for the next shriek.

"Malcolm ran away," says Duffy.

Everyone's eyes hook to him.

"We're all thinking it," he says, hurt.

"The whole family's gone. They're burying him out east," says Banks. Talking around the dead king's name. "Where they're from."

"They're not gone yet," says Duffy. "Not east, anyway. Just away from the house."

Piper levels him a look that's all contempt. "So what?"

His hand hovers away from the table for a second. He wants to hit her. Even here. Even though on a day like this it would bring her hand to her sabre faster than his fist could land. "So Porter ran, too."

I scoff and scroll down my phone. Text the coven: *Go.* Glance across the table at Duffy, still second-place even with Duncan dead. "You mean it was Malcolm and Porter together? Baby Malcolm killed his own brother?"

"No—" Duffy stammers. "But—"

"But what?" says Banks, sneering cold.

"Maybe—I don't know—"

Mack's phone buzzes first, on the table between us. Then Duffy's, and he jumps. Then Piper's and Banks's, both at once.

We all look down.

A text lights up Mack's screen: *Who's next?*

"God, *fuck* this shit," Piper yelps out, loud enough that every face in the room turns toward our table.

Banks grabs his phone and types fast.

"What are you doing?" Duffy's voice pitches high.

"What do you think? Texting this asshole back," says Banks.

"It's a private number," Mack says.

"So? That doesn't mean it won't go through."

Duffy grips his phone tight, like he's waiting for the screen to crack open and spill Duncan's blood across his blazer. "What if you piss them off and—"

Their phones buzz again: *Who can you trust?*

This time not even Banks punches back.

The third message comes through: *What if someone set Connor up?*

A picture comes with it: Malcolm running for the locker room, looking over his shoulder. Time-stamped last Monday, during the game. Just before Connor unraveled.

"That doesn't prove anything," says Piper.

The fourth message comes through: *What if someone set Porter up?*

There's no picture this time. We fill in the space with our careful sideways glances.

"Someone's fucking with us," says Banks.

"No shit," says Duffy. "And it's working."

The silence strains tight enough to shatter.

I shatter it.

I laugh.

"What the *fuck*," Duffy almost shouts. He drops his phone and it hits hard against the table. All of them stare furious at me. Even Mack.

"You're nervous," I say, teasing. "Guilty conscience much?"

"*Jade,*" Mack hisses.

I face him. "What? Do you have something to be afraid

of?" His eyes flash guilt and panic. I turn before he can break. "What about you?" I say to Duffy.

"No—no—" he says too fast.

"God, Duff, go to confession," says Piper. "Maybe it will help you sleep at night. I'm the one who shouldn't be getting this shit. I didn't *do* anything."

"You knew what they did. You were with them at Duncan's house," Mack tells her. "That's what it is. It has to be."

Banks makes a harsh sound that's half growl and half laugh. "You sure you're so innocent, golden boy?"

"You know I didn't do anything," says Mack. I can feel the fight in him—feel the guilt clashing and rising. *Guilt doesn't work on boys like them,* said Mads. But Mack was never one of them. The more his guilt pries him apart—the more he knows that someone thinks he's the same as his pack— .

—the sooner he'll bring the rest of them crashing down just to prove he's not.

It isn't fair.

I don't care.

And anyway, I'm making him stronger. The boy who always knew enough but never told them no.

"I didn't *do* anything," Piper says again, and she grabs her phone and says it loud and angry a third time as she types in the words.

"Who the hell did you cross?" I ask them. All of them at once, with a baiting smile.

"Nobody," says Piper.

But Duffy blinks wide and mutters, "We thought."

"Careful," says Banks. Still almost a growl.

Little lapdog Duffy laughs nervous. "It's her. It has to be. We might as well just say it."

My heart leaps up into my throat. I didn't think they'd guess it so soon. I thought they'd turn on each other, and leave it like that. At least for now.

"Watch what you're saying," says Banks.

"Oh, fuck off," says Piper.

"It's not her. It's some dick who heard too much when everybody was drunk and running their mouths at Mack's house. That shit got two of us killed already and it's going to take the rest of us down if we can't shut the fuck up."

Piper glares. "Was that a threat?"

"It's her," says Duffy again. "It's the girl from Duncan's party. God, I never should've let Dunc make me—"

"Bullshit," Piper spits. "You had a choice."

"It's not *her*," says Banks. "I'll prove it." And he types fast and grins up at us. "Asked her who gave her the drink. This is a fucking joke."

"*Jesus*, Banks." Mack pushes back from the table. "No, it's not."

"It's some second-string asshole watching like a creep from across the room," says Banks, and Piper and Duffy turn and stare. "That's the damn definition of a joke."

Mack knocks Banks's phone out of his hands. "I meant what happened at Duncan's," he says. "You fucked up."

Banks grabs his phone back and swings the screen in front of Mack. "Then text the bitch back and apologize if that's what you think this is about."

They all stay caught together. Anger flowing bright and fear snuffing it dim.

So I say, "Maybe it's *her*—"

Banks snorts.

"—or maybe it's some second-string asshole, or maybe it's

Malcolm losing his shit." I let my gaze wander off toward the doors, where two cops stand like sentries where before we could come and go unwatched. "Or maybe it's that detective playing you so hard you'll lock the handcuffs on yourself if you're not careful."

Mack finally looks away from Banks. "What do you mean?"

I scroll through nothing. Show them what a beautiful thing it is to be *innocent, innocent, innocent*. I say, "I mean it's none of us. Right?"

They nod. Hesitant at first and then too certain. A flagging lie, but it doesn't matter.

"So let's make them fuck off," I say. "Go somewhere they can't get to you."

"We're not running away," says Piper.

"Obviously." I give her a glance that withers her better than Lilia ever could, because Lilia never saw her with her secrets flayed open and her fear spilling out. "But Mack's staying on the boat this week. Let's go out on the water tonight. None of Malcolm's second-string boys this time. No telling anyone. Make it a wake for Duncan."

A pause hangs in the air. I can feel Mack nervous next to me. I take his hand in mine, guide his lips to mine, kiss him hard.

"Fuck them," I say.

Banks caves first. "Fuck them," he says, too loud.

"Fuck them," says Mack, right into my lips.

"Fuck them," says Piper. She slams her phone down.

And finally Duffy clears his throat and says, barely a whisper, "Fuck them."

The bell rings. Outside the birds stir, restless and all together. I can feel it in my wings.

RIFT

I walk Mack to class. I keep him silent. I tell him, *The walls have ears,* because it feels like just the right paranoid bullshit for the way they're all shattering apart today.

He nods like it's true.

I kiss him good-bye in the doorway to Magistra Copland's classroom, so everyone has to watch. So everyone sees how unbreakable we are. When I let him go he almost looks fearless.

I linger until he finds his seat. Wink and wave with the whole class watching. The ones who are left, anyway: too many chairs are empty. Too many names rang through the speakers all morning, calling one St Andrew's Prepper after another to run away and hide when their parents heard that two more boys were dead.

"Still think you're a twisted bitch," says Banks behind me. So close I can feel his too-hot breath on my ear.

I turn. The door swings shut. We're alone in the hallway, Banks and me.

"Almost as twisted as your fuck of the week," he says.

I scoff.

"I'm serious, new girl. You know what you're getting into with us. Sure you can handle it?"

"'Us'?" I say, and I drench it in disdain. "I thought Mack was the golden boy I was supposed to corrupt for you."

"Yeah," he says, "but there's all types of twisted."

"I'm sure." I turn again. "I'm late."

He lets me get ten steps away before he calls, "You know what happened at Duncan's party."

I spin on my toes and walk straight back to him. I don't know what he's doing. I don't have time to think it through. "You mean the part where you and Duncan and Duffy and Connor drugged some girl and raped her?" It echoes loud in the hall but the doors are closed and no one hears and even if they did they'd pretend they didn't.

His smirk digs in. I blink three times, fast, and see Duncan bleeding under my hands. Hold tight to every ounce of it so I won't sink my claws into Banks's throat right here.

"Good story," he says. "Where'd you hear it?"

"Like any of you could keep your mouths shut. Like telling isn't what got Duncan a knife in his throat."

"Damn," he says. "Nothing's too soon for you, is it?"

"Duncan was no one," I hiss. "No one's losing any sleep missing him."

"Think your golden boy might be," Banks says with his glittering carnivore grin. "Think your golden boy might be trying to atone for something all the Hail Marys in the world couldn't undo."

I think of three nights ago at Inverness. The shifting sounds downstairs and Mack's spiraling desperate words: *The whole ocean couldn't wash this blood away.* The water running all night. The streak of blood on our bedroom door, painted fresh for Banks to see—

"Whatever you want to say, say it." I push too close to him. "Unless you want me to go get Mack so you can say it to him, too."

"Your call," he says. Laughter barely buried. "Same story either way."

I wait. Teeth gritted and claws clenching my skirt too tight, but waiting.

He says, "Ask your golden boy what he was doing Friday night."

"He was with me," I say. "All night. Not that you'd know what it's like to be with someone who actually has a choice about sleeping with you."

"Not Mack's party," says Banks. "Duncan's."

"He didn't go."

"You sure about that?"

"He wasn't *there*," I say, and my claws dig so hard into my skirt I can feel the fabric tear.

"Ask him."

"I don't have to," I say, and for a splintering firing second the hall spins to white and I see Duncan and Duffy and Connor and Banks and the door slamming closed.

"Your golden boy isn't so golden," says Banks.

He winks.

I shove him. Hard. I'm half his size but he doesn't expect me to fight, so he stumbles and crashes loud into the lockers behind him. "Fuck!" he bursts out in a long slope of laughter. "Duncan was right about you."

"Fuck you," I snarl in his face. "Fuck you and fuck your dead king—"

"Young lady!"

I step back. Magistra Copland stands halfway in her classroom and halfway in the hall. Her watery eyes flick from me to Banks behind her glasses.

Banks turns his laugh into a cough.

"Is everything all right?" Magistra Copland asks.

"Fucking fantastic," says Banks.

She says, "Language, Mr. Banks." Her eyes flick to me again. She still has one hand holding the door and I can see past her into the classroom. Everyone is watching me.

I smile and smooth down my skirt. I say, "*Si fueris Romae, Romano vivito more.*"

She smiles back, frosty still, but thawing: "*Si fueris alibi, vivito sicut ibi.*"

Banks snorts and mutters, "*Veni, vidi, vici.*"

Her smile ices back over, slick enough to send him spinning into the ditch. "I'm sure you did, Mr. Banks, but let's allow Ms. Khanjara to speak, shall we?"

He says, "We shall." Daring me to snap again. Daring me to tell.

I give them my best innocent-little-flower gaze. "I'm fine," I say. "Mr. Banks wouldn't dare do anything—*unchivalrous.*" It's the most ridiculous word I can think of. "We were just having a little disagreement about—" I pause. "How would you put it, Mr. Banks?"

"Any way you'd let me, Ms. Khanjara." His charm has gone cold. He barely bothers hiding what he means.

I see dead Connor, dead Duncan, dead Porter. Dead Banks, soon. Next. Tonight, even if I still haven't found his glinting smile on the boy who gave me the drink.

I show him all my hate for a shining little second and then I look back at Magistra Copland. "About how we define certain concepts," I say. "Guilt, for example. Truth."

"Sounds quite philosophical," she says.

"Consent," I add. Sweet and deadly. Past the cracked-open door the whole class stirs. Mack pushes halfway out of his seat and hovers and sits again, fidgeting. A plain-faced not-it girl in the front row goes wide-eyed under her bangs. The girl behind her leans over her shoulder and whispers. They give me the sort of look you only give a queen.

A queen who won her throne in battle.

They know. All of them. What Duncan and Duffy and Connor and Banks did. Why two of them are gone and the other two are caught in fear thicker than quicksand, slipping under inch by inch.

"Well," says Magistra Copland, "I'm sure it was a very enlightening conversation."

"It was," I tell her. My eyes flit to the whole thirsting crowd behind her and I raise my eyebrows just enough to send them diving back behind their hands.

"Perhaps better suited to a different venue," she says. "You and Mr. Banks both have classes to attend; am I correct?"

I nod once. "Of course. Just—" I measure the angle of her chin. Measure the way Banks's shoulders strain against his blazer.

I take my chance. "May I speak with Mr. Mack? He'll be right back, I promise."

She hesitates. Casts a look at Banks and makes a prim little cluck in the back of her throat. "You may." She steps back and holds the door wider. Mack scrambles out of his seat and into the hall.

"Get to class, Mr. Banks," says Magistra Copland. The door shuts hard.

All our careful cordiality shatters. "Fucking bitch," Banks says, spitting venom but keeping quiet. "Wish Dunc were back to get her ass fired."

"What is it?" Mack asks me.

I step back and give Banks a hard stare. "You tell him."

"She knows," says Banks. The words leave a sick sticky trail.

"What did you tell her?" Mack breathes in stony and sharp.

"Just the truth. That you're not as innocent as you want everyone to think."

This time it's Mack who shoves Banks. "Your guilt isn't mine," he says.

"Good thing." Banks grins wide. "You've got plenty of your own to handle." He checks my face. I paint Duncan's blood across his eyes. I stay steady, almost.

Almost. Not quite.

Banks shakes his head. "You really don't want me to spell it out, do you, Mack?"

And I say, "We do."

He comes closer. "You've got it all, golden boy. The new girl. Connor's spot, and now Duncan's."

Mack is sepulcher silent.

"You've got it all," Banks says again. "Think you played dirty for it, though."

"*Fuck* you," I whisper, tight and burning.

"Playing the good boy," says Banks. Eye to eye with Mack. "But you're one of us. I know you, Mack. I've always known you."

He throws us both his winning-winner grin. "See you tonight, huh?" Then he heads off down the hall with a stride so hard no one would dare try to pass him. "And watch your backs," he calls over his shoulder. "Nobody knows who's next anymore."

He flanks right at the corner. The light shining in through the windows shades darker. Mack lets out a laboring breath. "Jade—"

"Don't," I whisper, and I take his face in my hands.

He flinches when my claws graze his skin. "He knows."

"Don't," I say again. "He doesn't know anything. He's turning on you. He's scared."

"So am I," he breathes out.

"No, you're not." I kiss him quick and fierce and three-in-a-row. "You're the king. You're the one they're afraid of."

"He'll tell." Mack's eyes shift to his hands. He sees blood and daggers. He's filled in Banks's broad swinging accusations with his own guilt.

"He won't." I press close. "We won't let him."

"Not Banks." He shivers. "I can't."

"Then I will."

"This thing we've done." He takes me in his arms. "It's made good into bad. He's my best friend."

"You know what he did to her," I say. "He'll do anything to get away with it. You heard him. He thinks he's innocent. He *said* it—he said you're as guilty as him."

Mack's eyes close tight.

"Tonight," I murmur into his darkness. Reckless, but I don't care. If the columns of St Andrew's cracked when Connor fell, they collapsed to ash and dust when Duncan took his last breath. We're buried in the wreckage. Grasping at the crown.

We'll fall, too, someday. I don't care, as long as they fall first. As long as they know who pushed them.

"Tonight." Mack's eyes open. "But far away from here. They're all watching too close."

"Far away," I echo. The thrill drips down my spine like water and blood. "So it's done?"

"It's done," he says.

The words drop like stones and sink to hell.

FLIGHT

I don't go to class. I kiss Mack good-bye and let his hand linger on mine and stay close by Magistra Copland's door until it seals shut behind him.

Then I fly away weightless, out of the shrinking stifling halls, down the front steps, clattering over the stone. The campus stretches wide and deserted from the palm trees to the parking lot to the radiation-glow green of the field.

I run into the lane. Fling my bag down and throw my arms out and spin and spin. Tip my head back to the blue-paint sky. Scream piercing and shrill.

The sky screams back at me and the sun blots out to black—

—and high above me, the thousand birds that perched on the roof all day have sprung into flight. A thousand sharp-winged blackbirds, all rising up together. All shrieking mad calls. Scattering apart and drawing back close. Their wings churn the air and ruin it.

I stand with my arms flung wide and stare up at the darkened sky. Watch the swirling flock sift and scream and soar away across the field and into the sun.

When the sky is rancid bright blue again I chase their shadows down the little hill. The door to the combat room is unlocked and I go in and sit against the wall under the silver-X sabres. Daring them to break loose and spill my blood.

I stare at the white wall on the other side of the room, far away and scarred with plaques. See tonight play out a thousand different ways until the wrong answers cut themselves free and die on the floor. Until the only right answer bows to me from the other end of the piste.

I know how Banks will die.

I stand and face the sabres on the wall. Run my fingers down the metal and find my reflection, warped but perfect, in the silver.

The girl in the blade stares back with murder in her eyes.

I love her.

THREATS

Sunset starts early today.

I watch the wolf-pack run fast across the field. Thick gold light paints them magnificently against the green. There are fewer of them than last week. They look over their shoulders in the halls, but when they play, they look to Mack. He wears the captain's *C* now.

He's earned it.

Just before they crowd into their final huddle Piper climbs the bleachers and sits one row below me, sideways and cross-legged with her blazer thrown over her shoulder.

"Captain," she says, dripping envy.

I keep my eyes on the field.

"Never thought your golden boy would grow up this fast," she says. She watches the pack with me for a spun-out moment. "It's all you, isn't it?"

I don't hide my smirk. I don't need to.

I let her think what she wants to think.

She laughs jealousy and it rains down onto the field. "You won't even deny it. Little succubus bitch."

I don't blink until she does.

"How'd you do it?"

I say, "He did it all himself."

On the field, the coach shouts and the wolves cheer hoarse and run in.

"I mean Porter," says Piper. "What did you say to him?"

I say it again: "He did it all himself."

Mack shouts and the team shouts back and they run for the locker room. Mack's eyes find me at the very top of the bleachers. I blow a kiss to him and his smile breaks bright.

"I swear I know you," says Piper. Her hand is on her sword. "And whatever your secret is—"

Her phone buzzes. Then her hand goes up fast, caging over the screen. She steals a flutter-fast glance at me.

"What?" I say. "Is Duffy sexting you from the locker room?"

"Shut up." She pulls her blazer on and stands. "See you tomorrow."

"What about the boat?"

Her shoulders hitch tighter. "Not coming."

I let the taunt gleam through: "Why not?"

"I'm not fucking coming, okay?"

She turns and takes the stairs two at a time with her sabre bouncing.

"Later, sweetie," I call in the same sugar-sweet voice she used on Lilia back when she thought Lilia's crown would be hers. Her heel catches on the last step and she stumbles. She doesn't slow down.

My coven told her, *You know too much. Stay home tonight or you're next.*

I follow her down the bleachers, but slow. Soaking in the dripping-gold light. I'm barely to the sidewalk when Duffy rounds the corner, rushing and still in his lacrosse clothes.

I laugh. All carefree melody. "What, is Piper pissed at you again?"

He spins so fast he almost hits himself with his crosse. "I have to go. She—I have to go."

"God, calm down." I take a few easy steps toward him. "You look like you just saw your own murder."

"Don't even *say* that." He stumbles back. His phone falls out of his bag and clatters to the pavement. I reach for it, but he yelps *No* and snatches it off the ground.

"Right," I say, drawn out. "So, see you at the marina?"

"No," he says. "No. I can't. I—"

He leaves the sentence hanging broken in the air. Turns and walks fast toward the parking lot. Looks over his shoulder and sees me still watching.

His walk turns to a jog and then a sprint.

My coven told him, *Duncan and Connor paid. Stay home tonight or you're next.*

So it's just three of us now, tonight.

Banks and Mack and me.

When Mack comes out I kiss him before he can say anything. He tries to speak and I say, "Not here." I wrap my arm around his waist and walk with him to his car. His boys keep their distance. Watching us—

the best of St Andrew's—

the king and queen—

—and thinking, *who's next*, and wondering if tonight it will be our names splashed across the messages that blink them awake.

I keep him there with me until there are only three cars left in the lot: his and mine and Banks's, far away. I slide back onto the hood of his car and pull him close. Weave us together. He doesn't hesitate anymore when I bring him to me—not since the night we killed Duncan.

He says, finally, out of breath, "Banks—I can't—"

"He's already dead." It's too much to say out loud but I don't care. He's seen his real self now. He can't pretend anymore that the two of us aren't the same. I bring my lips to his ear and whisper, "He deserves it."

Mack holds me close and kisses me like there's nothing else left in the world. And for this moment—

even now, with the sunlight shifting from gold to scarlet—

even now, with Banks waiting for fate to seal closed over his head—

even now, with the blood running thick—

—it's only us.

I watch him drive away. Stand alone with my long shadow and my hair glowing red. When he's gone I walk back and wait for Banks's car to thrum to life.

He pulls up just as my door slams shut. Rolls down his window and says, "Jade."

I lift my sunglasses. "Mr. Banks."

He turns away and laughs into the empty passenger seat. Looks back at me. "Can you give me a ride to Mack's?"

I wait.

"I'm serious. God, *fuck* this." And he shakes his head and says, low, "Just follow me and let me leave my car and then I'll ride with you to the marina."

I wait.

"Come on, Khanjara." He doesn't say it right. He says it the way politicians say the names of countries they hate. "Just this one thing."

"Why?"

"No questions."

"Fine," I say, smiling toxic. "No escort."

He revs his engine and the growl rips across the lot. "I got a text."

"So?"

"So I have to leave my car up at El Matador and get you to drive me to Mack's. Or—" He pauses. "Fuck it to hell. Or I'm next."

I stare.

"Fuck you."

"Play nice," I say. "You're the one asking for a favor."

"*Fuck* you," he says, leaning hard against it. "Are you in or not?"

I let him dangle until finally he looks half ashamed. Then I say, "I'm in."

We drive fast up the coast and the red almost-sunset pours down over my shoulders and the wind roars loud in my ears. And then we're there on the bluff above the crashing waves.

He gets out but leaves his door hanging wide. I stay facing the sunset. "So," I say, "are you coming?"

He looks at his phone. "Got another text," he mutters.

I climb over and perch on the passenger-side door. "Tell them to fuck off."

His eyes shift. He's thinking about it.

"Come on. Let's get away from this mind-game bullshit."

He scoffs. "You're not the one getting threats all day."

I let my eyes stray down. Bite the corner of my lip.

"Wait—"

I look up. Guilty.

"The bitch texted you, too?"

I show him the message: *When Banks asks you for a favor, say yes or Mack's next.*

"*Damn*," Banks breathes out. "This bitch doesn't play."

I laugh. Not the silvered knowing laugh I gave him when we first pulled up to the bluff or even the nervous laugh that might make sense for the worried flock-girl I'm playing. A high cheerful giggle that sings out before I can stop it.

Banks stares.

I breathe in deep. "Nothing," I say. "It's just—it's working, isn't it? You know somebody's going to break and go to the police."

His eyes narrow and then he laughs, too. Edgy and loaded. He says, "Duffy."

I say, "Definitely Duffy."

"Fuck," says Banks. "I'm finished. Let's go get drunk."

"Done," I say. "Except—" And I hold my phone up to him and throw it into the backseat. "Nobody's getting in my head tonight."

"Fucking cheers to that," says Banks. He throws his phone into his car and slams the door.

I slide back into the driver's seat and Banks jumps in. We look out over the water—

at the sun sinking—

at the waves rolling in huge and unsettled—

at the whitecaps breaking against the jutting rocks below us.

A beautiful breathless night is coming in.

I start my father's car and pull away. Banks glances back at the sun setting the water on fire. "El Matador," he says, and he laughs again. Darker than before. "Know what it means?"

Of course I do. It's why I chose it.

"No," I tell him, and I step hard on the gas and pull into the stream of lights.

He grins. The sunset coats him in red. He says, "The killer."

TETHERED

The sky has scabbed over to almost black by the time Banks and I walk out to meet Mack on the boat. We stopped for liquor. Banks is already drinking it.

"Mack!" he yells, loud and exalting and thrusting the bottle high. The lights gleam kaleidoscope-crooked through the glass.

Mack stays where he is, watching us from the upper deck with both hands gripping the railing.

So I shout it, too. Grab Banks's other hand and raise our fists into the air. "Mack! Get down here and let us on."

He lets go of the railing and comes downstairs. He slides

the gangway out, but then he crosses it and stands blocking our way.

"Come on," I say. "Let's go."

"This is a bad idea," he tells me.

"Fuck, man, we didn't drive to every corner of this whole damn state for you to flake," says Banks. "Let's go."

And I say, "Mack. Come on. You know we need this."

He takes me in. Windblown hair and bright eyes shining. I left my blazer and my tie in the car, and I'm barefoot with my shirt half-unbuttoned and my necklace dancing in the lights. "Jade," he says, "what if this is what they want?"

I laugh and say, "Who?"

He takes his phone out and juggles it back and forth. "The girls."

"What girls?"

Banks chugs from the bottle. "Hell, no. Not tonight, Mack."

And I say it again: "What girls?"

Mack looks at Banks. Banks wipes his mouth and says, "The three bitches in the masks."

I come closer to Mack and take his hand. "Were they here?"

The boys share a glance. "It's them," says Mack. "They're the ones texting us."

"Right."

He pulls his hand away from mine and shows me his phone. I already know what it says:

The more you win, the more you have to lose.

And then—

We know everything.

"Jade," Mack whispers. "They could ruin us."

"Dude. Chill," Banks butts in, like he wasn't angry and shaken an hour ago. Like he didn't drive winding miles up the coast because a ghost in his phone told him to. "We got messages, too, okay? I had to ask Jade for a ride or I'd be next. She had to say yes or you'd be next."

"Me." Mack still clings to his phone. "But not you?"

I say, "Not me."

The air rushes out of his lungs. "Good."

"God, you make me sick," says Banks with a laugh. "When's the damn wedding?"

I ease the phone out of Mack's hand. "We did what they said," I tell him, steady. I spin and crouch down by the locker next to the slip. "What's the code?"

He stammers and says, "Three-two-one-three."

I press the numbers and the lock clicks free. I drop Mack's phone into the locker and shut it. Decisive. In control.

"Let's go," I say again.

His eyes hover between Banks and me. "What if it's a trap? What if—"

"We're going," Banks yells. He cuts past us across the gangway. "It's a mutiny. You're outvoted, captain."

Mack looks out past the even rows of boats, glittering holiday-bright under the lights. "You're sure this is right?"

"Better than right," I say.

I cross the gangway. He brings it in after us and looks for answers in my eyes.

And I say, whispering close even though Banks is already shouting from the upper deck and too drunk to care what lover bullshit we're dawdling with—

"The more you win, the more you have to lose."

He nods, wordless.

I pull him away from the railing and hide us in a dark little alcove. "We've done too much to go back," I say. "We have to finish what we started or we'll lose everything."

"We already have." The shadows etch themselves dark on his face. For a split-thin second I hate that I've done this to him—that I've taken the gold that drew me close to him and tarnished it.

But he wouldn't be mine if I hadn't made him like this. He would still be nothing, knowing enough and hating them for it but never cutting them down.

I nestle him deeper into our dark. Run my hand through his hair and smooth it down. I say, "What's done is done."

The words sink in the way I want them to. He nods again: more certain this time. "I can't sleep," he says. "Not since Duncan."

"You'll sleep when it's over."

"When we're done," he says, all resolve now. All loyalty.

All mine.

He leads me out of the shadows and to the stairs. "Night is coming," he says.

His eyes stray up to where Banks chatters loud. His hand squeezes mine tight.

He says, "Let's go."

ADRIFT

The sea is rough tonight.

Safe in the marina we barely felt the breeze, but as soon as Mack guides us out into the open water the wind picks up and tears sharp and stinging at our faces. We head fast for the last red of the sunset. The cresting waves are bigger every minute. When they hit we stumble, Banks and me, and fall against the railing and each other and the wide window to the captain's room.

"Mack, get out here!" Banks shouts. He hands me the bottle and I drink—

—or he thinks I drink, anyway. I've hardly had a shot all night, but I've grabbed the bottle as often as he has. Laughed louder when he did. Stumbled more when he did.

"Mack!" Banks bellows again. He presses his face to the window. "Come on!"

Behind him, I shake my head. Barely, but enough.

"In a minute," Mack yells.

"Fuck," says Banks. "Where's he taking us? Japan?" The bow hits hard against a wave and he staggers into me. His knee knocks into mine and he steadies himself with one hand on my arm. He says, too close, "Can't believe Mack's the one who ended up with you."

I blink slow. "Believe it."

He holds on for another too-long moment before he takes his hand back and leans on the railing. He looks up, past Mack, past the highest deck, up into the stars. "You sure showed up at the right time to watch everything go to hell," he says.

"I just assumed things were always like this at St Andrew's."

He laughs. "Twisted. I keep saying it because it keeps being true."

"Thank you."

"No," he says, "thank *you*, Ms. Khanjara." He stretches his arms out along the railing. Slides one hand across my back. His fingers burn through my shirt and into my skin. "You're the only one who's not losing your shit."

Behind the glass, Mack keeps the course. The shoreline we left has faded away completely, and to the north only the dimmest lights shine from the cliffs. We'll head out to sea until they've all died to dark. Until we're past El Matador and too far away to see the shore even if we stayed out past dawn.

We're a tiny lonely light on the tar-black water.

"Not scared of anything, huh?" Banks asks.

"No." I flash a grin that glows bright.

"Damn," he says. I know he sees my fangs. "Never met a girl like you before."

That night at Duncan's house the dazzle-smiled boy said, *I've never seen anyone like you—*

We crash hard into another wave and I say, right as we hit, "Maybe once." A spell-quiet murmur he won't hear until he's all alone in the dark. Then, louder, "And you never will again."

"This shit," he says. "It'll be over soon."

It's the truth.

We stay where we are. The lights vanish one by one and I feel the birds from the rooftop circling. It's impossible, but they're there. Diving together in the black sky. Watching over me. Blotting out the stars so not even heaven can peek through.

Finally Mack lets the boat idle. He comes out onto the deck

and takes a long, deep drink. Then he kisses me and I feel the liquor hit my veins—

—except it isn't the liquor, and it isn't his kiss. It's the moment.

"What now?" says Banks. He scans the horizon. "Fuck, it's dark out here."

"Now the party starts," I say with the wickedest smile I've let myself show since I stepped through the doors to St Andrew's.

Then I say, "Truth or dare."

"Again? Fuck," says Banks, but he laughs.

"Have a better idea?" I say, all challenge and double meaning.

He scoffs. "Not as long as you're playing. It'll be my turn to ask next."

I pull Mack's arms tight around me. "I know."

Banks takes the bottle back and drinks. "Dare."

I say, "Jump."

He blinks. "You mean—"

"No," Mack says.

But I nod. "I mean in."

"Fuck no," says Banks.

I laugh. "Are you scared?"

"Hell yes, I am. You're crazy."

"Weak," I say, searing and digging. "God, you're a disappointment."

He riles. "You do it."

Mack grabs my hand and says, "Jade, don't."

I take the bottle from Banks and drink—really drink this time. Enough to dull my heartbeat so he won't see it tapping fast through my skin. Enough to see him the way he looked that night, I hope, when I see him for the very last time.

"*Don't*," says Mack, urgent.

"She won't," says Banks. "Calling it right now."

I pull out of Mack's grasp and run across the deck and down the stairs. The boys clatter behind me. I call, "Where are the lights?" and Mack fumbles at the wall. The stern deck floods with daybreak.

I back away from them until I feel the railing cold against my legs. "Where's the ladder?"

"On your right," Mack stammers out. "But you can't—"

I laugh. Burning bright with anticipation and every stupid reckless thing I'll risk. I'd do anything—

I *will* do anything—

—to get what I want. And I know exactly what I want.

I unlatch the gate. Unhook the ladder and send it clanking down into the water. Spin back to the middle of the deck. The boat shines white but it doesn't matter anymore, because now I know I can paint the white red.

I can take every single thing they tried to ruin and make it mine again. Make it a weapon that cuts them down and bleeds them dry.

I unbutton my blouse and let it flutter down to the deck. Unzip my skirt and let it fall. Stand there in jade-green lace and my silver crucifix. Bare skin and faded bruises but tonight, all the power is mine.

They stare. Banks leering and Mack strung tight in fear.

"Weak," I say. "You'll never be men. You'll be scared little boys forever—"

And I turn and run hard for the edge and leap.

SINKING

The water swallows me whole. Its teeth cut gashes into my skin and it's so cold that my mouth flies open and I gasp and then I'm choking. It's darker than any dark there's ever been. The water grabs my arms and my legs and pulls me down, pulls me apart, pulls me deeper—

I fight.

I will always fucking fight.

The ocean should know better.

I kick its grasping strangling fingers away. Pull hard with both arms. Mads said *you can't swim for shit,* but I can and she knows it and tonight I'm not weak like I was that day under the too-bright sun. Tonight I swing hard at the hands that hold me and the teeth that want me and the haze that drags me toward sleep—

I burst through the surface. Gasp so hard I see another sky of stars between me and the real sky. The boat blazes bright but ten times farther away than it should be. The waves lift me and drop me back down.

Mack yells from far away. I see them leaning over the railing. Two little shadows screaming, *Jade.*

But they don't jump in.

I fight. Breathe in deep and dig into the water and crawl for the light. It takes hours. It takes days. But I kick and I fight and then all at once, the lights are blinding and Mack and Banks are five feet away and yelling themselves hoarse. My hand hits the ladder. The shock—

the thrill—

—shoots up my arm and fills me up. I shout at Mack and Banks, shout at the sky and the shrinking stars, shout at my guardian flock and feel them scatter away into the night.

I'm safe. They know I can do what I came here to do.

My other hand finds the ladder and I climb up and stumble onto the deck. Dripping wet and with water caught deep in my lungs, but laughing. A wild shrieking laugh that peals brighter than the waves and the wind.

"Fuck," says Banks. And then, "*Fuck*, Mack, you know how to pick them."

It echoes from the white-sheets room, *Fuck, Dunc, you know how to pick them—*

—but the echo is dull and drowning and sinking to the bottom of the ocean.

"Jade—" Mack gasps. He runs for the cabin and comes back with a towel and wraps me in it. I shiver against him. I kiss his neck, kiss his jaw, kiss his lips.

Taste salt water and liquor and freedom.

Then I turn to Banks. I say, "Your turn."

"Don't do it," says Mack, and he means it.

It works better than anything I've said.

"Why not?" says Banks. He pulls off his shirt. "Think your girl will change her mind about which one of us she wants?"

"Don't do it," Mack says again. The worry rises in his voice. "The water's too rough."

"You didn't stop her. You're sure as shit not going to stop me," Banks says. He shouts loud into the dark. Climbs up onto the first rung of the railing and swings one leg over and balances there, one foot on each side, grinning back at us.

"Banks—" Mack calls out, pained and sharp—

The boat rocks and Banks almost falls but his grin stays

nailed in place. The same as it did when he slammed the door to the white-sheets room. The same as when he cut through the crowd with a drink in his hand. The same as when he stood with me under the lights, I think, and I can almost see him there—

Banks yells. The water swallows up his words.

Mack shouts, "Brody!" and he's a little boy again shouting for his best friend before he can dart into the street—

—but Banks is all wolf now. He howls at the sky and swings his other foot up to the top rail and flips backward into the dark.

Mack slams into the rail and shouts at the water. Keening. Torn apart.

"Jade, no, we can't—" he says. "We'll bring him back in—"

Far back, at the very edge of the circle of light, Banks comes up. Coughing hard.

I unhook the ladder. Pull it up. Feel each rung clank sinful and knowing. Clip it back into place. Lock the gate closed. The boat pitches. Banks tries to shout to us, but he goes under again and struggles back up.

"He's my best friend," says Mack. Pleading.

I turn on him. "You promised."

"I can't!"

"He's guilty. You know he's guilty."

"But—"

"He's not your friend anymore!" I shout it louder than I want to. "He's one of them."

"He's—he's—" Mack grabs for the gate.

I push his hand away. Another wave rocks us hard and we fall this time, both of us, onto the deck. I grab his hands and say it right into his face: "He knows what we did."

"He doesn't! He can't!"

"He knows! You heard him in the hall—when he said you played dirty, and you have your own guilt—"

His breath catches.

I say, soft and cruel, "He'll ruin us."

And I've won.

Mack's shoulders stoop but his jaw hardens. I hold my breath. Banks shouts, distant and drowned.

Mack says, "For you."

I say, "For us."

He stands up.

I say, "Take us home."

He turns away from the dark water behind us. Walks heavy to the stairs.

The wind whips up and slurs across every inch of my skin. The towel is splayed across the deck and weighted down with seawater. I pull it across my shoulders and tie the corners around my neck. It's as white as the sheets from Duncan's house, but I've turned it mine. Turned it imperial and ominous.

Banks is almost back now.

I stand up. The deck is slick under my feet. The boat rolls with the waves but I don't stumble. A lantern hangs next to the cabin door. I unhook it and wrap one hand tight around the ring at the top.

Then I find the light switch and plunge the deck into darkness. Another light still shines from the stern, and another high up from the roof. I hit every switch until only the stars shine down.

Banks shouts. Close. Afraid.

I walk back across the deck in the dark.

Banks shouts again—

"Light!" He breathes the water in and chokes and flounders. "I need light!"

I hit the switch on the lantern. It flares blue-white. I hold it out over the water with one hand. My cape hangs heavy against the wind.

"Jade!" Banks shouts. Right below me now. I have to lean out over the rail to see him. His arms flail against the slick stern. "Give me the ladder!"

I don't move.

"Fuck!" he shouts. He throws his arms up and tries to grab the rail, but it's too high to reach. His hand slaps against the deck. He won't hold on for long.

I lean over the rail. Lean close with the lantern circling us together.

"Jade! Help me! It's not a fucking joke anymore!" His hand slips and he goes under and struggles back up. "Jade!"

I kneel down and reach out. He grabs onto me so desperate that I can feel his whole soul caught between our hands.

"Help me get the rail," he says. "The ladder—where's the ladder?"

I say, "It's gone."

He coughs hard. "You—what are you—"

And I'm sick of him. Sick of his rough drunk charm and his rough drunk hands. Tonight he doesn't dazzle and he doesn't smile, and I don't know if he gave me the drink that night, and I'll never know, and it doesn't matter because tonight, *this* night, I'll kill him. "Shut up," I say. "You should've seen this coming."

"What the *fuck*," he gasps. I can still see the three long scratches I left on his arm. "What the *hell*—"

"You know what we did to Duncan."

He chokes. His hand slips closer to the edge. "You—" he rasps out. "You mean—"

"We killed him."

"Fuck!" he shouts, and then, dying desperate, "Mack!"

"He's gone," I say, and the engine thrums hot and thrilling.

Shock shines through his panic and his fear. "You didn't— you—"

I shout over the waves and the wind and the engine pulling me away from him—

"You know what you did." The waves crash around him and he swallows too much water. Our hands are clasped but I'm alive and he's dead and he knows it.

I say, "You met a girl like me once before."

I hit the switch on the lantern and the whole world goes as dark as the water.

I reach out too far to be safe. Bring my hand down to where the scratches start on his arm. Rip the scabs open again.

And he laughs a death-rattle laugh and he knows, he knows, he knows. His hand slips again. With one more wave he'll be gone. He chokes out one last word, lashed bloody and bare and finally understanding—

Revenge—

I let go.

His hand disappears into the dark.

The engine thrums louder. I stand up and look out to where the horizon should be. I don't even know where I'm looking anymore—toward home, or toward the cliffs of El Matador, or out toward the endless open ocean.

There's only darkness. Rolling and hateful and complete.

UNITED

We don't speak the whole way home.

Mack sits rigid behind the wheel. I sit one seat over in a sweatshirt that hangs loose around me. It's bright proud blue, with ST ANDREW'S LACROSSE bold across the front. On the back is a white X with one word, MACK, blazoned over it.

We don't speak, but his hand holds mine so tight I think my bones might break.

Back on shore, my coven will do all the things I planned. Mads pulled up as soon as we left the slip. Jenny and Summer climbed into my car and drove back to Mads's house, right behind her, and parked so the whole world could see that beaming shameless red car in the driveway. They grabbed up my phone from the backseat and texted my mother and father, *Staying at Mads's.*

Tomorrow, when they realize Banks is missing, every bit of proof will say I never went out at all. And his car will wait at El Matador with his phone blinking its little beacon, and when they find it the last message will say, *You know what you did to her. You and your dead friends.*

Guilt doesn't work on boys like them, but whoever finds his phone won't know that. And someday, when his bloated rotting body washes up in Malibu, they'll know it broke him.

He broke.

He drank too much and he swam too far out.

He stopped fighting.

Poor Banks.

It's almost midnight when we're back in the slip. Mack

shuts off the lights in the captain's room and we walk out onto the deck together. Banks's shirt hangs off the back of the boat, wrapped around the railing. I crush it together in my hands.

Mack stares at the gate I locked. Everything is as spotless as it was when we left. I say, "You never went out tonight."

He nods.

I say, "I was never here."

He nods. But then he says, "Jade—" and it's brimming full of all the loyalty in the world. To justice over mercy. To *her* over his pack.

He says, "Stay with me. I know I won't sleep. I'll see things. But if you're here—"

He says, "Stay with me."

I do.

WAKING

Mack reaches into my sleep and wrenches me awake.

"Jade—" he gasps, and light floods in and I can't remember where I am.

"Banks—" says Mac—

I remember.

I feel a smile shimmer across my face and last night comes flooding back, as dark and unrelenting as the waves that swallowed Banks down. I close my eyes again and sink back against Mack's chest.

"I saw him," says Mack. "He was right in front of me and he was soaking wet and dead and saying he knew—"

I murmur up at him, "What's done is done." Pull him back down with me.

He says, "I think I'm going crazy."

I feel him almost as close as we were last night here in the dark. I open my eyes. "You're not."

He says, "We'll never be forgiven."

"It doesn't matter."

His face changes. He smiles at me, but it's strange and sad and it doesn't match what he should be. He says, "I'll always feel guilty. I'll never be like you."

"We're the same," I say. Lying for him.

He shakes his head. "No." His eyes drift closed, but then he jolts up and grabs my arm so tight I can feel a bruise bloom under my skin. He says, all terror, "There's blood on your face."

I won't let him splinter apart. "No, there isn't."

"It's his," he says, but then he hears himself. He takes his head in his hands.

"Mack," I say, and I sit up and run my hand along his back. "When's the last time you slept?"

"Last night," he says.

I wait.

"Last night, sort of," he says instead. "I don't know. The night Duncan died. I can only sleep when you're here. I just see it all, over and over—"

"Stop."

"No." He buries his head deeper into his hands. "We're the villains. We are."

I get up and go to the window. Look out at the marina warming slow in the morning light. Last night blurs across it, bleeding together—

the bloody sunset off the bluff at El Matador—

Banks choking out, *Revenge*—

the engine thrumming to life and carrying us back to shore without him.

Mack is right: he'll never be like me. But he'll be close.

When we're done, he'll know it like I do. He'll feel the pride and the thrill and he'll understand.

He will.

BEHIND THE GATES

Mads says, *You're getting reckless.*

The gate swings closed behind me and I walk barefoot up the driveway. She waits inside until Mack's car pulls away. Then she crosses the grass and gets into the passenger side of my father's red car at the same time that I get into the driver's seat. I wear Mack's sweatshirt and my uniform skirt, still damp from the deck.

She says, *You're getting reckless.*

"No, I'm not," I say. I open my mirror and trace two fingers under my eyes to chase away yesterday's slipping mascara.

"You just brought him here. He could've seen us."

"He didn't."

"He could've."

I snap the mirror shut. "Fuck, Mads, it's too early for this."

She reaches over and takes my hand. She says, barely out loud, "Are you okay?"

I look away. Out past the sharp fierce spikes on the gate to the street with the trees bending across it. At the morning light pooling where the shadows don't reach. I say, "Every time one of them dies I'm better than I ever was."

She doesn't say, *Don't lie.*

I say it again: "I'm not reckless. You know how good that plan was yesterday. You know they'd never be able to prove anything even if they looked at me."

She says, "When."

I look back at her. "What?"

"*When* they look at you. They will. Four boys are dead—"

"Six," I say. "It will be six. And one girl."

Even this early her eyes are circled in kohl. She is always, always Mads. "Seven dead," she says. "All of them since you came to St Andrew's. All of them since the party at Duncan's house. And everyone knows what happened to you."

"To *her*," I say, sharp.

Her hand holds mine tighter.

I say, "I don't care if they catch me. They can do whatever they want once I'm done."

"What about Mack?"

"What do you mean?"

Mads watches close. She says, "You've left it so it all points to him. Duncan died at Mack's house. Mack's boat went out yesterday. Mack held the knife for you. That's your plan, isn't it? For after?"

The sun comes through the palms and stripes light across the windshield and our eyes. When I think of after—

of when I've ripped all their red-circled faces out and thrown the page away—

of when all the scorching white is drowned in an ocean of red—

of when their whole hungry pack is cut down to nothing and none of them will ever mix another drink, grab another girl's arm, crush a hand across her mouth so she can't scream—

—I can't see anything at all.

There is only now. The boys I've killed and the boys I'll kill.

Finally Mads gives me my phone and says, "Don't forget us. We'll be yours until it's over and we'll be yours after it's done."

I say, "I know."

I don't tell her there will never be an after.

THE HAUNTING

There are no birds on the roof today. The whole school—

the whole kingdom—

—is stifled under the ash from Duncan's crumbled reign, but the silence is loud and startling. The current under it rushes stronger than the riptides that pull swimmers out to drown past the rocks at El Matador.

Everyone is watching. The boys and the girls and the cops at the door.

Piper and I are the first to our table at lunch. The whole week behind us wears at her eyes. She's brushed her makeup on heavier to cover it, but I can still see the creeping dread underneath.

She says, worn through, "Fuck this."

"God, Piper, go to confession," I say, safe and mocking and the same words she said to Duffy a day ago. "Maybe it will help you sleep at night."

"Fuck this and fuck *you*," she says, "whoever you are—"

But then her fire burns out and she gives up. "Whatever. I don't know if you're a narc, or best friends with those bitches in the masks, or if you and Mack are all ganged up with Malcolm now—"

"Malcolm?" I don't hide my scorn. "You think he's the one fucking with you?"

She laughs through her teeth. "He's gone, isn't he? And he's guiltier than all of them except his brother."

That word, *guilt*, sits strange on her lips. "They're all guilty. They had a choice," I tell her like she told Duffy.

"Malcolm's the one with the dealer." She says it low, all defense and gutted sleeplessness. "Malcolm made the damn drink. Malcolm—"

She stops and waits.

"What?" I press, and I need to know exactly what she doesn't want to say about him.

"Why do you even fucking care?"

That night Malcolm stood at the bar, mixing the just-for-me

drink. Floated just outside the door and said *you know I trust my dealer*. But in between, in the static and the white—

"God, your priorities are fucked," says Piper. "His brother's dead and we all know Porter was too weak to do it on his own. So maybe Malcolm's playing into all the bullshit from before until somebody admits they were in with Porter."

All around us the murmuring-silent St Andrew's Preppers bow low at their tables. Keeping their heads down so they don't get swept up in the vengeance that's picking off their A-team one by one. I say, smile-slicked, "Mack thinks it's the girls in the masks."

"God," she says. "He might not even be wrong. Shit like that doesn't happen without a reason."

I let my smile go wicked. "You know what the reason is."

"Yeah, fine," she says in a huff. "Shit like this never happened before no matter what went down at Duncan's parties."

Her words knot tight together. I count them off—

Duncan

Duffy

Connor

Banks

—and I'm prouder of it than I've ever been of anything.

I say, "Maybe those girls will be back."

"Maybe you're one of them," she says. Almost on fire again, but a weak fire that won't last. "Maybe you know them. Maybe—"

Duffy sits down in, hunching and glassy-eyed. "Banks still isn't here?"

We don't answer.

Duffy says, like he can't stop himself, "God. No."

Piper sends a quick glare scything across the room. Against the far wall, the gray-suited detective stands watch. Sister María de los Dolores hovers close behind him.

I laugh at Piper and Duffy and their fear. "I'm sure he's just skipping," I say.

"Or he ran," says Piper. "Like Malcolm."

"Or he's dead," Duffy says, and the last bell tolls deep. "Like Duncan. Like Porter. Like Connor—"

"Shut *up*, Duff." Piper's voice grates harsh.

Duffy shakes his head and says, "Where's Mack?"

"Don't you fucking start," I say, tugging at his fraying splintering nerves.

"I didn't mean—I didn't mean—"

"So don't *say* it," Piper snips.

Then Mack comes through the doors and crosses the crowd to our table. Edges around the dead boys' empty seats and starts to say, "Jade—"

He stops. He stumbles back into the stone-and-wood arches that hold the low windows in place. His hand comes up, shaking, and his eyes lock on the seat next to me. His seat.

"What?" I ask, and something deep in my veins shivers colder.

"It's you," he gasps. Not to me or Duffy or Piper. To the empty chair.

Piper's eyes cut quick to mine.

I say, "Mack—"

"He's dead," he says. "He's *dead*."

"Mack—" I say again, and then I think to laugh. Too late, but better than nothing. "Mack! Sit down. Stop fucking with us."

He doesn't look away from the chair. He reaches out closer and then draws away horror-fast. "Don't you see him?"

I get to my feet and slip one arm around him. Whisper, "Stop talking. Right now."

He gapes fear into my eyes. "He's there. He's right there."

Duffy clutches at Piper. "Who is it? Mac—"

"No one." I say it slow and clear and only to Mack. "You're seeing things."

Doubt flickers across his face and vanishes again under the terror.

I turn toward all the perking-up eyes. "He's been like this," I say. "Since Duncan. He's not sleeping."

Piper and Duffy shift, nervous. The murmurs are rolling louder now, and across the room the gray-suited detective pins his stare on us.

I say, laughing too much but not enough, "We'll be right back."

I pull Mack away, to the very edge of the room. Hold his face in my hands. He won't look at anything except the ghost over my shoulder.

"Stop it," I hiss. "There's nothing there. Like this morning, with the blood—"

"He's here," Mack whispers. Behind him the detective starts across the room, slow but certain, with the sister shadowing him. "He can't be here. He's dead. He's *dead*—"

"Mack!" My claws dig into his skin. His eyes come to mine, sudden and at last, and the terror in them shocks through the space between us. The man in gray is halfway to us now, close enough to hear if Mack cries out too loud—

—and we can't end like this. We won't. Not before we're done.

I keep my hands on his jaw and in his hair. "Mack," I say again, but soft enough to sift through the ghosts. "We did what we had to do. Don't doubt us."

He shakes his head. "We're ruined. I'm ruined because he's dead—because we—"

I kiss him all at once, before he can say *because we killed him.* Kiss him with the detective closing in and the sister grasping for his sleeve. Kiss him hard enough to bring him back to me, hard enough to remind him that he killed for her, hard enough to save us—

"Jade," says Sister María de los Dolores. It floats over us like a corpse on the water. "That's enough."

And it is, because all at once Mack whispers against my lips, "He's gone. He's *gone.*" And he pulls me close and his relief drowns me as deep as the waves that drowned Banks.

"He was never here," I say, still coaxing soft. I kiss him again and he's real this time. For a soaring shining moment there is nothing else at all—

only Mack and me, fearless—

only Mack and me, bound by blood—

only Mack and me, sworn to each other.

"Jade," says the sister again.

My lips leave Mack's. His gaze is clear now. His fear still lingers but he's slashed it down and left it powerless. He is brave and mine. The sister and the detective stand waiting in their matching gray, but I don't care, because nothing they do can pull Mack away from me.

"Miss Khanjara," says the detective, eyes flicking between us. "Mr. Mack. Your friend Brody Banks never came home last night—"

"We're not saying anything without our attorneys present," I say. Sweeter than sweet with all my relief sinking in.

The detective looks at Mack. "Andrew," he says, and he doesn't know anything about us at all. "You and Brody go back a long way."

Beside me, Mack nods. His arm is still close against me and it trembles, just a little, and I slip my hand into his and hold tight.

"You're sure you don't know where he is?" the detective asks.

Mack takes a breath, stuttering at first but then even.

And he says, "You'll have to speak with my attorney."

I've made him perfect, right in the last desperate moment.

"Well, you heard them," says Sister María de los Dolores. "They've asked for their lawyers." Her stare hooks doleful into the detective.

He steps back and says, "We'll talk again." Looking too close at Mack's bruise-dark eyes.

The sister says, "Until then—Jade, *behave.*"

But she winks when she says it. Fast enough to miss and hidden under her wimple and the heavy sag of her cheeks, but there.

When they fade back across the room Mack sighs out guilt and ghosts. We should go back to Piper and Duffy, be our shining best selves, but right in this second I can't. Right in this second it can only be us.

Right in this second I pull Mack around the corner and tuck us in by a window where two walls come together.

Mack says, when we're alone, "I thought I was brave."

Somewhere far away there's the faintest rustle of feathers and wings.

"After Duncan," he says. "When I woke up the next morning I felt—*proud*."

His voice slips through the space between us and dances across my skin. His darkness and his light are circling each other.

He doesn't know which side will win.

"But I'll never be as brave as you," he says. "You've seen all of it. Everything we've done. And look at you." He traces two fingers across my cheek. "You're beautiful. You're *glowing*. There's no guilt on your face."

His fingers trail down my neck and over my collarbone. He takes the crucifix between his fingers. The silver links us together here in our stone corner.

His eyes flicker to the window. "Those birds yesterday—did you see them?"

I nod.

"I wonder where they went."

I think of the whole flock taking wing when I screamed into the sky. Their huge shadow rushing west to the water.

"I wonder what it means," he says. "I wonder how it ends."

"With us," I tell him, and I wrap my hand over his and close his fingers tight around the crucifix. "It ends with us."

CAUGHT

He sleeps, finally, after school. In my arms, with the curtains drawn tight. In my arms, with the little waves lulling us toward dreams. In my arms, with no one else to make him doubt.

In sleep he looks younger. The boy who wouldn't raise the knife until I locked his hands around it and told him it was the only way to keep his honor.

But I know better.

He sleeps because he isn't that boy. He's found his dreams and darkness.

He's found himself.

I lie sleepless in the dark with my good cruel king. My thoughts float and fly and swim. I should leave, but I don't.

When I finally stand he doesn't stir. I get dressed and fix my lips and my hair. I'm slipping almost out the door when Mack's phone buzzes on the floor.

The message is from the coven: *Not even her?*

I never asked them to send it.

I flare. I unlock his phone—*what's yours is mine*; that's what I told him when I leaned close last night and watched him unlock it. I delete their message and scroll back up.

He asked them, this morning, before he came to lunch with Banks's ghost hobbling behind him—

What do you know?

They said, *Everything you don't want told.*

He said, *You mean Duncan.*

They said, *Everything.*

He said, *I need to see you.*

They said, *You can't be trusted.*

He said, *I won't tell anyone.*

And they said, hours later and already knowing, *Not even her?*

He didn't answer.

But he didn't tell me.

The anger closes over me as hard as the rolling waves did last night.

They tell me, *Don't lie.* They say it all the time. Summer sweet and Jenny sharp and Mads silent. They all say it, even though they know I only lie when I have to. Not when it matters. They say, *We're yours.*

Don't lie.

They're the liars.

I type fast and thoughtless: *Don't ever talk to him again without talking to me first.* Then, *Meet me at the marina. Right now.*

Then I delete all of it.

I kiss Mack good-bye with my lips brushing his like hummingbird feathers. I leave him dreaming.

I go to my coven with a storm gathering under my wings.

LIARS

Summer had the secret phone this morning.

Jenny rats her out, Jenny the girl she loves, Jenny the girl she won't tell with words even though she's already told her a million other ways.

Jenny says, the second Mads stops her car, "It was Summer."

And Summer says, "Jenny!"

And Jenny says, "What? It fucking *was*."

Summer blushes pretty and perfect. She gives me her fluttery praying-mantis eyes. They don't work on me. She can't charm me like she can charm boys at bars and girls at parties and Jenny spinning circles in the boxing ring.

I say, "Get out."

Mads has her car pulled up at the edge of the marina. Her sunglasses are on and the engine is running. I was at the end of the dock waiting when she drove in. I could feel six eyes on me through the black glass. Feel the secrets they never should have spun without me.

Summer gets out of the front seat. The sunlight weaves across her hair and she shimmers like heaven and treasure but I don't care. I sit down where she was and she scrambles into the back next to Jenny. Jenny laughs, mean. I say, "Let's go."

Mads drives. I leave my window shut and turn the air-conditioning as cold as it goes. Colder than Summer can stand.

Jenny says, "I told you she'd be mad."

I turn and stare them down. "I have a reason, don't I?"

Jenny smirks.

And Summer says, timid, "So he didn't tell you we texted."

"He was seeing *ghosts*. He's on the edge and you're pushing him too far. You have to leave him to me."

"He didn't tell you," Jenny echoes. "We told you not to trust him."

"You should've fucking told me not to trust you, either!" The words fall between us, bloody and ragged.

Jenny and Summer steal a glance at each other. They don't speak.

Mads says, eyes on the brake lights crowding ahead of us, "You know you can trust us."

"No, I don't! You're all liars."

She says, "We don't lie when it matters."

Jenny buries her laugh behind her hands.

"He's not yours," I say. "He's mine. He's doing this for me."

And Mads says, "So are we."

I open the window all the way and let the heat of the deadlocked cars wash over us. I'm right, but Mads isn't wrong.

I say, over the humming waiting traffic, "Fine. If he needs you to meet him, you'll meet him. We'll use it."

Jenny says, "That's a terrible fucking idea, by the way."

"Summer should've thought of that before she started chatting him up all on her own."

"It's a risk," says Mads. "We don't know what he'll do. It's not like it was before."

"It doesn't matter," I say. "We're almost done. If this is what he needs we'll make it happen. So when he walks away he'll know the only way he has left is to finish what he started."

"What *you* started," Jenny sasses.

"Exactly," I say. "Me. Not you. And what I'll finish by Friday night."

Mads says, "Ambitious."

I don't say, *They're closing in.* I don't say, *It's now or it's never.*

I say, "You know I am."

The traffic moves a halting foot forward. We coast until the river of lights goes red again. I say, "Tomorrow morning. Before dawn. He'll believe anything we want him to believe. He thinks Banks is haunting him. If you want him to, he'll think you're haunting him, too."

Jenny grins. "We are."

It sings true from one of us to the next to the next.

I'm angry with them still, but they're mine. And soon, when the boys are dead and St Andrew's is washed clean, we'll be bound back together without this simmering between us.

I say, "We'll make him as bold as he needs to be. He'll come for them. All of them."

"For Duffy," says Mads.

"For Malcolm," says Summer, mine again.

"For Piper," Jenny finishes.

I place one hand between Mads's seat and mine. She takes it. Jenny and Summer join in so all four of us are locked together.

And they know it without me saying it, because they're mine:

He'll kill them all for me.

TOIL AND TROUBLE

Day turns to night and he never tells. Not about the things Summer said without me, and not about the things we say together, all four of us casting our spell.

I trust him more and less.

But I trust Jenny and Summer and Mads with everything again. We have a plan and I'm alive the way I've only felt since we swore to kill the boys. Since we circled them in red and built plots like scaffolds that we'll climb all the way to immortality.

It's my most reckless plan yet and Mads tells me so three times, but she loves it.

They all do.

We meet so early it's still all night. At Summer's house, the way we always do before a party, because the vanity in her room stretches broad enough for all four of us to sit under the dressing-room lights. I arrive exactly when Mads pulls up. She and Jenny wait for me and we walk up the driveway together. Summer lets us in without a word and we slink up the stairs past the cleaning ladies still washing another party away.

The three of them paint themselves lethal and beautiful. Cheekbones carved sharp and lips curling. Hair gathered high. Black dresses and white masks. Dusted with gold.

Last night we told him where to be, and when. *Or we tell,* we said. *Everything.*

He'll be there.

We arrive two hours before he will. Weave in through the back with the cars parked far away. Lock the chain back over the door so he wouldn't be able to break in even if he tried. The theatre is long-dead, its gilded flash rotting the same way it was when Summer's father bought the building. *He wants to fix it up for premieres,* Summer said, *but keep it edgy. So he can pretend he makes art films instead of slashers.*

Unfixed, it's perfect for us.

By the time Mack arrives—one pair of headlights glowing muted far down the block—our stage is set. My coven is all in place and I've swung another door open. I lit his path with thin candles, waxy and crooked and burning nervous below cobwebs and neglect.

He's alone. I'm sure of it, because from my high window I can see that no one pulls up behind his car or follows him out. And because I know I'm all he has left.

He stops in front of the theatre. He's dressed all in black with his jacket collar pulled high around his neck. He almost looks sinister. I love him for it.

His gaze drifts up from the foundation to the roof. He looks straight into my eyes for a long moment without knowing it. Far off a dog howls and rattles at its chains.

He digs into his pocket and finds his phone. Types something. Puts it back away and straightens his shoulders. My phone is on silent, but I check it, and I'm right: he wrote to me.

No matter what happens I'm yours.

When I look back he's gone.

I slip down from my perch and then up again, moving silent into the rafters. My coven waits below me in darkness so thick it would catch me if I fell.

I hear his footsteps. I wait, silent and shadowed.

The footsteps stop.

My coven says—

We know.

I smile so bright it almost breaks through the dark.

My coven says—

We know.

Summer pulls the ropes. They groan and creak and the curtains open. She said, *I don't know how long it's been since they had a show here. Fifty years? My dad thinks it's brilliant. Everybody else thinks it's crazy.*

But it's just what we need—my coven and me. A dead theatre on a dead street where the streetlights are broken and the doors are nailed shut. As haunted as anywhere in LA, even before we crept in and made it our lair.

The curtains clank to a stop. Dust puffs and floats like smoke. They sit all in a row on the almost-empty stage, draped across mismatched chairs with the velvet molting off and the springs stabbing out. Jenny is on the left, spinning a bottle in her hands. Summer floats up to the chair on the right. And Mads sits ruling in the center with a gold crown on her head. Glowing in the shaky light of the dozen candles we lined up at the edge of the stage.

A white sheet hangs high up behind them: a stretched-smooth waiting screen.

Mack stands below it all, with ten rows of broken seats between him and my coven. He can't see me, but he can see my coven real and ready: the spirits he summoned.

They speak again, louder, rising—

We know.

Jenny holds the bottle out to him. Shakes it bright and tempting in the candlelight.

And then Mack says, "What do you know?" His voice is bolder than I thought it would be.

Jenny laughs mad and wild and raucous and throws the bottle straight into his hands. He doesn't catch it. He lets it shatter on the floor.

Summer says, too inviting, "Don't be afraid. It's just a drink."

Mack shifts and stands taller. "Tell me what you know."

And Jenny says, "You killed them."

"I didn't—" he says, and the fear blooms bright in his eyes. "I didn't."

Mads laughs. Not wild like Jenny or teasing like Summer. Low and knowing. "They needed killing."

Mack breathes in sharp and stays that way, frozen in guilt and flame.

Then he lets go.

He says, "How do you know?"

Summer spins her phone and says, hypnotic, "She remembers."

It lights into him all at once—the truth all of them already know, no matter how much they won't let themselves admit it. Because they're *innocent, innocent, innocent* as long as they tell themselves they are. As long as they can tell themselves *we'll remember* and *she won't*. Because to them it isn't real and it isn't wrong and *that little whore with the jade-green eyes* would never come for them.

Because *that little whore with the jade-green eyes* is no one at all.

Because she's *just a girl*, alone and trapped and powerless with their hands locked over her mouth—

—and they're the golden boys today and the whole world tomorrow.

His legs go unsteady and he falls hard into a seat. Clutches onto it. His eyes light up dizzy with the dozen shivering flames. "It's too much—I can't—"

"Kill Duffy." Jenny says it, shrill enough to pierce skin. "Or his guilt is yours."

"I can't." Mack is gasping and gray. "The police. They're coming for me. That detective knows something."

"He can't hurt you," Summer soothes. "Not the way we can."

He sits caged in wood and faded velvet. Sleepless and guilty and terrified, but holding onto the boy I've made him. He says, "Only Duffy?"

They wait.

"Only Duffy," he says again, bargaining. "That's all."

Mads watches him. She is stone-still and remorseless. "Everyone who shares the guilt shares the blame."

He flares up and stands and faces her down. "And what if I won't? Everything is different now. I've killed for what they did to her—"

"You've killed," Jenny echoes back. "We'll tell."

"But it was *right*," he says, and the flames dance and dance. "That girl—"

"*That girl*," says Mads. She stands. Stalking and strong. Towering tall at the very edge of the stage.

"She wasn't the first," says Summer, slithering up beside Mads.

And Jenny comes up, too, and says, "You knew."

"But I didn't—"

"But you did," says Summer. And she and Jenny stoop down and blow out one candle and then another until only one flame is left. Summer holds it, kneeling on the stage.

Mads says, "You knew enough."

A taunting, tempting pause.

Summer blows out the last candle.

"Wait—" Mack calls.

They rise up lithe and weightless, coiling away and vanishing behind the curtain. Out in the dark Mack trips and stumbles. "Wait—" he calls again—

Far off to the side, hidden in a pile of broken scenery, a projector beams to life. The light shines bright onto the sheet that hangs down over the stage.

I have everything I need waiting ready on my phone. Today the story is all mine.

It comes to life, unflinching. Flung across the sheet at the center of the stage and blown bolder and brighter and larger than life. It's the party at Duncan's house, pieced together from all the million pictures the glittering St Andrew's Preppers posted that night. All silent and in black-and-white, from the dead-king masks along the walls to the pack, grinning hungry together.

The pictures fly faster and blur and then they freeze—

—and now they're circled in dripping red.

Connor first.

Then Duncan.

Then Porter.

Then Banks.

Then Duffy.

Then Malcolm.

Then Piper—and Mack startles out a cry.

Then the screen goes white.

Mack's voice trembles out again: "No. I don't want to see any more. Stop—"

The last face fills the screen. A plaster mask, not the one I stood behind before the night shattered, but the closest we could find. It sneers hard and proud the way only a dead king can.

Sneering like the dazzle-smiled boy.

Mack says, "I'll do it. I swear—"

But my coven is already gone, already running invisible to Mads's car. It's only him in the dark and me in my rafters and the story spinning out in white.

"You can't," Mack cries out, half-strangled. "I'll do it—"

A red X slashes across the mask, one line at a time. It drips bloody and triumphant.

The mask disappears and for a long choking second only the red X marks the white sheet—

—and then I tap my finger down on the screen.

The light goes out.

The silence is better than the most thunderous applause in the world.

In the stunned dark I glide down barefoot from the catwalk. I pull the curtain shut again and the old rope bites my hands. A sliver of glass stabs into my foot. I don't flinch.

I wait.

In the theatre, Mack shouts, "Hello?"

No one answers.

He stumbles closer.

It's time.

I pick up an old broken table we pushed off the stage for their show. It's lighter than it looks, but heavy enough that it takes all my strength to send it toppling. It crashes into a row of music stands and they fall loud and angry.

"Stop!" Mack shouts, and the stage tremors as he jumps up.

I bloom into the innocent flower he thinks I only play for everyone else.

I step into my shoes and clatter across the stage too fast. Slip and fall and let out a flock-girl shriek.

Mack shouts, "Don't move!" He grabs at the heavy hanging velvet.

I breathe in, scared, and let a frightened little cry slip out. I hate it so much my lips curl back when I hear it. I shout out, brave but still trembling, so he can be braver—

"I have a knife! I swear I'll kill you!"

The stumbling at the curtain stops. Mack calls, "Jade?"

I say, "Mack!" The dust falls so heavy that I breathe it in and cough.

"Jade!" he shouts, desperate and raging and fighting only for me. He flings the curtain apart and in the solid black, the glimmer of the candles at the back of the theatre paints me his.

"Jade—" he gasps out, and he pulls me into his arms and holds me so tight I almost can't breathe. "Did you see them? Did they come this way?"

I find my phone and shine the flashlight into the dark. Backstage is a cluttered wreck. The light catches on the huge webs that hang down from the catwalk. A spider skitters back up its silk. I shudder. "Who?"

His flashlight comes on and he says, "The girls in the masks."

"No," I say. "What is this place? Did they tell you to come here, too?"

He edges closer to the props crowding the wings. "I asked them to meet me."

"Why didn't you tell me?" I ask, and the anger in my voice is exactly as real as he thinks it is.

"I thought they'd hurt you."

"I didn't *do* anything. They can't hurt me."

He brings me back to him. "Because of me," he says. "I thought they'd hurt you to hurt me."

And I laugh, a pealing silver bell that destroys all the dark around us, because he isn't wrong. Summer said, *Don't fall in love. Not with him,* and she meant it. She knew he'd keep it from me, *for* me, if she told him not to tell. She knew it would make me pull away from him.

It's because she loves me, but it's hardly an excuse.

I say, "Mack. Nothing they do will ever hurt me."

He kisses me so sudden I drop my phone. So true he drops his. And it's the two of us in the cobwebbed dark, victorious over the girls in the masks and the threats on our phones and the police combing through Inverness to see how Duncan really died.

We don't need anyone else.

Finally he says, "They called you here?"

"Yes," I say. I find my phone in the dust and show him my coven's texts from an hour ago, when the stage was set and he was already on the way. They sent the address and told me, *Be here in one hour or we'll tell Mack's secrets.* "I came in and there was a light at first but then it went out, and then something knocked everything over behind me—"

"You didn't see anyone?"

I shake my head. "I thought they called me here so I'd be out of the way. When you texted me I thought maybe they were meeting you somewhere else—"

"No," he says. "They were here. But Jade—" And all at once all the worry is gone from his face. "They're on our side."

He laughs. A real laugh. Not sleepless and second-guessing. He says, "They want us to do this. What we're doing."

He still can't say it, so I do. "You mean kill the boys?"

He nods. "We have to. We're *right* to."

So I laugh, too. "Because three girls in masks said so?"

He takes me into his arms. The dust sifts up around us and shines in the flashlight-glow.

He says, "They're not just girls."

TYRANNY

Duncan and his pack thought they were untouchable.

Mack and I really are.

We walk in together. We're all the power Duncan promised and all the glory we deserve. We are united. Our uniforms are starched so sharp they'd cut anyone who tried to touch us. Our strides are so strong the crowd falls back.

We are terrific and terrifying. We are conquerors of St Andrew's and of fate. We show our faces proud when all the rest of our pack has run fast and fearful.

The ones who are still alive, anyway.

The whole world whispers even though they won't say it out loud to the detective in his gray or the KTLA reporter the sisters chased down the stairs. They whisper—

Duncan—

I heard his family's paying the school to be silent—

Malcolm—

he ran because he knows he's next—

Connor—

it wasn't an accident—

Porter—

somebody made him do it, and then they made sure he'd never talk—

Banks—

they got him, you know they did—

Duffy—

he's gone too now, and why did he REALLY run—

The same cruel current shivers through it every time: *they deserve it.*

They're glad to see the pack fall.

Some of them even say—and it's girls, not even flock-girls because they're afraid to straggle out of line; it's the not-it girls who say it and the flock-girls who listen too long—*what if it's her?*

They never give her a name, but they know who they mean.

They want it to be her, I think. The girl from the party at Duncan's house.

Or from the party before, or the one before that.

It's a ruined kingdom that we rule but I wouldn't have it any other way. So I walk in with Mack, the king and the queen stepping bloody and bold and resolute through a battlefield where the dirt is wet and red.

They're afraid of us because we aren't afraid of anyone.

The old theatre is a secret we've buried together. We left the way Mack came in, past candles burning low. I blew them out and left them smoking in the dark. When we broke out the sky was glowing with dawn. The street was empty. It was just the two of us in the apocalypse and the daybreak.

He said, "Duffy. We can't let him live."

He said, "We'll finish what we started."

And we kissed in the red-gray light with cobwebs still hanging from our shoulders.

When we get to the statue Piper stands alone in front of it. She says, "Isn't this lovely. Mack and Jade, stealing from the corpses."

I smile sweet and curl closer against Mack. "So did they come for Duffy yet?"

She doesn't bother faking nice anymore. "He ran," she says. "Like half the fucking school."

I laugh. Beside me, bound to me, Mack says, "Of course he ran."

"Shut up."

I shrug. "Well, you're not surprised, are you?"

Her eyes narrow to slits.

"But it's still embarrassing."

"Shut *up*," she spits again. "He's with Malcolm. He told me."

"Are you sure it was Duffy?" I ask. I'm reckless again. It

doesn't matter what she thinks anymore, because there's no one left to listen. "Are you sure it wasn't the ghost girls on his phone?"

"Fuck you," she says. "I don't need him."

I ease closer to her. Let my serpent-self coil around her and bind her tight. "You're scared," I say.

"I'm not."

"You are."

"Whatever," she says. "You're fucking twisted. I knew it the first day you walked in." Her eyes slash over to the men standing guard across the commons: on one side two security guards, brand-new and in bold St Andrew's blue; on the other, two policemen with their badges winking in the dusty light. "I told that detective about you."

"Leave Jade out of this," says Mack. "She's the only one who doesn't have anything to do with it."

But I stay fearless and flawless. "I'm flattered."

"I told him it's no fucking coincidence that some bitch shows up on parole and everyone starts killing each other."

"You know Duncan killed Connor," I say. Not watching her; not watching the guards or the dwindling leftover flock-girls. Watching the boys instead. Watching their teeth. I want Malcolm back so I can tempt him until he stops chewing at his lip, stops pressing his mouth tight, stops hiding the smile that will give him away if he's the reason Banks never dazzled through the static. "You know Porter killed Duncan."

"Yeah, and I know nobody was killing anybody until you came in with your smirk and your first-date fucking and started playing your games—"

"Piper," says Mack, and he's more the king than Duncan ever was. "Don't say another word about her."

She smiles through her fear, grim and gritting. And she leans close and says, "I think maybe you're the guiltiest of all of us, new girl."

The bell tolls from the chapel.

I whisper to her, soothing, "I didn't do anything I shouldn't have done."

Piper hisses back, "Neither did I."

She pushes past us and stalks into the commons. The guards and the starlings watch her go.

She's all alone and she knows it. All alone with fate closing in.

Mack says, "Is Duffy really with Malcolm?"

I spin my crucifix. "I don't know, but Piper does."

"We need to find out," he says, all edge. "We need to finish this."

"We will," I say, and I love him for it, and I love my coven for turning him into the hardened king he is. I step back until I feel the statue behind me. Her arms cradle me close. I pull Mack to me under her dead white eyes. "I'll talk to her tonight. I'll make her tell."

"If she won't," he says, low, "maybe she'll have to be next. To bring Duffy out."

Behind me, the Virgin Mary's head bows lower. Praying for lost Mack and the soul he's shaded darker every day since he met me. I say, "We can't be rash. They're all watching."

He says, "We're running out of time."

"Only if we're careless," I say. "I'll talk to her tonight. Then we'll know how to bring both of them down."

He sighs. He says, "Soon."

And I breathe it back to him: "Soon."

GUILT

Patience wears us thin but doesn't break us. I let the minutes slip through my fingers like sand. Let the rumors slide over my wings. Stare back when boys stare.

Let them talk.

I want them to know. But not until we've done everything we swore we'd do.

I wait until the day is almost over. Until the light we saw break outside the old theatre has died again and I'm safe in the dark. Until I've left Mack at the marina wrapped in promises.

Until I've made my plan for Piper.

I get ready at home, alone, in my room. My parents are out and the house looms dark and silent. I take the folded paper out of my pillowcase and smooth it flat on the vanity. Four ragged holes cut through the page.

I'm as ready as Mack is. Tonight, Piper will break. She'll tell me where Duffy is hiding. She'll tell me enough that by midnight I'll be back home and planning his last breath and hers.

She'll tell me the truth: Banks, or Malcolm. So at last I can rip the memory free—

—and then rip it apart with my bare hands.

Tonight I dress in white.

Mads had my fencing things ready for me when I drove up this evening, back from Mack's. She met me at the gate and it slid open between us, striping black between our eyes. She held out the heavy white suit and the mesh mask and the sabre. I took them.

She said, "You're ready?"

I said, "Yes."

The gate slid closed and I drove home to dress for battle.

My armor waits on the bed while I comb my hair and fix my makeup. A ritual, the same as getting ready for a party. The same as getting ready for a murder. Watching myself, not looking away, until I know exactly who I am.

I take off my robe. My skin is smooth. The bruises are only shadows now.

The boys are nothing.

I fold the paper and put it away again.

I walk into my closet, to the very back of the very last row, and dig behind my long red homecoming gown. It's exactly where I left it—the dress I wore to the party at Duncan's house. Short and white and shining. A bad girl pretending to be good. A bitch and a siren and a party-crasher.

Sweet sixteen.

It's washed clean, but the hem is torn and three rows of sequins hang dangling by a thread. They gleam bright anyway.

I put on the dress. It slides cold and heavy over my skin.

The girl in the mirror is defiant. She is merciless.

She is revenge.

My coven texts me from the secret number: *Come to the combat room, dressed to fight. Or you're next.*

I fold the skirt close around my waist and put on my armor. The dress scratches when I tuck it underneath the heavy cloth, but I don't care. When I'm ready I hold my mask in one hand and my sabre in the other. My face is carved from stone.

I drive to school under the high streetlights with the windows down and my sabre and mask on the seat next to me. I don't think anything at all. Not about the boys. Not about that night. Not about their blood.

Tonight I'm only the queen.

I park in the darkest corner of the lot, far away from everything. The school shines bright. The spotlights pierce through the flowers and cast the stone rough and dangerous. Piper's car is already here.

I walk the very edge of the lot, hidden in the shadows. Mask in one hand and sword in the other. My footsteps are cold and even. The fields and the court are shrouded tight in darkness, but I don't need light. As soon as I pass the bleachers I can see a dim yellow glow at the window of the combat room.

She's here.

I don't pause outside the door. I push it open and walk straight in.

Piper stands ready in the middle of her favorite piste—the one farthest from the door. Her mask is already on.

I feel the thrill rising up in me again. I won't kill tonight, but I'll break her apart anyway. Turn her and her stupid second-rate boy against each other so when it's time to kill again, they'll both know they brought it on themselves.

They're weak. Even Piper, standing strong on the strip with her weapon in her hand.

"Jade," she says. I can hear the sneer in her voice. "I should've known."

"Did they call you here, too?" I ask.

"'They,'" she mocks. She takes a wired-tight step forward. "If there's a 'they' at all."

I'm on the piste now, walking straight toward her. Under my jacket, the sequins scratch at my skin like new feathers pricking free. "What do you mean?" I ask her, so innocent I know she'll hate me for it.

And she says, "It's you."

I stare through her silver mask and into her eyes.

"I don't know what you did at your old school, but you didn't just fuck a teacher," she says. "If you were even in school, and not some juvy psych-ward prison."

I say, "Interesting story."

Her hand shifts on the hilt of her weapon. She's ready to fight. She wants to fight. "You're a twisted bitch, and not just the way Banks talked about you when he wanted to fuck you for it."

She says *talked*, not *talks*. She knows he's dead as well as I do. But everyone knows, even if they wouldn't say it out loud like she would.

"You're twisted for real," she says. "Like, god-complex twisted. Sadistic-twisted. You came in here and you saw what they did to Connor and you thought, here are some people I can play some good fucking mind games with."

She's all intensity. She wants her moment.

I slash it apart with a laugh straight out of a country-club dinner party. All silver and gold and breathy handmade cheer. I say, "Amazing. You're twice as unhinged as your boyfriend."

She shifts her weight back onto her heels. "Whatever," she says. "Maybe I'm not right, but I'm close. You're doing this. You're playing us all against each other and it's working so well you're almost the only one left. You and your precious Mack."

I step across the line so we're toe to toe. "It's not my fault you chained yourself to the weakest boy at St Andrew's."

She spins away. "Fuck you."

And I say, "Likewise."

She says, "There were never any girls in masks. You got Mack and Banks to make it up."

"If you say so."

"It's been you this whole time. Texting us and laughing in our faces."

"If you say so."

She turns back to me. "You're going down for this. Connor and Duncan and Banks, too. Their blood is on your hands even if you never picked up a knife."

We're so close my nose almost touches her mask. I whisper straight into the screen, "Is it on my hands, or theirs?"

We stay frozen. Deadlocked and deadly.

Then our phones buzz, mine in my hand and hers along the back wall below the heavy military swords. She springs away and darts for hers and I check mine, careless.

It's the coven: *En garde.*

"Or maybe it wasn't me," I murmur.

But she steps back onto the strip and says, "They want us to fight."

Now it's my turn to mock her: "'They'?"

"Whatever," she says. "Maybe it's Mack. Maybe it's your bitch from the psych ward."

Our phones buzz again: *Prête.*

I slide my mask into place. She turns silver and shining behind the woven metal.

"I'll win," she says.

I step back to my line and bring my weapon up.

Our phones buzz one last time. Piper reads the message out loud: *"Allez."*

Her eyes spark bright behind her mask.

We let our phones fall to the side of the piste.

I pounce first, but she's ready. She throws a lightning-quick skyhook and her sabre scrapes my waist just before my attack lands. She yells loud the way she did the day I watched her practice. Spins away from me with her chin thrown high.

She's a better fencer, but I'm a better fighter. Tonight, the points that count won't be won with sabres.

We step back to the line.

"You could give up now," says Piper. She's confidence and flash.

"So could you."

"I'll win," she says again.

"Like Duffy won?"

"God, shut *up*," she snarls. She lunges before I'm ready. I parry but she presses forward and then she yells again. There are no lights or judges to keep her honest. I let her gloat.

"They're texting Mack, too," I say. "The girls you think don't exist. So I care because maybe they're you."

She laughs. I attack. I score and she shouts and I laugh back at her and say, "My point. You know it was."

"Fine," she says with her little concession-nod. Then, "We're over. Duff and me."

"Do you think that's smart?" I say. I keep my weapon pointed at the floor. Keep Piper caged until I've said my piece. "A weak ally is better than no ally at all when someone's killing everyone in your pack."

"It's *not someone*," she says, angry enough that it makes her lie bright and bold. "Connor fell. Porter lost his shit and killed Duncan, and then he took himself out of the game. And yeah, your bullshit made them do it, but you won't get to the rest of us. It's over. *You're* over."

"What about Banks?"

"What *about* him?"

"He's gone," I say.

She has her sabre back up. She's itching to lunge again. She says, "He's hiding out. Like Malcolm and Duffy."

"Hiding," I say. "Because they have something to hide."

"*God*," she half-shouts. "Who the fuck do you think you are? The patron saint of stupid sluts who drink too much?"

I bring my sabre up fast and run for her. She hits my blade away and I lunge and miss and stumble almost into the far wall.

"They're guilty," I say, and I turn back to her. "Duncan and Duffy and Connor and Banks. They know what they did."

She laughs angry and bitter. "They don't care what they did. It doesn't fucking matter. Everybody knows what happens at Duncan's parties and you're the only one who gives a shit. She sure as hell wasn't the first."

My blade flicks back up. We're facing the wrong way and not even on the piste, but I don't care. "But she'll be the last," I say—

—and it's too far and I know it as soon as I say it and my lungs pinch tight—

—and she knows.

She pulls off her mask. Her eyes are wide. She's twice as shocked as Duncan was when I leaned close over him while his blood drained out into the sheets.

She says, "You're her. You're *her*."

She grabs at my mask and yanks it off and stares hard into my eyes. "You're her," she says again, slower, filling up with knowing.

I don't lie. Not when it matters.

She springs back and brings her weapon up again. Like it's instinct. Like she'll slash the truth away.

I take three strong steps toward her. I drop my sabre. I don't need it. We stand face-to-face, eye-to-eye, girl-to-girl. I say, "Fate's a cruel bitch to girls like you."

"It wasn't my fault," she says. "I didn't do anything."

"Exactly," I hiss.

She steps back. Her face is the same color as her jacket. Her makeup is garish against the shock-white. "It was you. All of it was you."

My plan is shattered. I've veered so far away from the path I carved out that there's no way to claw back on. My rage is bleeding up through all the careful calculating and I've lost my edge, I know it, and all the sleepless reckless ruthlessness is rising up against me, but I can't think about it—not now—

And I say, "Not just me. Mack, too."

I've thrown it hard to pin her down. To make her mine again and buy me enough time to cage her up until I can call him or call my coven or scare her silent—

—but she doesn't step back. She steps forward. Hard and fast and dauntless. She shoves me and I stumble back into the wall. She says, "So what's your plan for him? Drag him along to watch his friends fall apart, and then get some JV asshole to kill him, too?"

"Of course not." I'm half-shouting in her face. She has me locked against the wall and she'll never back away. And she's almost right, and she would've been right a week ago, but he's killed for me and for *her* and he isn't like them. Not anymore. "He's the only one of all of you who doesn't deserve a knife in his throat."

Her eyes fill up slow and delighted. "You don't know," she says.

"Fuck you," I spit, and I push her away.

She doesn't lose her footing. "You don't know," she says again. And she grins damned triumph and says—

"Your golden boy is as guilty as all of them."

You knew enough, I told Mack, and I was right. But he hated them for it. He killed them for it. He burned their kingdom down.

I stand my ground. "No, he's not."

"Jade," she sings. "Poor little Jade. He's the one who gave you the drink."

It hits me hard in the chest, in the heart, in the teeth. The whole room glows searing and brighter until the lights explode and the ceiling catches fire. And I'm back in Duncan's house with the music pulsing loud and the lights spinning. Back with the plaster masks of dead kings' faces.

Back with the dazzle-smiled boy hidden behind the static—

And I know it as sure I've ever known anything.

She's telling the truth.

Then I'm screaming and screaming and screaming. There's a blade in my ribs ripping through me and spilling my blood, and I hate her so much that nothing in the world will stop it—

I push her so hard we both fall. She shrieks and I scream again—

and everything spins, everything flashes too bright—

and I see him in front of me, I hear him, and he's saying, *Elle*—

saying, *Pretty name*—

saying, *But not as pretty as you—*

I struggle to my feet and I kick her hard, and again, and she's shrieking and scrambling away and into the wall. The blood rushes in my ears, louder and louder—

and the dazzle-smiled boy says, *They know everything—*

and the dazzle-smiled boy says, *They'll ruin us—*

And Piper pulls herself to her feet with one hand clutched against her ribs and the other grasping at the wall. She coughs. She gasps. She says, "It was him. It was him. It was him—" and she won't stop—

and she said, *fine, go fuck some roofied slut* and she left me there—

and she says, *it was him, it was him, it was him—*

and my hands grab at the swords on the wall. Grab the top blade and pull with all my strength. The wires snap. I fall hard to the floor.

it was him it was him it was him—

I stand up and stagger with the sword hanging heavy and blunt from my hands.

it was him—

And Piper is still shrilling and scrabbling against the wall, grabbing at her stupid needle-thin sabre with its blunt button end and she's nothing, she's no one, she's helpless and hopeless—

I swing the sword with all my strength.

it was him—

The metal slashes against her side and cuts through her jacket like it's nothing, like it's ribbon, like it's skin—

and she falls and the gash spits red—

I promise. I've never loved anyone more—

And I scream.

And I raise the sword.

And blood flies from the blade and paints the wall and even in my rage I see the beauty, and it's devastating.

I scream. I hate. I rage.

I swing the sword again with all of it, with all of me, straight for her neck.

I scream.

it was him—

I kill her.

RUIN

Mads finds me in the white room with the spinning lights.

She runs blurred fast across the floor and my vision twists and twists until the floor is over us and the ceiling is below—

My hands clutch the sword tight against my chest. The second sword hangs swinging over my head from one wire.

The floor is red.

Piper lies next to me with her amber bird-eyes fixed on the ceiling. Her right hand is still caught around the handle of her sabre. Her mouth is a shocked little circle.

Mads says, *Jade.*

Kneeling in Piper's blood. Kneeling in front of me, in front of the splattered beautiful red arc on the wall above us, in front of the sword that hangs over me and the sword that killed Piper.

I say, *It was him. It was Mack. The boy who gave me the drink*—

—and my hands grip the sword so tight it almost cuts through my gloves.

I say, *I lost control—I ruined everything—I'll kill him, Mads, I have to*—

Mads says, *Jade, oh, Jade*—

—and she is life but I'm death. I'm drowning in Piper's blood, and in the wild and violent sea that carried Banks down. In what we've done.

And in what we've left undone.

I've lost control. I've lost myself.

My face is wet but I don't cry. I don't cry even when I kill, even when I'm locked in a room with four wolves, even when I drown in the truth and the ruin I built with my own hands.

I slash one glove across my cheeks and it comes away wet but red.

It's Piper's blood.

I don't cry.

I say, *He's no one*—

I say, *They're nothing*—

I say, *They'll never make me anything I wasn't before*—

And then I'm crawling away from the wall, scraping long red gashes into the floor. Crawling to Mads.

I don't cry.

My shoulders shake. My lungs wrack. I feel the horrible sounds that rip themselves out of my throat and bury themselves in Mads's shoulders.

I don't fucking cry.

Finally I stop shaking. Finally I stop making the sounds that ruin me. Finally every muscle in me aches and hollows and I'm so tired I can see sleep hanging from the ceiling and crawling out of the two bright gashes that set Piper free. I say, slurred and catching—

"What do I do? What do I *do*?"

I don't have a plan. I don't have anything. I want to curl close to dead Piper and slip under into the darkness she already knows. Burrow down into the red and the nothing—

Mads says, "We'll call Jenny's father. Self-defense—I don't know—"

I unfold. I am outside myself. The way I would have been that night if there was any justice in all the world—

I stand up. The sword is impossibly heavy. "No," I say, and it echoes high.

She stands up after me. She's a shadow in black and I'm a ghost in white and red. She says something and I say, "No." And I say, "What's done is done."

I let the sword fall against the floor. It thuds hard—

the door swings shut—

—and little red drops scatter onto the white.

I stare at Piper lying dead and done. Piper who said, *I didn't do anything.* Piper who said, *You're her.* Piper who said, *fine, go fuck some roofied slut.*

Piper, the girl I killed.

I crouch down next to her limp, lifeless body. The room spins and hums and I hear feathers and wings and my own pounding heartbeat.

My vision floats up high into the rafters and I look down

on us. Down on the bright-lit white room. At Mads in her perfect dark black. At me balanced on my toes and bowing reverence to a dead girl who was never worth saving. At Piper in her sea of red.

That little whore with the jade-green eyes takes Piper's hand and slips it away from her sabre. Holds her gloved fingers tight and drags them through the red. Brings them to the space where the floor is still white. Writes five letters, shaking and huge:

DUFFY

—and lets Piper's hand fall defeated next to the last trailing letter.

That little whore with the jade-green eyes steps back. Picks up her mask and her phone and her sabre: everything that proves she was here. There are no footprints and no fingerprints. Just angry wide-flung drops of red and a heavy sword on the floor.

That little whore with the jade-green eyes backs all the way to the end of the piste. The room fades in and out.

Mads follows me silent to the door. I open it and she slips out into the night.

I stare across the endless miles between Piper and me. She stares and doesn't see.

She walked out that night.

She left me there with them.

I step out into the dark with Mads and let the door swing shut behind us.

ESCAPE

Mads drives my father's red car fast, so fast, weaving through the crawling traffic and flying hungry along the shoulder, never stopping, never slowing down. Her hands grip the wheel tight. Her jaw is set so hard it could break stone.

I sit in the passenger seat on the bright silver sunshield Mads found in the trunk. It shines all the freeway-light back up around me and webs me in white and red and gold. Piper's blood drips down and paints the shield the color of Mack's lies and her truth.

The sky glows with city lights. The stars hide their fires the way he wanted when he knew they knew too much. The cars blare loud and angry at Mads speeding furious between them.

Nothing is real.

It's a night that won't end.

It's darkness and light and blood—

—so much blood—

It's wings that follow us all the way home, swooping low, whispering my name, whispering *you're her*—

I don't remember how to scream.

HOME

Hancock Park is dark and blurred. The branches hang so low the car snaps them apart. The jacarandas are all in bloom for a bright shouting moment and then when I blink the dripping petals are gone again and the branches point and writhe like snakes—

My house is as empty as I left it. Windows staring blank. Birds in the eaves. Mads has the lights off the way we did when we left Banks to drown. She pulls my car into the garage and the door clanks down heavy behind us. The chains grind. The air is still and cold.

Mads is on the phone with our coven, saying words in broken bloody pieces—

get my car from St Andrew's and get here now, to Jade's—

get rid of the phone—

stay in the shadows—

don't stop for anyone—

—and her hands shake black bags free from the box by the door.

Come on, Jade, give me your shoes, give me your mask—

And I do.

Stand up.

And I do.

We have to get rid of this—

She folds up the bloodied sunshield.

I take off my gloves. Unzip my jacket and slide my arms free. Step out of the white pants heavy with red. Stand in my hanging sequins and my bare feet and feel my lungs flutter—

Mads says, *You have to go wash off the blood. I'll be right there—*
Jenny and Summer are coming—
We'll be right there—
We'll get rid of all this—

And I slide ghostly up the steps and into the house. It's dark. Everything is dark. My breath is too loud. Rasping like Duncan, cracking like Connor, choking like Banks—

and I hear glass shattering and the croaking bird that sat on the oleander branch above the gates of Inverness—

and all their ghosts cling close to me; all their hands grab at my dress, grab at my ankles, grab at my skin—

It's too dark. I need light. I need to see them, chase them away, chase them out of my house—

I need light—

FIRE

They keep the candles in the tall cabinet in the dining room. I find the drawer in the dark. I find a candle, pale and narrow and new. I find the matches. I strike one and it flares and fades before my fingers find the wick.

Strike a second and it sparks and dies and falls to the floor.
Strike a third and hold it close until the wick catches

fire and the match burns all the way to the end and I smell scorched blood.

I walk up the stairs with the candle held tight in both hands. It smokes the air clean so no ghosts can show their rotting faces and bare their loosening teeth.

My room is dark. My bed is empty. Outside the window a thousand birds cluster so close all the starlight is snuffed out.

In the mirror on my vanity I am a glowing dead girl. My face is striped in red. My dress catches the candlelight and dances bright and broken.

Blood drips down the candle instead of wax.

There are voices all around me, whispering—

god damn, she's feisty—

fuck, Dunc, you know how to pick them—

give her a minute, she'll be gone—

I've never loved anyone more—

And my hand is on my knife, the good long knife from my sister's wedding silver, and my knife-hand digs into my pillowcase and the candle drips blood onto the sheets. I find the folded paper with my four dead boys gouged out. It's time to cut Piper free but she doesn't have a picture because *she didn't do anything—*

The blood drips down my hands, down my arms, down my dress. I grip the candle and the knife and the paper, all my weapons against the whispering dark and the blood that marks me guilty and dead and *her—*

The birds watch from the windows.

The bathroom lights up bright with the tiny flame. I balance my candle against the curving neck of the faucet and stare into the mirror at the girl from the St Andrew's Prep party on my sweet sixteen.

Revenge-black hair.
Blood on my face.
Blood on my hands.
A long silver knife—

BLOOD

I wash my hands.

The water rushes fast and clear. I leave it ice cold, as cold as my heart, as cold as murdered Piper with her sabre on the floor.

The girl in the mirror watches dead-eyed and soulless. I hate her. She is weak. She is guilty. She trusts. She shouldn't.

Downstairs voices echo. And I see her—

—the girl who fought and couldn't fight.

I look at my hands. They're shivering and clean and wet. But the blood blooms back out of them like the summer-flowers breaking blue and sticky outside, and I see her—

—the girl who said *I'm going to kill them.*

The birds shriek and the tall clock from Inverness groans. Outside an engine fires hot and Porter speeds hard onto the freeway and crushes to dust between metal and pavement.

I drown my hands under the water and feel it close deep and unforgiving over my head. The blood flows thick and I see her—

—the girl who held a dripping knife and all the power in the world.

I pull my hands free again. They're redder than before. My dress is stained and torn and the bruises are back. I taste Duncan's blood on my teeth. I feel it drip down my legs. The circle of red spreads thick around me and I see her—

—the girl who let go, who lost control, who lost the power I ripped out of their chests.

I lean over the sink and splash the cold water onto my dress, onto the stains, and the damn spot won't wash out—

and it marks me guilty, marks me *her,* marks me lost.

I'm not done. I can't be done. But I am, I *am*—

And I bring my hands out of the water and rub them fast together and still the red bleeds out. Duncan's blood and Piper's, soaking into the page on the floor. Soaking into the red X over the dazzle-smiled boy, there all along and I never ever saw it—

And I laugh and laugh and try to scream and can't because their hands press against my mouth and the lights are bright and spinning.

I want the dark back but the candle blazes and the blood blooms and the light sparks off the knife resting hard on the porcelain—

I betrayed her. The girl who needed the girl I am.

The door hangs barely open and I'm alone in the room and I can't move, and my face bleeds and my throat bleeds and my dress is ripped and ruined.

My hands are still red. They'll never be clean. The smell of blood rises so strong I feel it digging into my lungs and I grip the knife and say to the girl in the mirror—

Wash your hands—

Go to bed—

What's done is done—

And the knife clatters and the room shakes sideways. The floor hits me hard in the face. Cold and smooth and wet.

My hands run red, but hot now instead of cold. Blood pours quick from two long gashes—

one for the girl alone and trapped—

one for the girl who betrayed her and left her unavenged—

—and my hands are red with guilt and ruin.

The candlelight is bright and brighter but my eyes are slipping closed. My lips are numb and it's over, it's over, it's over. I don't have to fight anymore. The little laughing girl with the too-big eyes and the tiny gold earrings sits next to me with my blood all around her and she giggles and smiles and stares in wonder—

And she says,

Sleep well.

And I fade.

MOURNING

Everything is white. The ceiling and the walls and the lights.

It all seeps back to me. Through the fog that laces my thoughts. Through the blackbird-feathers across my eyes where they won't open all the way.

I remember the floor rushing up and my wrists pouring red.

I struggle and my eyes open wider. The fog settles heavy into my head and a dull throbbing pain presses itself just over my right eye.

My father says, *She's awake, she's awake—*

—and my mother's hands clasp onto mine.

I feel it like the blade against my wrists: shame and fear and fury.

I've broken them. All their Stanford dreams and their little girl who always lied but always loved. Fought and won but never got caught.

Never lost.

Always chose.

My eyes burn hot and I struggle against the fog—

against the creeping darkness that tries to keep me silent and still—

—and I sit up.

My mother's makeup is tracked through with tears. My father hasn't shaved. They wear last night's going-out clothes.

The light pours through the window on the far wall but I think it's wrong. It's still night. Endless and unbroken. I wear a scratching white hospital gown. Needles poke into my arms and ooze venom under my skin. My wrists are bound tight in white bandages.

I close my eyes against all of it. The dark flutters with a thousand wings.

They speak. I answer. I've hurt them worse than I ever hurt the wolves.

But they say, *You're safe.*

They say, *No one will ever hurt you again.*

They say, *It's over.*

They stay with me. They let me not-speak and I stop

trying to tell them I'll fix it. My throat feels strange and raw. My thoughts tangle in themselves. They've given me pills—the people in white and blue who drift timid behind my parents. They've spilled poison into my arms through the needles.

They're keeping me dull and dead exactly the way Duncan's boys did that night. The way Mack did when he gave me the drink.

I sleep and wake. The light changes from white to gold.

I sleep and wake. The light changes from gold to red.

I speak again. Finally. I tell them, "You can go home. You can rest."

They say, "We won't leave you."

I say, "I need to sleep. I want you to rest. I don't want you to have to look at me like this."

My mother says, "It isn't your fault. It was never your fault."

My father says, quiet, "You did nothing wrong."

For the first time since I woke up still alive something stirs in me and says, *fight*.

I will still be their daughter after this.

They kiss me on the top of my head and make me promise I'll call them if there's even one thing I need. They promise they'll be back in two hours even though I tell them to rest longer.

They leave me in the white-sheets room with the sunset glowing red.

I stare at the sky and fight the fog. It's fading, but I'm still not whole.

When a new nurse comes in with dinner on a pale blue tray and pills in a paper cup I smile dry-lipped at her. She half-smiles back and checks the screens next to my bed. She's different than the rest of them: no shiny plastic courtesy and no pity in her eyes. Her scrubs are bright wild pink and a spiny tattoo peeks through her hair: *Vive sin miedo*. She tells me there will be a woman in to talk to me when I'm ready. I say, because I can, "Do I have to?"

She nods. "Rules. But take your time."

She leaves me alone.

When her squeaking-rubber footsteps have died away I drink the tea and leave the food. I drop the pills into the watery applesauce and swirl it together until they disappear.

Out in the hall, drifting lazy through the white, a low voice says, *Elizabeth Jade Khanjara*. Another voice answers, fading too much to hear.

I sit up and swing my feet off the bed and onto the floor. My vision shivers up. My legs are unsteady. I stand anyway. Walk, one step at a time, to the door. Holding tight to the rack of tubes and screens.

The hall stretches long outside my room. At the very end, two men in guns and badges stand chests-out, talking low to the nurse in her pink.

The men look up. One of them says, hands sliding to the silver cuffs on his belt, "Just a couple of questions."

"Absolutely not," says the nurse.

The other cop scoffs and shakes his head. "Then we'll stay right here until we can."

"Outside," says the nurse. She glances over her shoulder at me. "Other side of these doors."

She follows them out the door and looks back through the narrow window set into it. On purpose, waiting, until I slip back into my room.

They've come for me, but I'm not done.

I sit back down on the bed and unhook the ugly plastic phone and call the only number I know by heart. I tell Mads what to bring. I say, *Cedars-Sinai. Emergency room door. Drive fast.* I hang up before she can say anything. But she hangs up, too. I know it.

I wait. I count down from sixty twenty times. Five minutes to get the things from my room and run back across the fourteenth green, and fifteen to drive to me. The fog burns away. The pain in my head throbs bright and the gashes on my wrists sing themselves awake.

Tonight I'll fly.

After twenty minutes I leave the white-sheets bed behind me. I float silent to the door with my blinking screens. To the left, the hall stretches out to the sealed-shut doors with the two men guarding them, shoulders blocking out the windows, backs to me. To the right there's a siren-red EXIT sign over a stairway door. Past it, another nurse walks away.

She disappears around a corner.

I yank the needles out of my arms and I run. I fly. I soar on the wings no one will clip. The screens beep shrill but I'm at the stairway door already and through it and running down and down and down. The echoing zigzag gray makes my head go light and my hands clutch at the railing but it doesn't matter, because I will always fight.

I always fight.

The stairs dead-end at a heavy door and I crash through it and stumble out onto cigarette butts and sidewalk. My eyes skim across the parking lot and the buildings jutting high until I see the glowing beacon, EMERGENCY, calling me to my coven.

I dash breathless-fast down the sidewalk and across the pavement. A car honks and a man in a white coat shouts. I'm faster than they are. I am on fire.

I'll never be theirs.

When the sign shines just above me an engine roars. Mads's black car peels away from the curb and pulls up shouting and defiant. I swing myself into the passenger seat and slam the door and behind me Jenny and Summer yell, "Drive, drive, drive!"

Mads screams out of the parking lot so hard her tires burn the pavement away to nothing.

They shriek my name, *Jade Jade Jade*, and I love them. I love them more than anything.

Mads squeals across an intersection with the light flashing to red. She says, "Where are we going?"

And Summer shouts, "Anywhere!"

And Jenny shouts, "Away!"

And a third voice says, not quite shouting: "We're free."

I turn and she's there, pale and with a cigarette between her fingers but the circles almost gone from under her eyes.

Lilia.

I say, "How did you—"

"She fucking *texted* us," says Jenny, and she throws her arm around Summer's shoulders to pull Lilia's hair.

And Lilia sasses back: "You texted me first."

"Summer did," says Mads. "We didn't."

Summer beams at her and me and all of us. "I did. Lilia and Malcolm and Duffy and Mack."

"Piper," Lilia says. "Dead with Duffy's name spelled out.

And then you on a stretcher, and there was so much blood, but I *knew*—"

"You didn't know," says Jenny, and we turn a corner, and the sunset pours out into our eyes. "You flipped your shit when Summer said *who's next*—"

"She knew," says Mads. "She told Summer she wanted in."

I look at Lilia who faded every time Duncan grabbed her arm.

Lilia who took her blue war-paint and carved *GUILTY* onto a dead boy's banner.

"So where are we *going*?" she asks, alive the way she was when I cut three marks into her skin. "I ditched rehab for this."

We scream with laughter, all four of us. Laughter that hurts deep under my ribs but raises a proud fist against everyone who isn't us.

I say, when we stop, "Duncan's house."

They gasp delight and Summer says, "You're back, you're back, oh god. You're back. I was so fucking *scared*, Jade."

Jenny says, "I told you she'd be fine."

And Summer says, "Don't act like you weren't freaking out as much as I was last night."

"Useless bitches. Both of you," says Mads.

"Thank fuck I'm here," says Lilia.

They are perfect.

I say, "Do you have my phone?"

Jenny hands it to me.

She made me say, last night, when I was bleeding myself to death and the ambulance was shrieking up the street, *I know*.

I said to Mack, *You gave her the drink.*

I said, *I hope someone kills you the way you killed Duncan.*

The dagger in my ribs digs deeper.

I look at my coven and not at his desperate unwound replies and I say, "So everyone knows Piper's dead?"

"Everyone knows." Lilia scrolls and blows smoke. "And everyone thinks it was Duffy." She shows me a picture: the gray stone of St Andrew's, hemmed in with police cars. A news van parked half on the sidewalk. Boys with thousand-yard stares.

Jenny opens her window and shouts out into the bleeding sky, "He think she's on his side. Malcolm does, too. They think she's fucking *harmless.*"

"Jenny, God!" Summer grabs her and pulls her back. Jenny falls half into her arms and stays that way. "We're harboring fugitives."

The wind rushes loud and I say, just to Mads: "And Mack?"

"He's sorry." The car surges faster.

"Sorry I'm dead, or sorry I'll kill him?"

She shakes her head.

Jenny shuts the window and Lilia lights another Parliament. Summer sighs into Jenny's bleach-pink hair. I look out at the night flooding in over the lights and the cars and the city.

When I think of Mack the space between my ribs aches hollow like the gasping wound in Duncan's chest. I didn't love him—not the way he thought he loved me.

But I loved who we were together. *Power,* said Duncan. *Twisted,* said Banks.

And for one high wild instant, it was true.

I say to my coven, "Mack will die tonight."

It sinks in and clings to our skin and our hair. Filling up the silence as we hum for the hills. Until Lilia's cigarette is a burnt-short stub and she throws it out onto the road.

Then her cold hand finds mine and she says, "Are you really all right?"

I say, "Yes."

Mads says, low, "Don't lie."

Their hope and their sorrow and their rage swirl tight around me. My beautiful deadly girls with their loyalty so strong nothing could break it. And Lilia, one of us now, hardening from glass to diamond.

I say, "I'll be fine. When this is over."

It's the truth.

Summer sighs stars and wistfulness. Jenny elbows her. Mads says, "We're yours."

They are, even Lilia. Like Mack never was. And I wonder, spun up in their vow, if he told me all along—

when he said, *maybe I'm worse than all of them*—

—if the darkness I saw gleaming out from under his dull gold was something he tried to hide from me, not something I had to dig free.

I wonder what I really saw when I looked at his picture on the page Summer printed. If I saw his light or his darkness.

Or the dazzle-smiled boy.

The sky glows red. Bloody and bold and resolute.

Mads says, "Tonight. It ends tonight."

OUR NIGHT

Thirteen days past sweet sixteen my claws are sharper than they ever were before.

We're all flash tonight. Jenny and Summer and Mads and me. We're vengeance and poison we spilled in a theatre so dark the truth hid like a spider where no one could see it. Red lips, each our own color. Jenny's pink and Summer's rose and Mads's scarlet and my blood-red. Deadly smiles and whitest-white teeth.

My hair is black again. Revenge-black and sharp and short, shorter than it should be, but I don't care because it's still mine and nothing else matters. And my eyes are hidden behind sunglasses so dark no one will ever see through them until it's too late, and Summer swears I'll trip and fall and never walk again, but I don't care about that, either.

Tonight I'm fate.

Tonight Jenny and Summer and Mads and me, we're four sirens, like the ones in those stories. The ones who sing and make men die.

Tonight Lilia is ours, unfurling her wings, and we're five instead of four.

Tonight we have knives where they think our hearts should be.

Tonight we're walking up the driveway to our best party ever. Not the parties like we always go to, with the dull-duller-dullest Hancock Park girls we've always known and the dull-duller-dullest wine coolers we always drink and the same bad choice in boys.

Tonight we're going to a St Andrew's Prep party.

Hosting it, technically.

And nobody turns down girls like us.

We break down the door. We let us in. Our teeth flash. Our claws glimmer. Mads laughs so shrill-bright it's almost a scream. The dead kings wake. We all grab hands and laugh together and then everyone, every St Andrew's ghost we've killed is back and every boy we'll kill tonight *knows*, far away where they are, and I know they see it—

for just a second—

—our fangs and our claws.

THE SET

Duncan's house is haunted but ghosts can't hurt me anymore.

It's blackout-dark when we drive in. The house shirks back into the hills like the family that ran when their perfect son—Duncan the captain, Duncan the king, Duncan the Dartmouth-bound—died exactly the way he deserved.

The neighbors won't look, but we stay hidden anyway. Mads parks far past the dead-dark driveway and we flit shapeless and shadowed through the trees. They wouldn't see us even if they looked.

We kick through the giant windows along the back of the house. The ones we broke with crosses on Friday night but they fixed on Saturday before anyone could wonder why two girls burned with enough rage to rip their whole house down.

The alarm beeps and the phone rings deep in the dark. Lilia answers it and recites the code dead Duncan gave her. She says, lilting and hundred-proof, "You know how boys are. Never careful enough."

They set the stage, my four siren sisters. They know how to summon the boys we need:

Duffy.

Malcolm.

Mack.

Two weeks ago they were weighted down weightless with solid gold armor. They were a wolf-pack stalking the hills, invincible. They knew consequences were for other people.

Tonight they've seen death creep close. They've seen blood soak into the dirt under Inverness and birds line the peaks of St Andrew's.

When their dead king's widow whispers to them they listen. When she says *Come to Duncan's* they obey.

Lilia tells Duffy and Malcolm, *Mack's coming. He killed them. He'll kill you, too, if you don't stop him.*

She tells Mack, *They're coming. Do what Jade wanted.*

And they bring out the poison and I dress for my final act.

I wear my homecoming gown. It's the same fatal red as my lipstick. My makeup is so very, very perfect it will make them afraid just to look at me. My hair shines sleek. My nails are gold. Mads's sunglasses hide my eyes.

When I'm ready I unwrap the gauze from around my wrists. The stitches crawl up my arms and my skin is bruised and dark, but there's no blood on my hands.

I put on the long black gloves I wore to Summer's party

on New Year's Eve. The silk slides over the stitches and hides them away. I step into high black heels with shining red soles. I straighten my crucifix.

I set the golden crown on my head—the crown Mads wore when she told Mack *you knew enough*. It fits me perfectly.

My coven kisses me good-bye. They leap back through the window we broke and their wings poke dark out of their backs. They turn to birds in front of my eyes and fly away, all of them. They won't be here when Duffy and Malcolm and Mack go cold. They won't be here when the police come and I tell them, crying and wide-eyed and *innocent, innocent, innocent,* what Mack did.

How he killed all the boys in his pack because they knew his secret.

How he tried to kill me.

I am alone tonight. The way it needs to be.

I am here where it began and where it will end.

I'm ready.

THE KING

Malcolm and Duffy drive in first, together. They pull in with their lights blazing and the bass thumping loud enough to rattle the broken glass, but not loud enough to cover their fear.

They walk up the driveway side by side. Uneasy allies.

Playing bold, but I can smell their sweat and feel their skin prick with goosebumps.

They walk around to the back, the way Lilia told them. Weaving through the trees in the dark. Stumbling and saying *shit* and *what was that*.

I'm hidden where they won't look, but where I can see.

They step out onto the wide stretch of concrete and suddenly they're in the day again. They shade their eyes against the light shining down in a square around the pool. The broken window gleams. The house yawns dark beyond it.

"Shit," says Malcolm. "Where is she?"

And Duffy yells, "Lilia!"

The dark swallows up his voice.

"I don't like this." Duffy digs for his phone. "This doesn't feel right."

They wait too long. The darkness presses closer.

"Fuck," says Malcolm with his dead brother's eyes set into his little-boy face. "It's Mack, not Lilia. It has to be."

Duffy turns away and clutches one hand to his mouth.

"Fucking golden boy." Malcolm laughs on his gallows. "Killing his friends over some bitch at a party."

Duffy's face shines with sweat and sickness. "Let's get out of here. We can go to the cops—I don't know—"

Their shadows spin. An engine hums and quits on the other side of the house.

"*Fuck*," says Duffy, and his shoulders wilt.

Mack strides in all boast and courage. His feet are sure, even in the shadows. When he steps into the light the lines carve deep into his face. He has nothing left to lose.

"Look at you," he says.

I've never seen anyone like you—

His voice thrums through the stitches on my wrists. His neck wants my knife.

"*Look* at you," he says again—

There's no guilt on your face—

"You're paler than Porter was when we caught him with the knife," says Mack. "You're scared."

Duffy shies away, but Malcolm bristles with Duncan's old ghost and says, "What, and you're not?"

Mack laughs haunted. "Not anymore."

Malcolm says, "You killed my brother."

Mack looks him in the eye and doesn't lie. "He deserved it."

"Bullshit," Duffy bursts out. "No, he didn't—"

"So did Connor and Banks," says Mack. "So do you."

The two wolf-boys share a taut glance. Malcolm says, finally, "It's both of us against you."

Mack shakes himself loose. He's unstrung. I almost don't recognize him anymore. "Kill me," he says. "I don't care."

Duffy's and Malcolm's eyes meet again and they shiver, both of them.

"You're afraid," Mack says again. I hear my own words in it—

you're a fucking coward—

—and he is. A coward who hid behind their guilt. A coward who wants them to carry the shame of what he did.

He says, "I'm not afraid of you."

He says, "We're all dead anyway."

THE KNIGHTS

I know the dark house better than I should. Duncan has only been gone for six days, but the rooms have settled heavy into themselves. The emptiness has its roots deep in the marble.

I slip away to the kitchen and find the poison my coven fixed. It's amaretto. Gold rusting to red. A sweet sick intoxicating smell, like bitter almonds.

I pour three drinks here where Malcolm stood, mixing poison.

Where Mack took it and brought it to me.

Where the dead boys stood together with their hungry yellow wolf-eyes prowling across the crowd in the heat and the light and watched the glittering girl in the too-short dress spin and spin.

I leave the bottle on the counter.

I carry the three glasses all together, holding them against each other. The poison swirls beautiful and dizzying. I stand at the window, just beyond the light. The boys are frozen, waiting to swing and fight. Waiting to die.

I hate them with a rage so bright it's deadlier than the poison in their drinks.

"It's over," says Malcolm. "The cops are coming for you."

"I don't care," says Mack.

"She was nobody," says Duffy. "You killed for some drunk bitch—"

Mack swings his fist hard into Duffy's jaw. Malcolm yells and yanks him back. And Duffy cries out scared, cowering down, clutching at his face. He falls back and Mack swings again, for Malcolm.

And little-boy Malcolm shouts at him: "Give up!"

Mack lunges again. Malcolm ducks and fights back and his knuckles crack against Mack's cheek.

They fall back, staggering and panting and with Duffy's blood speckled on the concrete. Mack is wild-eyed and Duffy heaves and Malcolm says, *Give up.*

Mack says, *No. I won't. For Jade.*

My name on his lips is the last cue I need.

I shriek glass-shatter and murder and they freeze where they are. The almond smell curls all around me. Hissing. Eager.

Mack raises his head. "What was that?"

Malcolm says, "It's just Lilia."

"Fuck," says Duffy. He drags one hand across his lips and leaves a streak of red from his nose to his ear. "That wasn't Lilia. It was—"

It's on all of their faces.

"Jade," says Mack, half hope and half horror.

"No," says Malcolm. "She's dead."

It's time.

I step out of the shadows and through the jagged glass teeth that reach up around my ankles. Into the sun. The spotlights burn down onto me and I feel my crown glowing so bright the boys squint and go blind.

I am a queen in a golden crown and a dress the color of blood, holding death in my hands. I am everything the girl in the white-sheets room wanted.

Mack gasps my name, *Jade*, and goes so weak he falls.

Malcolm and Duffy back away with fear on their faces.

Mack says, *Jade*—

I laugh.

Malcolm says, "They said you were dead."

I smile and my fangs scrape against my lips. I say, "I was."

Duffy says, still shaking himself free of my ghost, "Did Lilia call you here?"

I say, "You're guilty."

Duffy scrambles and says, "We're not. It's Mack."

I step closer. "So you're innocent?"

"Yes," he says, so flustered furious I know he believes it. So certain he could swear it—

to his lawyer, to a jury, to God—

—and never think he was lying. Because to him it was nothing.

She was nothing.

I slink closer to him. I can't believe he ever thought Duncan wanted him for anything other than keeping a harmless servant at his right hand so he'd always be safe from a revolution. Not like he was with Mack, even with him circling just out of reach of their little pack of four.

I say, "It was Mack."

From the ground he cries out my name.

I say, "Mack. Shut up."

He says, "Jade."

I say, "You know what you did. You know what it means."

And his eyes flare with pain. "No, Jade, I never—"

"You did," I say. I breathe in deep and smell the sweet bitter almonds coiling all around me. "And this is the end."

I bow my head. Graceful and gracious.

I turn my back on him and my shining beautiful gown swirls around my feet. I soak it in—

the satin cool and close on my skin—

the gold-red drinks in my hands—

the shattered windows and the dead-dark house—

—and I breathe out again and it turns the night so cold the green grass frosts and the palm trees go black and withering.

I go to Malcolm and Duffy. "Golden boys," I say. It's all melodrama but I love it. "He killed Duncan. He killed Piper. He killed his own best friend. He almost killed me—"

Mack says *No* but it didn't matter to them and it doesn't matter to me.

I say, "Tonight he'll pay."

Their eyes are horror-huge. They knew it already, what Mack did, but they didn't believe it.

I say, "He was going to kill me. I knew too much. Like Piper."

Duffy trembles with hurt and hate.

"I saw him come in that night with Duncan's blood on his hands—"

Malcolm's fists clench.

"I swore I wouldn't tell. He held Porter's knife to my neck and he made me swear. And then when it all fell apart he came for Piper and he came for me." And I tell the truth: "He left me alone. He left me for dead."

They're staring at me like I'm freedom. They're drunk off my words.

Duffy says, "You're braver than anyone, Jade."

I don't bow my head this time. I say, "I know."

Malcolm turns almost into Duncan again. Taller and

broader-shouldered with his gray eyes glinting. "We won't let him hurt you," he says. "It's over."

I laugh the brightest bird-wing laugh I've ever laughed and it soars over the iced-black palm trees and the dark house and the hills. "You're king now," I say to Malcolm. "Like Duncan wanted. You'll keep us safe. Both of you."

Duffy reaches for his phone. "I'll call the cops," he says. "Before Mack tries anything."

Mack says *Jade* but we leave him bleeding on the ground. Let him suffer the way he should.

I say, "Wait. Let's drink to him first. To the end of him."

Duffy breathes out shaky and leveled. "I'll fucking drink to that."

He takes a glass.

Malcolm says, "To Mack's fall." He takes the second glass and swirls it over his head. The light dances through the cut crystal. "Amaretto?"

I nod. "My very favorite."

From the ground Mack says, "No—"

I say, "And to the golden boys."

Duffy and Malcolm say, "To the golden boys!"

They raise their glasses and I raise mine. The crystal clinks together with so much singing shrieking power I can't believe they don't see the death's-heads floating in the amber.

Mack struggles and says, "No, don't, don't—"

I laugh.

I bring my glass to my lips. The poison crawls close.

Malcolm and Duffy drink deep. Duffy shouts, "It's over."

Malcolm says, "We won."

Mack says, "No—"

I spin again and tower over him. "What? Do you want to drink with us?"

His traitor-green eyes shine and he says, "No—"

I say, "Why not? It's just a drink."

He says, "Jade, no, I didn't—"

I hold out the glass. There is death in Mack's eyes.

He reaches a shaking buried hand out to take it. He knows exactly what I'm giving him. He's ready to die.

But that would be too easy.

I let the glass fall and shatter on the ground. The poison splashes between us. Burning into the concrete and spitting onto my gown.

Mack's head drops. Malcolm and Duffy laugh giddy and guiltless. I tip my head back and stare up into the sky. The stars blaze bright.

This is the end.

THE QUEEN

Duffy falls first. Duffy the follower, leading at last.

He hits the ground and his whole body wracks and shakes and shudders—

—and next to him Malcolm panics and falls to his knees and says, "Duff—what is it—what's wrong—"

Duffy is contorted and strange and his jaw cracks against itself. He can't speak. He can't fight.

Then Malcolm realizes. He jumps up and shouts at Mack: "What did you do?"

Mack stares hollow.

Malcolm says, "Jade! He did something—where did you get the liquor—"

I take his hands in mine. The black silk glides smooth over his skin. I whisper to him, "Give it a minute. You'll be gone."

"Fuck!" he shouts. "Fucking bitch! It was you all along—"

He yanks free and grabs his phone and I knock it out of his hands. It flips across the concrete. He ducks for it but then—

—then it's his turn. Little-boy Malcolm, who stood at the counter and mixed the drink for the brother he wanted to be.

I watch them both for a drawn-long moment. Writhing. Dying.

I don't feel anything at all.

I turn away from them and face Mack. He stares ruined and guilty.

I can't remember how it felt before. I don't know why my pulse fluttered feathery under my skin when he said *I've never loved anyone more,* or why it meant anything when we fell together into his bed the night I made him kill Duncan.

He is the dazzle-smiled boy.

He is the one who will end it. He knows it as well as I do. He sees his death on my face. He wants it.

But it won't be his until he's had his heart ripped out and frozen.

It hurts more when someone you love is holding the knife, I said to Jenny and Summer and Mads when we sat in my room on Saturday morning with the lacrosse boys in our hands.

I was right.

I was a prophetess even then.

I tell Mack, "I'll be waiting."

I walk away from him. Through the broken glass. Past the broken boys still dying slow and horrible. Through the broken window and into the dark.

I don't need light.

I walk back through the kitchen and pick up the poisoned amaretto. Cradle it close and carry it with me into the low broad room with the dead-king masks guarding the walls. In the cold shadowed silence one ghost spins alone. Her hair is long and platinum-blond. Her dress is short and shining.

Deep in the dark, a clock chimes. Twelve bright gold clangs.

It's Friday again.

I walk the path Connor dragged me down that night. I can't feel his hands clamped onto my arms anymore. I can't feel the haze. I can't feel the thudding heavy bass that followed us all the way to the end of the hall even when the music bled dull into the melting walls.

The door is open. The air is charged and sparking.

I turn on the light.

The room is empty. Everything is perfect and undisturbed and no one would ever know anything happened here. No one would know how they sneered and shouted and crushed me down.

No one would ever know what happened to *that little whore with the jade-green eyes.*

I could say, *It never happened.*

But I don't lie when it matters.

I walk one foot in front of the other to the edge of the

white-sheets bed. I sit down. I set the poison on the clear-glass nightstand. I fold Mads's sunglasses next to the bottle. I close the silver crucifix in my hand and yank hard. The chain breaks against my neck and I drop it on the glass.

Silver was never my color. My color is gold, like the crown on my head. Black, like the gloves that bury the stitches I don't need.

Red like my dress. Red like my lips. Red like the blood of the boys I killed.

Footsteps echo on the marble. Staggering but steady.

I asked Duncan, after he kissed me hard and hungry, *Do you believe in fate?*

He said, *No.*

I said, *You should.*

And I told Mack all along, *It had to be you. It had to be us.*

It was a lie to drag him closer and bind him to me. I didn't believe it. I knew I was fate, my coven and me.

His footsteps scrape closer.

That night, when Duncan saw me across the room and whispered to Duffy—

when Malcolm mixed the drink and Mack brought it to me—

when Connor dragged me biting and clawing into this room—

when Banks said, *fuck, Dunc, you know how to pick them*—

when Piper slammed the door shut with Porter guarding it and they left me to the wolves—

when I fought and fought and fought and lost—

—it was fate.

It was spelled into our stars when Mads dyed my hair and

Jenny bought the contacts and Summer gave me the dress and we swallowed vodka and cruelty and went winging out to crash the St Andrew's Prep party on my sweet sixteen.

I said, I spat, I swore: *You picked the wrong girl.*

They did.

They had to.

It could only be me.

Not the first—

—but the last, the last, the last.

They picked the right girl.

WHITE

Mack says, *Jade.*

I don't turn to him. I sit with my back straight and my crown shining and my dress painting me proud and unruined.

Mack says, *I love you.*

I say, "I know what you did."

He says, "I didn't."

I say, "You know you'll die tonight. You know I've made this all your fault. You might as well tell the truth if you're going to waste your time saying you love me."

His shadow casts over the white. His breath comes ragged.

He says, "I didn't know."

He says, "Jade, I'm begging you. Look at me. You know me."

I say, "We're nothing to each other. I'm just a girl you wanted to fuck. You're just a boy I let fuck me because I wanted to see how many of your friends I could make you kill."

He says, "That's not true."

I say, "Then we're both liars."

The bed sinks lower with his weight. He is here with me, where they were.

He says, "Banks told me what he put in her drink—"

And I laugh so mirthless and merciless my crown slips. I reach up and straighten it. I still won't look at him.

"No," he says. "Not that night. He told me the morning Piper told you. When you found me in the hall—when we swore we'd kill them—"

It's a lie. It's a slithering stupid lie and I'll never believe it. I won't let him live. I won't let him take his neck out of the noose or his name off my list.

He keeps his guilt.

He says, wrenching with pain I don't understand at all anymore—

that I never understood—

—he says, "Jade. I promise you I'm not like them. They made me guilty."

"You knew who they were," I say. "You knew what they did."

"I wanted to stop them. I always did, Jade—I told you how much I hated them—"

"You knew," I say again, and it burns in my throat like liquor and poison. "And you went to their party and took their drink and went up to the girl they told you to talk to, and then you left her there alone—"

"No." His hand finds mine. I pull hard away. "It wasn't like that," he says. "I was with her on my own. And then somebody ran into us and spilled her drink, and I went to go get something else and Banks was on his way by, and he said—he said, take this. And he gave me his drink."

Every word he says makes the walls warp uneven the way they did that night. Every word sits in my stomach, heavy and hollow. "They planned it," I tell him.

"I know," he says. "I should've known. If I could go back to that night—"

"You can't," I say, and the walls settle smooth. "What's done is done."

He takes my hand again.

I pull away again.

He says, "I'm guilty. I know I am, and it's killing me—"

"*You.*" The sound curls on my lips.

"I'm guilty," he says again. Slower this time; deliberate. "I was going to turn myself in tonight. Tell the police what they did and what I did. Not for me. For—"

His voice catches and bleeds raw.

He says, "For *her.*"

Something flutters low in my lungs.

He means it. The guilt is real and rooted in, and he killed for me and for her. He hates those boys and he's glad they're dead.

He said, *I wanted to stop them.*

But he didn't.

I lift my chin and turn to him.

He looks into my eyes—

—jade-green instead of brown. The eyes he looked into that night when he said, *I've never seen you before. I've never seen anyone like you.* When he stood with me, a dazzle-smiled boy with a dazzling girl, hiding away from the boys who saw us and knew only their golden boy could do the cruel thing they wanted.

He knows.

He says it, stricken: "You—"

And his hands take mine and I don't pull away. His warmth and his weakness burn through the silk—

—and I am still ice. I am still savage and wicked. I am the little girl who pushed the boy off the playground castle. I am all the things I was before he knew me. I am the girl who lost and the girl who won.

He says, "You're her."

I say, "Yes."

He says, "Jade—"

He says, "Elle—"

And the furious feathered wings fill up my lungs and they beat fast and faster—

He says, *Elle*—

—and I am her again, here in this room where they thought they ruined me.

Here in this room without them.

And he says *Elle* and *I love you* and *I'm sorry* but I say *get out* and *leave* and *go* until he isn't there at all.

Until it's only the girl in the shining white dress, so close I can smell the bleach in her hair. So close I can feel the hands pressing down on her mouth.

She was alone here in this room but now—

—now I'm here with her.

Now I've killed for her.

Tonight she will walk out and never come back.
And I cry for her.
I cry.
I am the girl I saved.

RED

The sirens find me.

I hear them when they're still far away, climbing the hill to dead Duncan's house. They come close and closer.

I stand up steady in the white-sheets room. The girl with the jade-green eyes.

And I leave.

I turn on every light as I walk out. The light in the hall that shivered and dripped when Connor pulled me away from the crowd. The light in the kitchen, over the bar, shining down on the poison and the ghosts of the boys who mix drinks for girls they think they can ruin. The light in the looming broad room where I spun and shone. The lights far up in the dizzy-high entryway where we shrieked laughter sharp as daggers and cast our curse on the night. The lights on the porch, setting it bright and empty against the shadows in the yard.

I don't have to hide anymore.

Let the light blaze down.

I find Mack at the door. We hold hands with blood dripping

through our fingers. Listening to the sirens howling louder. Watching St Andrew's blue spin across the wide winding street and the trees and the grass.

It was fate. They had to come for us.

Mack takes me in his arms and says, "I'm sorry. I love you."

I don't say it back, but I kiss him. Kiss his bloody bruised lips and taste the faintest clinging trace of bitter almonds.

The first police car pulls into the driveway. Men shout. The sirens wail so loud I know dead Duffy and dead Malcolm can hear them from hell.

Mack says, "Jade—Elle—"

And he squares his shoulders so strong no one would ever know he's broken. He says, "I killed Duncan. I left Banks. I brought Duffy and Malcolm here. Let me pay my debt."

I kiss him again. I whisper into his ear, a serpent hiss that blossoms soft—

"It was me. All of it. Connor. Duncan. Porter. Banks. Piper. Duffy. Malcolm."

I say it cruel and proud.

I say, "I killed them. The debt is mine."

He says, like he said the night Duncan died—the night I was his and he was mine—

"Are you sure?"

I decide.

I say, "Yes."

I kiss him.

And then I say it—

a whisper into his ear—

You knew enough.

He pulls back. "Jade—" he says, and his eyes wash out with doubt and guilt and fear. "If I could go back—I'd do anything in the world if I could change it for you—"

And I say, "For her."

"I love you," he says.

"Not for the girl you love," I say. "For the girl you left."

Outside footsteps pound hard up the stairs and a man shouts, *LAPD*—

I kiss the boy who killed for me. Kiss him good-bye, one hand in his hair and the other clinging to his with the neck of the amaretto wound between our fingers.

The cop slams hard on the door.

My lips part from Mack's. I breathe it into him: four words, beautiful and deadly.

The debt is yours.

I open the door. I walk out onto the stage-lit porch. The cops shout, *Don't move.* They shout, *Hands up.* They shout, *On your knees.*

I don't listen.

I walk down the steps and onto the green lawn. They throw a blinding spotlight across the grass and circle me in. They shout. Their guns come up.

High above me the sky is made of birds.

I raise my hands.

The lights spin. My crown shines brighter than the sun. My wings stretch out so wide they cover the whole valley.

I am ruinous and unruined.

Shadows fly. They circle me, four of them, shouting and shouting with their guns up.

I say, "What's done is done."

They grab me all at once. They try to knock me down. They yank at my hands and I feel my gloves slipping and my stitches bursting open and my blood soaking into the silk.

They say, *Elizabeth Jade Khanjara*—

They say, *You're under arrest*—

They say, *You have the right to remain silent*—

From far back behind the house one of them shouts for medics, but it's too late to save Duffy and Malcolm. It was always too late.

They say, *The hell is she smiling for*—

They say, *Wipe that smile off your face, you're in serious shit*—

They drag me away. Cameras flash. My heels rip through the grass. My dress shines dizzying in the lights. They lock silver handcuffs onto my wrists. They pull me across the grass toward their cars. They try to make me fall.

I don't fall.

They push my head down and shove me into the car and slam the door. A metal grate cages me in. They've trapped me but I don't care. Nothing they can do will ever bring the wolves back to life.

I lean close to the shining bars of my cage. The cop in the front seat twitches. He smells like cheap cigarettes.

I say it right into his ear—

What's done cannot be undone.

He flinches away from me. He says, "You're going to be sorry you did whatever you can't undo."

I think of dead Connor and how everyone swore it was an accident. Dead Duncan and the knife in Porter's hand. Dead Porter who drove deathwish-fast onto the freeway. Dead Banks with his car waiting at El Matador. Dead Piper with Duffy's name scrawled in her blood. Dead Malcolm and dead

Duffy celebrating drunk and stupid with bloody knuckles and the guilt that finally caught up to them.

I think of Jenny's father with his front-page headlines and his murderers who walk free. *You'll be a celebrity,* said Summer, starry-eyed, just before they turned to birds and flew off into the night. *You'll be his goddamn dream client,* said Jenny. *You're the girl who wins,* said Mads. And Lilia said, *For every girl who wants revenge.*

I think of the four boys in the white-sheets room. Walking out. Stalking proud through the halls of St Andrew's with everyone knowing exactly what they did that night and every other night.

But never again.

The radio gasps static and the scared-stupid cop mumbles into it. The passenger door swings open and another cop climbs in. The door slams.

The car slides back down the driveway. The sky glows bright and breathes with feathers and freedom. Mack watches from the door.

The dazzle-smiled boy who killed for me. Dizzy from my kiss and *innocent, innocent, innocent.* A bottle of poison hanging from his hand.

He is alone in the dead king's house.

Far away my coven flits and flies and watches over me. They are mine and I am theirs and I will never lie to them again.

Far away my mother and my father stand tall for me. They will love me always. They will see the little laughing girl always. I am her, still, even with blood on my hands.

I am free.

I am everything I have ever wanted to be.

We drive away from Duncan's house. Away from the spinning lights where they picked the girl fate had already chosen.

I look back, just once, before it all disappears—

—and Mack lifts the bottle to his lips and drinks the poison down.

I smile with my fangs showing.

I am the queen and the killer.

I'm not sorry.

TELL US WHAT YOU THINK

EDITORIAL
Naomi Colthurst
@NaomiColthurst
NColthurst@penguinrandomhouse.co.uk

MARKETING
Alesha Bonser
@AleshaBonser
ABonser@penguinrandomhouse.co.uk

PR
Simon Armstrong
@boypublicist
SArmstrong@penguinrandomhouse.co.uk

#FoulIsFair

To the early readers whose superb instincts pointed me in exactly the right direction: Ellen Bryson and Lydia Netzer.

To the authenticity readers whose insight and input were essential in making this story intersectional: Haarthi, Namrata, Neha, Quinn, and Kat. Any missteps are my own, and everything done right is because of you.

To the coven, past and present and always: Liana, Cat, Emily, Sony, Katie, Jessica, Michelle, and so very many more. Sisters, by something more than blood.

To all who survive, every day, in spite of everything: those who forgive and those who fight, those who seek justice and those who seek revenge, those who have stood up with the whole world watching and those whose stories will never be told. You are strength and you are power.

ACKNOWLEDGMENTS

I am so wildly, wildly grateful for everyone who has made Foul Is Fair what it is. My deepest thanks—

To Sarah Burnes, for believing in Jade from the very beginning, for your fierce and fearless advocacy, for your aggressiveness and warmth and brilliance, and for those four perfect words on September 28th.

To Sara Goodman, for understanding this book all the way down to the bone, for your assurance and your razor-sharp notes, for your energy and drive, and for never accepting anything but the best.

To Naomi Colthurst, for seeing Jade exactly the way I see her, for your wit and your eagle eyes, for your thoughtful and incisive ideas, and for loving the lines I thought everyone would hate.

To everyone at the Gernert Company (especially Julia Eagleton) and Wednesday Books (especially Jennie Conway), for your enthusiastic and endless support.